CF

Praise fo

DEA

"The second Chili Cook-off mystery is a spicy blend of a feisty heroine, colorful casino performers, and a deadly chili contest. The highly likable cast of characters and their hilarious hijinks make this series a blue-ribbon winner."
—*RT Book Reviews*

"Cozy mystery lovers will be delighted to read this spicy mystery. It is a fast-paced page-turner of a read . . . with engaging characters." —*MyShelf.com*

"Witty dialogue, numerous suspects, and a strong development of characters highlight the strength of writing by an author . . . [who] continues her record of entertaining readers with insightful characters and laughter."
—*Kings River Life Magazine*

CHILI CON CARNAGE

"Maxie is an edgy firecracker of a main character, and I can't wait to see the trouble she gets into on the Showdown tour. I'm also anxious to meet her dad, the infamous Texas Jack Pierce. I've always found that chili gets better with time, and I predict that this fun new series is going to continue to get stronger and stronger!" —*Mochas, Mysteries, and More*

"This is a fun mystery in a unique setting, and Maxie's dedication to finding her father promises that there will be an enjoyable future for readers in this new series."
—*Kings River Life Magazine*

continued . . .

"I am always excited when I find a new book by Kylie Logan. To not only find a new book but a new series is heaven. She draws you right into the story and you can't help but read the book to the very end . . . This is a fun, fast-paced read . . . If you like your mystery hot and spicy then you should be reading *Chili con Carnage*."
—MyShelf.com

"The mystery aspect of the novel was well-thought-out and planned. Maxie is a sort of no-nonsense character and her investigation proves that . . . I'm looking forward to the next book in the series as much for the family drama as I am for the mystery . . . A great first effort!"
—Debbie's Book Bag

"As the first in a series, this is a solid mystery, introducing readers to an interesting setting and a unique cast of characters."
—CA Reviews

Berkley Prime Crime titles by Kylie Logan

Button Box Mysteries

BUTTON HOLED
HOT BUTTON
PANIC BUTTON
BUTTONED UP

League of Literary Ladies Mysteries

MAYHEM AT THE ORIENT EXPRESS
A TALE OF TWO BIDDIES
THE LEGEND OF SLEEPY HARLOW

Chili Cook-off Mysteries

CHILI CON CARNAGE
DEATH BY DEVIL'S BREATH
REVENGE OF THE CHILI QUEENS

Revenge of the Chili
Queens
33305234097388
4am   01/28/16

REVENGE OF THE CHILI QUEENS

KYLIE LOGAN

BERKLEY PRIME CRIME, NEW YORK

BERKLEY PRIME CRIME

An imprint of Penguin Random House LLC
375 Hudson Street, New York, New York 10014

REVENGE OF THE CHILI QUEENS

A Berkley Prime Crime Book / published by arrangement with Connie Laux

Copyright © 2015 Connie Laux.
Penguin supports copyright. Copyright fuels creativity, encourages diverse voices,
promotes free speech, and creates a vibrant culture. Thank you for buying an authorized
edition of this book and for complying with copyright laws by not reproducing, scanning, or
distributing any part of it in any form without permission. You are supporting writers and
allowing Penguin to continue to publish books for every reader.

BERKLEY® PRIME CRIME and the PRIME CRIME design are trademarks
of Penguin Random House LLC.
For more information, visit penguin.com.

ISBN: 978-0-425-26244-3

PUBLISHING HISTORY
Berkley Prime Crime mass-market edition / August 2015

PRINTED IN THE UNITED STATES OF AMERICA

10 9 8 7 6 5 4 3 2 1

Cover illustration by Miles Hyman.
Cover design by Diana Kolsky.
Logo design by © Paseven/Shutterstock.
Interior text design by Laura K. Corless.

This is a work of fiction. Names, characters, places, and incidents either are the product of
the author's imagination or are used fictitiously, and any resemblance to actual persons,
living or dead, business establishments, events, or locales is entirely coincidental.

PUBLISHER'S NOTE: The recipes contained in this book are to be followed exactly
as written. The publisher is not responsible for your specific health or allergy needs
that may require medical supervision. The publisher is not responsible for any adverse
reactions to the recipes contained in this book.

If you purchased this book without a cover, you should be aware that this book is stolen
property. It was reported as "unsold and destroyed" to the publisher, and neither the author
nor the publisher has received any payment for this "stripped book."

Penguin
Random
House

Oscar and Ernie have already had a book dedicated to them so this one is for Casey!

Acknowledgments

I am one lucky author.

Each year, I get to spend an entire week with my brainstorming group. In the fall of 2013 we spent that week in beautiful Chautauqua, New York. Among the trees quickly morphing into gorgeous shades of red and bronze, the four of us took long walks, shared meals . . . and talked. We talked and talked and talked. In our brainstorming group, each member has two sessions during the week in which to discuss any aspect of her current work in progress or some future planned book. Sometimes we come with full-fledged ideas that just need some fleshing out. Other times, we come to the table with problems with characterization, or questions about plot. In my case that fall, I'd started writing *Revenge of the Chili Queens* and had a few chapters done, but I was at a loss for what else was going to happen in the rest of the book.

Brainstormers to the rescue! We talked out my plot and what had happened in the two previous books in the Chili Cook-Off series. We made notes and threw out possibilities and finally, we made a trip to the store, bought a poster board and a pack of sticky notes and got to work, writing down scene ideas and plopping them into what looked to me like an endless amount of empty chapters. It didn't take us long before we had the skeleton of the story and after that, the details just naturally fell into place.

Thank you, brainstormers Shelley Costa, Serena Miller, and Emilie Richards. You saved my chili on this one!

I'd also like to thank my family, especially David, who was left at home that brainstorming week with a new-to-us cat and a dog we'd just taken in to foster. I'm happy to report that everyone made it through the week in one piece!

As always, my thanks to the folks at Berkley Prime Crime and to Northeast Ohio Sisters in Crime, a great group of sisters and misters who are always supportive and enthusiastic.

CHAPTER 1

They say there is nothing hotter than Texas in July.

They are not only dead wrong, but that collective *they* owes me an apology, a clean blouse—since my white cotton peasant shirt embroidered with bright flowers was already wringing wet—and a tall, icy margarita.

Those perfect-haired, big-smile, smooth-talking weather forecasters on TV didn't offer much consolation. They said the record high temperature for San Antonio in October was one hundred degrees, and that it looked like over the next few days, that record would be broken.

By the way, that record was set way back in 1938.

Didn't it figure.

See, 1938 or thereabouts was exactly what we were trying to recreate there on the plaza outside the famous Alamo.

The year 1938, and the reign of the San Antonio Chili Queens.

"Are you just going to just stand there, or do you plan on doing some work tonight?"

My half sister, Sylvia, zipped by and tossed the comment at me, dragging me out of dreams of the AC back in the RV we used to travel the country with the Chili Showdown, the event that wandered from town to town all over America, hosting chili cook-off contests and showcasing chili in all its glory, as well as chili fixins and all the must-haves that go along with a good bowl of chili, stuff like beans and sauces. Too bad she was carrying a head-high stack of plastic bowls and she couldn't see the look I shot her way in return.

Work?

In this heat?

The words I grumbled are best left unreported.

But never let it be said that Maxie Pierce isn't one to pitch in. Especially when that pitching in meant reenacting the role of one of the city's famous Chili Queens, those wonderful women who were part of a tradition here in San Antonio for more than one hundred years. The Chili Queens cooked pots of steaming chili in their homes, then, once the sun went down, carted them to plazas around the city to feed the customers who couldn't get enough of the bowls of spicy goodness. For all those years, the Chili Queens were at the center of San Antonio nightlife. Along with them, the plazas filled with diners and musicians, with talk and singing and music that continued into the wee hours of the morning.

Of course I would work. But not because Sylvia asked me to.

Chili, see, is in my blood. Just like it's in the blood of my dad, Texas Jack Pierce, a man who's been missing for a few months and whose place Sylvia and I had taken behind the counter of the Hot-Cha Chili Seasoning Palace where he sold dried peppers and spices and chili mixes that were famous from one end of the country to the other. So it's only natural, even though I'm not from San Antonio and nowhere near old enough to have ever had contact with any one of the original Chili Queens, that I definitely feel a connection.

I bet there were plenty of nights they melted in the Texas heat, too.

I lifted the hem of my flowing black skirt and headed into the nearby tent where Sylvia and I would be serving chili to the crowds of people gathered that night for a charity event.

Read with the Chili Queens.

That's what they were calling it, and this night—a Monday—the event was raising money for a local literacy center. On Tuesday, we'd be there with a bunch of warm-and-fuzzy types collecting money for an animal shelter; on Wednesday, the food bank people; and on and on through the week. The whole celebration ended on Sunday evening with a beauty pageant back at the Chili Showdown at the fairgrounds.

Charities aside and beauty queens ignored, I had a proud tradition to uphold.

Chili. It's my life. And I do everything I can to promote it in all its wonderful, glorious, spicy-good incarnations!

The thought firmly in mind, I sidestepped a stack of

folding chairs that still needed to be set up around the tables under the tent designated for the Palace, and headed over to where Sylvia—dressed the way I doubt any real Chili Queen ever would be, in a flowered sundress in shades of pink and purple—was doing a last-minute check of our prep area.

"Chili. Spoons. Bowls. Napkins." Just as I walked up, her jaw dropped and her baby blues bulged. "Napkins. There are no napkins. Where are the napkins?"

Rather than tell her not to worry (because Sylvia was going to worry no matter what; she's just that sort of high-strung), I spun around and headed over to where we'd stacked the supplies we'd brought over to Alamo Plaza that afternoon.

"Napkins," I mumbled to myself, and dug through a mountain of packing boxes in search of them. I found what I was looking for and gathered pack after pack of napkins into my arms.

"Need help?"

At the sound of the voice, I stood and found myself looking up into a pair of luscious dark eyes, a cleft chin, and a smile that lit up the quickly gathering twilight.

"Help?" I am not easily upended by good-looking guys. It must have been the heat that caused my voice to crack. "I've got it. Really." As if it would prove my statement, I hugged the packs of paper napkins closer to my chest. "Thanks."

The man turned his smile up a notch and added a wink to go with it. While he was at it, he strummed his right hand over the strings of the guitar looped around his shoulders. "No problem, senorita." He made me a small bow that was corny and gallant all at the same time. "I'm at your service."

I gave him a quick once-over, but it didn't take even that long for me to realize he was one of the entertainers who'd been hired by Tumbleweed Ballew, the administrative power behind the Showdown, to add a bit of authenticity to the evening. He fit the part. Tall, and with hair the color of the crows I'd seen around the city. "You're . . . ?"

"Glad I stopped over." Another of his smiles sizzled in my direction. "You're Maxie, right?"

"You know me?"

"I've heard about you. But aren't you supposed to be . . ." I'd given him a quick enough once-over, but when he looked me up and down, he took his time. "I was expecting the chili costume," he said. "From what I've heard, it's really something, and you . . ." Another once-over made heat rush into my cheeks. "You're something in that costume."

I wasn't about to deny it.

"I'll wear the Chili Chick costume at the Showdown over at the fairgrounds every day this week," I told him. "But in the evenings when we're here as part of the fundraisers, we're supposed to dress like the old Chili Queens. This outfit . . ." I put a hand on my long, black skirt. "It fits with the whole Chili Queen thing. A giant red chili costume, fishnet stockings, and stilettos? They don't exactly go with the re-creation."

"Maybe not, but . . ." He let go a long whistle. "It sure is something I'd like to see."

"So stop at the Showdown." Believe me, I wasn't being

forward. The whole point of me wearing the Chili Chick costume and dancing outside the Palace was to draw in customers. And this guy would be a customer, right?

"I'll be there," he promised. "But only if you've got plenty of spice."

He was talking about chili and the dried peppers we sold at the Palace, but the way his eyes sparked gave his words a certain little spicy kick of their own.

I told myself to keep my mind on peppers. "Abedul peppers to zia pueblo peppers," I said.

"And selling pepper and spices, business is good?"

"We're smokin' hot!"

Another long look and he grinned. "I have no doubt of that. So . . ." Another strum of the guitar strings and he stepped away. "I'll stop in at the Showdown this week to meet the Chili Chick, and later when I have a chance, I'll come back here and get a sample of the chili you and your sister are handing out. But only if your chili is good."

Who was I to miss an opening as perfect as that?

Heat flickered in my smile. "My chili is very good."

His eyes gleamed. "I bet it is. I'll be back later for some," he said, and he strummed the guitar again and walked away.

"Chatting? You're chatting?"

Sylvia's high-pitched question came from right behind me and made me jump.

"You were supposed to be getting the napkins." She grabbed them out of my arms.

"I was doing a little PR," I told her. "Drumming up business."

"With the entertainers. Who are working here just like we're working here. So you know he didn't pay his one hundred dollars for the ticket to get into the event and sample all the different chili, and how much you want to bet he's not going to leave an extra donation even if he does come back here to our tent?"

I peered around the plaza, and in the glow of the thousands of twinkling white lights that had been strung between the tents of the fifteen organizations that were handing out chili in honor of the Queens, I saw the guitar player stroll over to the tent directly across from ours and accept a bowl of chili from a hot young cutie standing near the entrance. The banner over their heads announced that it belonged to Consolidated Chili Corp.

Call it gut reaction—my eyes narrowed, my mouth pulled into a frown.

"Get over it!" This from Sylvia, and this time, she wasn't talking about tall, dark, and luscious Mr. Hot Guitar Player. If I ever needed any proof that she was not worthy of working at the Hot-Cha Chili Seasoning Palace (I didn't), she provided it when she looked where I was looking and poked me in the ribs. "They're a huge corporation and they give people what they want."

"Mass-produced canned chili?" The very thought made me shudder. "They don't belong at an event dedicated to the memory of the Chili Queens."

"I heard they donated a bundle to be part of the week's festivities. You know, for the publicity," Sylvia informed me. "And look . . ." She wedged the stack of napkins under her chin so that she could retrieve something from the big square pocket on the front of her sundress. "They're handing out the cutest stuff. You know, as a way to advertise the big Miss Consolidated Chili pageant that will happen over at the Showdown on Sunday." She dangled a bottle opener in front of my eyes.

It took me a moment to focus and see that the bottle opener had *Consolidated Chili* written on it in red letters.

"And coasters," Sylvia added, pulling one of those out of her pocket, too. It was made of heavy cardboard and featured a picture on it that I—along with millions of other people—instantly recognized thanks to the commercials on TV. A can of Consolidated Chili's chili.

"Tacky," I said. "And not at all in keeping with the spirit of the evening."

"Maybe not, but it's plenty clever," Sylvia insisted. "So's their marketing strategy. You're dressed as a Chili Queen. There are a couple descendants of the real Chili Queens over there." She couldn't exactly point, since she had all those napkins in her arms, but she looked across the plaza at another of the tents. "There's even a tent being run by a couple drag queens."

This, I thought, was hilarious, but Sylvia just rolled her eyes.

"None of that was good enough for the Consolidated folks. They've got beauty queens handing out their chili samples. Real, honest-to-goodness beauty queens. I saw Miss Texas Spice. And Miss Chili's Cookin'. Chili's Cookin', isn't that cute? It's one of the names of the chilies they sell."

"Trashy and flashy." I ought to know, since I'd been

called the same things myself a time or two. I didn't take it personally. At least not when the criticisms were aimed my way. I did take it personally when some big megacorporation stepped in and started messing with tradition and taste and everything else that's near and dear to the heart of every true chili lover.

"They even have some bigwig here tonight overseeing the whole thing," Sylvia added, standing on tiptoe so that she could crane her neck and get another look at the Consolidated tent over the heads of the workers who scurried around. "I didn't see him, but I sure saw his limo. Big and black and shiny with a Tri-C license plate. Tri-C, get it? Consolidated Chili Corp. A big, shiny limo sure beats our RV and our food truck all to heck!" Sylvia gave an unladylike snort. "All these years, Jack has been wasting his time with the Showdown when he should have been concentrating on building a bigger business. Look what it did for those Consolidated Chili folks! And look . . ." In her megacorporation frenzy, she dropped the plastic-wrapped bundles of napkins so she could point. A tall man in a dark suit had just entered the Consolidated Chili Corp tent, and even though I couldn't see his face, I could tell by the set of his shoulders and the angle of his white ten-gallon hat that he was someone to be reckoned with. Then again, the way the Consolidated Chili people started fawning and gawking and milling around him pretty much told me that, too.

I folded my arms over my chest when I raised my chin and leveled her with a look. "They can act like big shots all they want. And they can pretend they're upholding some long Texas tradition, but anybody who knows anything about chili knows the truth. There's nothing better in the world than honest-to-goodness chili and nothing better than real people making it, not machines and cans and conglomerates." My lips puckered at the thought. "And there's nothing better than the Showdown, Sylvia, don't you forget that. Jack was doing what Jack loved to do. What he still . . ." Like I often did, I teared up thinking about Jack. Over the last couple months, I'd tried my best to find out what happened to my dad, but so far, I'd had no luck.

I bit my lower lip to control myself before I said, "There's nothing better than traveling with our friends and fellow vendors. Nothing better than meeting chili lovers and spreading the word about chili."

"Whatever!" Sylvia rolled her eyes. "You keep telling yourself that, Maxie. Me, I'll keep dreaming of that wonderful someday when I work for some real company like that Consolidated Chili." Thinking, she cocked her head. "They must need PR people, right? I've got plenty of experience as a food writer. And they must need admin types, too. Obviously, we wouldn't have done as well as we have with the Palace these last couple months if it wasn't for me. You have no head for business."

"You have no head for business." Yes, it was juvenile of me to repeat her criticism in a singsongy voice, but hey, Sylvia and I had been fighting all our lives, and maybe on some ethereal plane, even before. See, my mother had won Jack's heart when he was still married to Sylvia's mother. Sylvia had spent her life convinced that it was my fault.

His back was still to me as I watched the man in the dark

suit and the big hat make his way through the crowd in the Consolidated Chili tent, and the way everyone bowed and scraped, I was surprised I didn't see anybody kiss his ring. "You think real business is about some stuffy executive everyone sucks up to? That a real company is all about beauty queens and little bottle openers?" The irony of my questions was lost on Sylvia. Which is odd, since I'm the one who would normally find a bottle opener plenty useful, and she's the one who usually thinks things like that are vulgar. Then again, I guess vulgar takes on a whole new meaning when it's being orchestrated by some mega-rich corporation.

"I think real business is all about making connections with people," I told my half sister.

The nod she gave me in return was filled with pity. "Like the connection you were trying to make with that guitar player? I see disaster ahead. Again. You're always picking the wrong kinds of guys."

"And you're so good at picking the right ones? Like the one who got killed back in Taos." Oh, there was a story there, all right, and it wasn't a pretty one, since Roberto (whose name wasn't really Roberto and who wasn't really a Showdown roadie like we all thought he was and who, not so incidentally, turned up dead) was once engaged to my oh-so-perfect half sister. "Do me a favor and keep your advice to yourself," I told her.

Her shoulders went rigid. So did that simpering little smile that was second nature to her, even when she was saying something hurtful and cruel. Which was a lot of the time.

"All right. If that's the way you want it. But oh, Maxie, when will you ever learn?"

Good thing Sylvia gathered up those packages of napkins and walked away. Otherwise, I would have had to point out that I had already learned. I'd learned from Edik, the guy back in Chicago who emptied my bank account and broke what I have of a heart. Just like I had learned from a string of losers before him.

Speaking of guys, Nick Falcone, a former LA cop and now the Showdown's head of security, picked that moment to stroll over to the Consolidated Chili tent. Yeah, Nick was delectable. And as cuddly as a cactus.

I'd bet anything he was after one of those little bottle openers.

Or one of those perky beauty queens.

I didn't really care, right? I mean ever since Edik, I'd sworn off relationships.

Tell that to the sour thoughts that pounded through my head while I set up folding chairs, covered tables with plastic tablecloths, and—while Sylvia wasn't looking—added some dried Aji Amarillo peppers and ground pasillas to the too-bland-for-me pots of chili she'd made for tonight's event.

By the time I was done, the sun had set and the fundraising event had officially opened to the public.

We were plenty busy, and for that, I was grateful. Aside from the fact that the donations guests left in the big pottery-ware bowl we had near our serving station were helping to raise money for a good cause, I was talking up the Palace and people were learning about the Showdown. Lots of them said they'd come to the fairgrounds over the next few days to buy spices.

I knew I could thank the Aji Amarillos and the pasillas for that.

"Whoo heee!" Wiping a big red bandana across his forehead, Tumbleweed Ballew plodded into our tent and helped himself to a bowl of our chili. He gave me a wink. "Hotter than a Lone Star barbeque tonight! But that's not going to keep me from trying your chili. I've tried every single one of them."

"Even Consolidated's?" I asked him.

Tumbleweed has big ears and heavy jowls. He frowned and shook his head, and his jowls flapped. "Canned!" The way he harrumphed said it all. "But I'll tell you what, those ladies from the Women's League, their chili ain't half bad." He glanced beyond the Consolidated Chili tent to another setup where the lights seemed brighter than ours and the line for chili looked longer. And better dressed.

"No matter," he said with a twitch of his shoulders. "I know yours will be the best, Maxie, honey." Tumbleweed downed a spoonful, smiled, and nodded. "Sylvia didn't have nothing to do with this bowl of goodness!"

"She had plenty to do with it," I said, but only because Sylvia was within earshot and because I'd tell Tumbleweed the truth later. Tumbleweed and Ruth Ann, his missus, were the heart and soul of the Showdown. They scheduled our stops, they lined up city permits, they did all our advertising. All the years I traveled the Showdown circuit with Jack when I was a kid, Tumbleweed and Ruth Ann were the people I thought of as the ideal family. Even back then, I figured they'd been married for longer than I'd been alive, and since they didn't have any kids of their own, they took me and Sylvia under their wings. Or at least they tried. Sylvia being Sylvia, she never got close to anyone who traveled with the Showdown, and me, I was usually too busy getting into trouble to listen to much of what Tumbleweed and Ruth Ann had to say.

Which didn't mean I didn't adore both of them to pieces.

Smiling, I glanced around at the twinkling lights and listened to the smooth cascade of flamenco guitar that came from somewhere over near the Consolidated Chili tent. I thought of Mr. Hot Guitar Player, but there was no sign of him over there, just another of the entertainers who'd stopped to play and smiled broadly when the little clutch of people around him applauded. "It must have been something, huh?"

Tumbleweed didn't have to ask what I was talking about. Like I said, we'd known each other a long time. "It was a wonderful tradition. The Chili Queens were the center of San Antonio social life. At least until the late 1930s when the city shut them down. Said they were a health risk. Imagine that! Imagine giving up a scene like this that played out at plazas all over town. People gathered every evening to eat and laugh and talk. You don't get that kind of community now and it's a shame, ain't it? These days, it's all about how fast you can do something, not how well you can do it. It's all about texting and e-mailing. There aren't enough connections between people. Look around!" We both did, drinking in the wonderful atmosphere along with a huge helping of humidity. "Just think of how the world would be a better place. You know, if we all got out every evening and talked to our neighbors and got to know one another and—"

As sweet as it all was, Tumbleweed never got a chance to finish what he was going to say. That's because we heard a woman scream from across the plaza. That scream was followed by another voice—also a woman's—whose pinched falsetto could have shattered glass.

"She's crazy. I told you the gringo was crazy! This crazy woman, you see what she is trying to do. She is trying to kill me!"

CHAPTER 2

Like I was going to miss out on something as juicy as a death threat in the middle of a charity event?

I gave Sylvia a quick "I'll be right back," and just like a whole bunch of other people who'd been nearby and heard the carrying-on, I raced across the plaza to see what was up.

I found the center of the commotion not far from the main entrance to *Read with the Chili Queens*.

Read with them?

It looked to me like the two Chili Queens who stood toe-to-toe just inside the entrance to one of the tents were more interested in duking it out. Oh yeah, they had fire in their eyes. And chili ladles coated with tomatoes and spices and all kinds of greasy goodness in their hands.

The woman on my left was short and husky. Her silver

hair was pulled back and tucked into a neat bun, and her beefy arms were slick with sweat that sparkled like sequins when the overhead lights twinkled. She wore a long black skirt, like mine, and a red shirt. Both were covered by the white apron looped around her neck.

The woman who stood opposite her was taller by a head, with salt-and-pepper hair cut stylishly short and shaggy and a chin as pointed as the look she gave the other woman. She wore a white dress like a nurse might wear, with an apron printed with blue and red flowers over it.

"I'm crazy? Me?" Like the chili that dribbled from the ladle in her hand, the taller woman's words dripped malice. So did the look she tossed at the other woman. "You're the one who—"

"Loco! I told you! I told you she was nuts!" As if to gather support, the shorter woman took a moment to glance at the gathering crowd. When she stepped back and pointed her chili ladle at the other woman, the taller woman flinched, squinted, and stepped back, too. She bent her elbow and cradled the long handle of her ladle in one hand.

Across from her, the shorter woman mirrored her stance.

I held my breath and waited for someone to shout out *En garde!*

Before anybody could, Nick Falcone showed up. Didn't it figure? The guy who fuels my fantasies also ruins all the fun.

Nick stepped between the two women, and I had to give him credit; while the rest of us were waiting there, tense and perspiring and anxious to see who would twitch her ladle first and fling the first splats of chili, Nick was his usual cool-as-a-cucumber self. Navy suit (in this heat, was the guy crazy?), starched white shirt, killer tie in swirls of green and a blue that (not coincidentally, I'd bet) matched his out-of-this-world eyes. His expression was as suave as his outfit, like he was chatting up these two adversaries at a cocktail party instead of diffusing what looked like it might turn into a rip-roaring chili smackdown.

"Ladies." Nick nodded toward one woman, then the other, and believe me, I think he knew exactly what he was doing when he added one of his signature hotter-than-a-ghost-pepper smiles. Hey, when you've got that kind of talent, you've got to work it. "What seems to be the problem?"

"Problem?" the short woman blurted out. "Martha, she don't know the meaning of the word *problem*."

"Shaking in my shoes over here, Rosa," the taller woman snapped, and as if to prove it, she gave her shoulders an exaggerated wiggle. "As always, you scare me to death!"

"I should." Rosa's dark eyes spit fire. When she stepped forward, so did Martha, and Nick held both his arms out to his sides to keep the women from getting any closer to each other. Or maybe he was just trying to make sure his suit didn't get any chili on it.

He looked at the crowd in that steely sort of way cops (and, apparently, former cops) always do. "Excitement's over, folks. Time to head back to the party."

It wasn't a request.

And nobody was about to argue.

One by one, the partygoers drifted away to the other tents.

Except for the one who wasn't about to cave. Or miss one second of the excitement.

I think the moment Nick let go a breath that was all about praying for patience was just a heartbeat after he realized that I was still hanging around.

"You want to tell me what you're doing here?" he asked me.

My shrug should have said it all, but in case he missed it, I told him. "I figured you might need my help."

His smile was tight and not the least bit friendly.

Which was the only reason I was forced to remind him, "You know, the way you needed my help back in Taos when that Showdown roadie was killed. Or like back in Vegas when we were having the Devil's Breath chili contest and—"

"I probably don't need your help this time," Nick said.

"But you might." As if to prove it, I stepped into the tent where Rosa and Martha were still shooting death ray looks at each other. "If this has something to do with chili, let's face it, Nick, I'm probably the only one who can help. So ladies . . ." I glanced from Rosa to Martha and back again to Rosa. "What's shaking?"

Nick's grumble echoed back at us from the walls of the Alamo just beyond the perimeter of this particular tent. Even though I'm not much for history and don't know the exact story—I mean, not all the facts and all the details and the whole blow-by-blow the way a lot of people I'd already met in San Antonio did—I still recognized the iconic building made of creamy-colored stone. It was smaller than it looked in the pictures I'd seen online, and spookier looking, too. But then, the way I heard it, the famous battle that happened here in 1836 lasted thirteen days and killed something like eight hundred people.

Spooky went with the territory.

While I was studying the building with its arched facade and distinctive columns on either side of the main doorway, Nick was concentrating on the matter at hand.

"You're causing a commotion." I didn't think he could possibly be referring to me, so I let him keep talking. "Someone want to tell me what's going on?"

"This gringo here," Rosa began.

"She thinks she's God's gift," Martha spat out.

And Nick held up both his hands again.

"One at a time. Or we're never going to get anywhere. I was over there," he said, "at the Consolidated Chili tent, and—"

"You're kidding me, right?" Disgusted, I threw my hands in the air. "Don't you know what those people are? Who they are? Purveyors of cheap chili. Cheap canned chili. You call that authentic? You call that in keeping with the traditions of the San Antonio Chili Queens?"

"This little girl, she's right," Rosa said, and just like I did, she shot a look back toward the tent. Even as we spoke, a woman with very big blond hair in a very short and tight black dress, a very sparkly tiara, and a banner across her chest was handing out bottle openers and chili samples to everyone who walked by—including, I noticed, the hunky guitar player I'd met earlier. Rosa's top lip curled and left a smudge of ruby red lipstick on her teeth. "They have no business here."

"They shouldn't even be allowed in this sacred place," Martha said, and for one moment, I actually thought the two women had found common ground and could put their differences aside.

That is, until Martha added, "Not this close to the Alamo where my ancestors—"

"Oh, here we go again!" Rosa groaned. "Now she's going to make us listen to the list. Davy Crockett and Jim Bowie and William Travis. Yeah, yeah. Whatever! If I hear her say one more word about—"

"Oh, like we should listen to you?" Martha screeched. "What would you . . ." She pointed her chili ladle at Rosa. "What would you tell us about, Rosa? Your ancestors? The ones who fought for Santa Anna?"

"At least my ancestors lived to tell their story. And while they were at it, they taught their families the right way to make chili, too. That's why my great-grandmother was the greatest of the Chili Queens."

"Ha!" This from Martha, and I can't say exactly what high dudgeon is, but I'd heard the phrase and I knew it had something to do with being really pissed, and if ever there was a dudgeon that was high, it was Martha's. "My great-grandmother, she knew how to make chili. She was the greatest of the Chili Queens. Everybody knows that."

"Everybody knows that each and every Chili Queen had her own secret recipe and her own special way of serving her chili." I refused to get caught up in the squabble, so I kept my voice light and airy when I sailed past Nick. While I was at it, I gave him a look that pretty much told him, *See, if it's about chili, I can handle it.* "I think it's cool that you're both related to real Chili Queens. It's an honor to meet you. Both of you."

Martha's bony shoulders shot back.

Rosa lifted both her chins.

"I can't wait to try your chilies," I said, because really, in case Nick didn't notice, since the subject of chili came up, they'd both lowered those lethal ladles and were actually looking a little less like they were going to kill each other. "As a matter of fact, I'm going to have some right now. Whose tent is this? Which one will I be trying first?"

Rosa sniffed.

Martha snorted.

"Whose tent?" Rosa hissed. "They're actually making us share a tent. Share? With this gringo?"

"At least I know my way around a kitchen," Martha shot back. "My restaurant is the best place in town for chili. I use my great-grandmother's authentic recipe," she added as an aside that interested me no end. I knew it meant nothing to Nick. Then again, when it comes to chili, he's something of a Philistine. "We use the freshest ingredients, and we make the best chili in the world."

I was pretty sure this wasn't true, since my dad made the world's best chili and mine ran a close second. Not to worry, I knew this wasn't the moment to point this out.

Rosa, however, did not have the same diplomatic savvy as me. She rolled her eyes. "You might know your way around a kitchen if you weren't so busy sitting up front at the hostess station and drinking palomas all day long," she told Martha. "Now my restaurant . . ." She swung around to include me and Nick in her intense gaze. "You come to

Rosa's and you'll have authentic chili. Just like the Chili Queens used to make. The *real* Chili Queens," she added, and she wasn't looking at me when she emphasized that *real*.

Martha's mouth puckered.

Rosa's eyes spit fire.

It was Nick's turn to groan.

"I'm having chili." Aside from the fact that I knew it was the best way to lighten the atmosphere, I really did want to try the chili, so I breezed past everybody and over to where pots of chili simmered away. Without waiting to be invited, I grabbed a ladle, filled a bowl, and plunked down in the nearest chair.

We may not be as snooty as so many wine lovers, but chili tasters have their rituals, too. I spooned up a nice, big scoop of chili, closed my eyes, and breathed in deep.

"Comino seeds," I purred, and don't think I didn't notice that both Rosa and Martha smiled like those beauty queens over at the Consolidated Chili tent. I called it *comino*, not *cumin*. Right away, they knew I wasn't a poser.

"And serrano peppers," I added. When they're ripe, serranos are red, and hotter than jalapeños. "And ancho," I said, just so Martha and Rosa would know I wasn't just some pretty face who didn't know what she was talking about when it came to chili and peppers and the way tastes and spiciness and textures combine to create a really great chili. Ancho peppers are dried poblanos, and I knew they'd give this chili a subtle sweet smokiness.

I took a bite and nodded; I was right. While I was at it, I smiled at the two women, who were looking a little less angry and a lot more proud of their part in the tradition that is chili. "Beef and pork. And suet. Oh, ladies!" I was relieved when they smiled back. "If this is what real Chili Queens chili tasted like, it's no wonder the plazas were full of patrons every night. It's heavenly."

Martha smirked. "It's my great-grandmother's recipe."

Rosa looked as if she'd bit into a lemon. "Which she probably stole from my great-grandmother."

And guess what, I didn't want to hear any of it, not when I was mid-bowl of a mighty fine chili. Just as they started in on each other again, I hightailed it out of their tent and left Nick to handle these two warring Queens.

And yes, I took my bowl of chili with me.

I finished it right before I got over to the Consolidated Chili tent, but by then, Mr. Hot Guitar Player was nowhere in sight. That guy in the ten-gallon hat was, though. I got just a glimpse of his backside as he slipped into the shadows at the back of the tent.

I turned to head the other way, and Miss Hotter than a Chili Pepper (really, were they kidding, there's a beauty queen title that dumb?) offered a cute little bottle opener. Big points for me. I managed a smile when I told her a polite "No, thank you."

I have my standards, after all.

Eager to get away from the land of canned chili, I circled around the Consolidated Chili tent and over into our tent, where I saw Sylvia dishing out chili and looking just the slightest bit harried.

Aside from having standards, I also have a conscience, even if it's darned inconvenient at times.

I was all set to go and help Sylvia until something across the way caught my eye.

It was Mr. Hot Guitar Player, and he was deep in conversation with one of the women from another tent, a woman who reminded me of a cayenne pepper—long and skinny and hot.

Cascades of red hair. Tasteful pearls. Manicure; expensive dress and shoes; glowing, polished complexion that showed she had a good aesthetician and visited her often.

I wasn't surprised when I glanced to the sign above the entrance to the tent and saw that it belonged to the San Antonio Women's League.

Oh yeah, this lady was all about style, class, and money.

She was also as high in her dudgeon as Martha and Rosa had ever been.

Only in a much more calm and dignified way.

When she crossed her arms over her chest and the goldenrod-colored sleeveless dress she wore, two spots of color erupted across her high cheekbones.

Mr. Hot Guitar Player said something to her, but from this distance—damn!—I couldn't make out a word.

Whatever he said, she didn't like it. Her lips pinched. The color drained from her cheeks. She put a hand on Mr. Hot Guitar Player's arm, but he shrugged her off.

What they were talking about was none of my business, but hey, that had never stopped me before. I sidestepped my way through the crowd, hoping I might be able to catch at least some of the conversation.

I actually might have succeeded if the local celebrities

who hang out at all these sorts of functions didn't pick that exact moment to show up. A hum went through the crowd, and a whole bunch of people surged toward the entrance when a sleek white limo pulled up. I recognized the basketball player who got out first. He was hard to miss, since he was head-and-shoulders taller than everyone else around him. He was followed by a woman, who was followed by a camera crew from a local station, and there was a big guy bringing up the rear. His toothpaste smile told me he was a politician.

What with the crowd and all, I lost sight of Mr. Hot Guitar Player, and by the time the celebrities went over to the Consolidated Chili tent (I gritted my teeth) and my path was clear again, he was nowhere to be seen and the lady in the golden dress had moved over to the other side of the tent to hand out bowls of chili.

"Nice dress, but she needs more bling."

I glanced to my side and the woman who towered over me, and since I'd seen her around the tent being run by the drag queens, I guess that wasn't a surprise. She looked glorious in fawn-colored gaucho pants, a balloon-sleeved blouse, and a vest studded with colorful beading.

She was looking where I was looking, and I was looking at the woman in the gold dress.

"Who is she?" I asked.

"Evelyn, Eleanor, Edith. Something like that." She twitched wide shoulders and batted eyelashes that were long and thick and nothing like what my eyelashes ever looked like. "And I'm Ginger." She extended a hand and we shook. "I hear when you're at the Showdown, you're an adorable chili pepper. Teddi and I . . ." She looked over her shoulder back toward her tent where another woman—this one in a pencil-thin black skirt and a frilly red top with a plunging neckline—was greeting customers and handing out chili. "Teddi and I will be sure to stop in. Maybe we'll see that good-looking guitar player there?"

I didn't have to ask Ginger how she knew. I guess the way I scanned the crowd told her I was looking for some-one. And the way I'd watched Mr. Hot Guitar Player with Evelyn/Eleanor/Edith said something, too.

"He said he'd drop by later for chili," I told Ginger.

"Then, sweetie, you'd better get back over to your tent." She offered me a glittering, toothy smile. "You don't want to miss him!"

She was right, and I took her advice. I got back over to our tent just in time to help Sylvia handle a new rush of chili lovers who (by the way) all agreed that our chili had just the right combination of sweetness and punch.

"Kind of like us," I told Sylvia.

She pretended not to get it.

The rest of the night went by in a swirl of chili, chatter, and mariachi music. None of which, I noticed, was provided by Mr. Hot Guitar Player. In fact, I didn't see him again until just a few minutes before the event was set to end.

He didn't show up looking for chili, though.

And he wasn't there to connect with me, either.

When he raced up to where I was putting the last of our chili into containers that we'd take back to the RV and use the next day, his face was red and he was breath-ing hard.

"Hey!" I tried for casual, but that was a little hard seeing as how his mouth was hanging open as he pressed a hand to his heart. "What's wrong?"

"It's Senora Loca!" As if even he couldn't believe whatever it was that had just happened to him, he shook his head. "I've got to talk to . . ." His cheeks pasty and a ribbon of sweat on his forehead, he looked around. "Is there security anywhere nearby?"

"Well . . ." I scanned the crowd. "Somewhere."

I guess he thought he didn't have my complete attention, because Mr. Hot Guitar Player grabbed my hand and held on tight. He felt like a wet fish. A trembling wet fish. "Well, I need to find someone, and fast."

I can be excused for being a little off my game. It was late, and still hotter than blue blazes. Mr. Hot Guitar Player had caught me flat-footed. I stammered, "I saw him . . ." and waved in some vague direction that was sort of kind of back toward Martha and Rosa's tent.

Apparently, Mr. Hot Guitar Player was looking for something a little more definitive than that.

The next second, I caught sight of Nick and pointed.

"There he is," I told Mr. Hot Guitar Player. "Nick Falcone. I'll call him over and—"

"Nick Falcone?" Like my hand was on fire, the guitarist dropped it and turned as pale as a ghost. That is, right before he spun on his heels and staggered away.

"Hey, you didn't try our . . ." I made an attempt to call out after him, but even before the words were out of my mouth, I knew it wasn't going to work. Whatever the problem was, the guitarist was too worried to care.

"Chili," I added, just for my own satisfaction. I got back to work and promised myself that as soon as I was done with what I was doing, I'd head out to see if he'd found Nick and what I could do to help.

Easier said than done when we were in full cleanup mode.

By the time a team of Showdown roadies showed up to help with tearing down and stowing our tables and chairs, there was no sign of either the guitarist or Nick, and I was way too tired to care if I ever saw either one of them again.

"What a night!" How Sylvia could possibly look as fresh as the proverbial daisy when I felt as if I'd been rinsed, wrung, and hung out to dry, I didn't know. She flopped into a chair and took a long gulp from a water bottle. "I can't believe we have to do it all again tomorrow. And for the animal-loving crowd." A shiver scooted across her slim shoulders. "I hope they're well behaved."

"As long as they're not lifting their legs on the potted flowers we should be okay."

She didn't laugh.

But then, I didn't expect her to.

Instead, I got a bottle of water, too, and glugged it down. It was so cold, it hurt my throat and froze my stomach. It was fabulous.

"You coming with us?" I asked Sylvia, rubbing a kink from my neck. "Ruth Ann and Tumbleweed and a bunch of us are going to the River Walk. You know, to check out San Antonio nightlife."

"Not a chance!" She stood and stepped out of the way of the roadie who came by with a big push broom. "I'm heading back to the RV, and if you're smart, you will, too. The Showdown opens at ten tomorrow, and then we have to do this again in the evening. Honestly, I don't know what Tumbleweed was thinking when he volunteered us for these charity events."

"He was thinking publicity," I told her. "Like we should always be thinking publicity. Like Jack always did."

I wouldn't exactly call the look I got a smile. It was more of a sneer. "Notice how he's not around to do it anymore," she said, and when she saw my shoulders shoot back and my hands curl into fists, she threw out her hands as a way of telling me not to go off half-cocked. But of course, it was already too late for that. "You know what I mean," she said. "He's gone on to other things. Better things. He's not here because—"

"No one knows why he's not here. That's why we have to keep looking for him."

"No signs of foul play." She repeated the words we'd heard from the cops back in Abilene where Jack was last seen. "You know as well as I do exactly what he's up to. He's off with some woman. Probably another one of his floozies."

Don't think I missed the not-so-subtle implication here. When Sylvia starts throwing around words like *floozy* (who talks like that, anyway?), it's her way of getting a dig in at my mother. Who, by the way, is anything but, and was head over heels in love with Jack. At least while it lasted.

Three cheers for me; I realized all this and didn't bite at Sylvia's bait.

"Going to the River Walk," I told her, with an *adios* sort of gesture over my shoulder that she might have interpreted another, less friendly way had the light been better and had she been paying more attention. I'd told Ruth Ann and Tumbleweed I'd meet them near the gigantic sculpture on the plaza that commemorated the men who died during the Alamo siege, and I headed that way, but I never got that far.

That's because a couple things happened to derail me.

For one thing, I was nearly run down by the big, black, and very shiny limo with Tri-C license plates that zipped by.

Once I steadied myself from jumping out of the way and my heartbeat slowed down, something that glinted in the glow of the twinkling lights from the Consolidated Chili tent caught my eye. I closed in on it and found that it was one of those little bottle openers, and though I had no intention of keeping it as a souvenir, I bent to pick it up so that the cleanup crew wouldn't have to.

There was a coaster a little way off, too, and I went to retrieve that along with another little bottle opener that was close by.

In fact, when I looked around, I saw that there was a trail of Consolidated Chili promotional handouts scattered down the path that led toward the porta-potties that had been set up for the event, and from there, around to the other side of the plaza. The glow of the twinkly lights didn't penetrate here, and I peered into the darkness lit only by the soft, ghostly light trained on the Alamo.

I guess that's why I wasn't sure I was seeing what I was seeing even when I saw it.

I froze in my tracks and peered into the darkness, letting my eyes adjust to the play of light and shadows.

And that's when I knew my eyes weren't playing tricks on me.

It was Mr. Hot Guitar Player, all right.

He was sitting butt to ground with his legs splayed out in front of him.

His guitar was smashed to smithereens, the pieces of painted wood on the ground all around him.

Except for the strings. Those were wrapped tight around his neck.

CHAPTER 3

Sylvia has Nick on speed dial.

In the past, just thinking about her cradling her phone in her hot little hands and his number stored somewhere in its little cyber brain has annoyed me no end, mostly because I've always speculated about why she'd need to call him— and fast—and wondered if she did call, if he'd pick up.

That night, though, I was glad for the speed dial. The way my hands were shaking, I never would have been able to use my phone and call Nick myself.

I did, however, insist on talking to him once I raced back to our tent and had Sylvia make the call. When Nick answered, I heard laughter in the background, the clink of glasses, rattling ice cubes, and blaring music. I'm no expert, but it sounded like a Broadway show tune.

There was no use telling him I was sorry to interrupt whatever he was doing, because it wouldn't have made any difference and he wouldn't believe me, anyway, so I cut to the chase.

"We've got another body."

After Taos and Las Vegas, he knew I wasn't joking. He told me to stay put, and he called the local cops. He timed it just right. By the time Nick got back to Alamo Plaza from wherever he'd been off to, the boys in blue were with him.

I led them to where I found the dead guitarist, and since nobody said I had to leave, I stepped back and watched two cops bend over the body while another couple set up a bank of generator-operated spotlights.

As much as I hate to admit it, there are times I wish I wasn't so darned curious about things like murder.

This was one of them.

If I hadn't been so intent on seeing what the cops were going to do and what they might find, I wouldn't have seen what the glaring spotlights revealed: Mr. Hot Guitar Player didn't look so hot anymore.

Those dark, luscious eyes of his bulged out of his head. His mouth was twisted open. But it was the look of his neck that would haunt my nightmares from now until forever. The strings of his broken guitar were twisted tight around it. They cut into his skin and left a thin, bloody necklace, as if someone had measured him for a new shirt and drawn out the circumference of his neck with a red Sharpie.

"Maxie."

When Nick called my name, I jumped and tore my gaze from the body and the blood and the broken guitar.

He motioned me over to where he was talking with a blonde wearing a dark suit.

"This is Detective Anita Gilkenny. She'd like to know how you knew the deceased."

Since my shrug didn't explain, I was forced to spell it out. "I didn't. He stopped over at our tent earlier this evening. He said he'd be back for chili. But he never showed. Not until—"

My words dissolved in a rush of memory.

The guitarist running up to me late in the evening and blurting out something about Senora Loca.

And security.

The guitarist had asked for security and had run the other way when he saw Nick.

The realization settled into my brain and my throat went dry and my blood went cold and my mind reeled, and it's no wonder why. If the guitarist was in trouble, I could see him coming up and asking for security.

But I didn't understand why he didn't stick around. Or why he'd blanched at the sight of Nick.

Like he knew him.

While these thoughts raced through my head, I took a second to flash a look at Nick, but whatever was going on behind that chiseled face and those remarkable blue eyes of his, there was no hint of it in his expression. He glanced at the corpse, his face a mask.

I glanced at the corpse.

And thought of a million questions.

All of which I'd ask him when Detective Anita Gilkenny wasn't around.

No big surprise, Detective Gilkenny had questions of her own. "Until . . . ?" She looked at me hard. Her eyes were blue, too, but not the intense shade of Nick's. Hers were pale and streaked with gray, like an old bruise, and her complexion was pasty white.

"Until the end of the evening," I said. "That's when I was leaving and I walked over here and—"

"Do you know his name?" the detective asked.

I gave Nick a chance to speak up. He didn't.

"I guess Mr. Hot Guitar Player doesn't cut it, huh?" I asked the detective. She didn't think it was funny. But then, if there was one thing I'd learned in the course of the murder investigations I'd been involved with, it's that detectives are not exactly the laugh-riot types.

"I have no idea," I said, just as a uniformed officer over by the body called out, "No identification on him. And seventeen dollars and seventy-five cents in his pockets. All in change and small bills."

Detective Gilkenny scratched a line about all this in a little notebook. "If you didn't know him," she asked, "why were you looking for him?"

"I wasn't. I was looking . . ." I remembered the little trail of Consolidated Chili giveaways; I'd left them all on a table back in our tent when I went to find Sylvia and her phone, but I didn't bother to mention it. There was no use explaining—again—how the very idea of *corporate* and *chili* in the same sentence offended me to the core of my being and how I thought it was my duty to ditch the horrible souvenirs before they could taint anyone's opinion of real chili.

"I was looking for Tumbleweed and Ruth Ann," I said. "We were supposed to go out and get something to eat."

"And that's when you found the body."

Since Gilkenny was the one who made the comment, I didn't bother to look at Nick, even though I could feel those blue eyes of his on me.

"That's when I found the body."

"And the victim . . ." As if I could actually forget about the body over there in the glare of the spotlights, the detective looked that way. "He never came back to your tent for that bowl of chili he said he wanted?"

"Our chili is really good. His loss, huh?" I asked the question of Nick and got nothing but stone-faced silence in return.

"No," I turned away from Nick and told the detective, because it was, after all, the truth. "He never came back for his bowl of chili."

"And you don't know who he is."

"Like I said, not a clue."

"And you don't know anything about him."

I didn't, did I? And yet . . .

I looked past Nick and the detective to where the body still lay, avoiding another look at the man's face and this time concentrating on the pieces of the shattered guitar scattered on the ground around him.

"I'm pretty sure he didn't know how to play the guitar," I said.

Nick raised his eyebrows. From him, that's pretty much the equivalent of jumping up and down and asking what in the world I'm talking about. I wondered if it was because he thought my question was crazy. Or if it was because he knew I was right on the money.

Detective Gilkenny wrote another line in her notebook. "You said you didn't know the man. What makes you think he wasn't a musician?"

"There were plenty of musicians here this evening," I pointed out. "You heard them, Nick. There was a whole mariachi band that played for a little while. And there were strolling musicians all night long. But this guy . . ." I told myself not to do it, but I couldn't help it. Once again, I glanced at the dead man's face. "He wasn't playing music. He was just hitting the strings. You know, strumming." As if I had a guitar in front of me, I brushed my fingers over the imaginary strings. "He wasn't playing music. He was pretending to play music."

Gilkenny made another note and grumbled, "So maybe he didn't really belong here." She glanced over at me. "Did he seem to know anyone?"

This, I couldn't say. I mean, I had seen him talking to the beauty queen at the Consolidated tent. And to the lady from the Women's League. But that didn't mean he knew them, did it? In fact, the only one he seemed to know was Nick.

But that was Nick's business, not mine, and so far, he was keeping his mouth shut. This, of course, was plenty intriguing, and believe me, I intended to ask him about it. Later.

"He knew who I was," I said, thinking back. "At least he knew my name."

Gilkenny's straw-colored eyebrows did a slow slide up her forehead. "So you did know him. Otherwise, how would he have known your name?"

Oh, she was thinking just the way I was thinking. Only not about the person I was thinking it about.

That person stepped forward, and he pretty much said what I would have said, only coming from me, I was afraid it would have sounded a little too conceited. Poor Detective Gilkenny was as plain as I was flashy. There was no use making her feel any less attractive.

"Maxie has something of a . . ." I knew Nick didn't really need to think about it, so when he cleared his throat, I think he was just trying to soften the blow. "A reputation. You know, with chili lovers," he said so the detective didn't get the wrong idea.

It was true, and since that reputation was chili expert, chili lover, and Chili Chick, it was a reputation I was proud of.

"It's her job to promote her dad's spice and seasoning business," Nick added. "So lots of people know her."

"Like this guy." The detective nodded. "What did you talk about?"

"He asked how business was. He said he'd heard our chili was good. He said he couldn't wait to see me in my Chili Chick costume. Small talk."

Before the detective could ask anything else, a woman came around the corner, the same woman I'd seen having an intense discussion with the victim not too long before. Then, I'd seen her only from a distance, but up close, I saw that my initial impression was right on the money. And money was exactly what I was talking about. She was tall, lithe, and gorgeous, and her clothes screamed quality.

But money or not, nothing could soften the blow of

seeing a body. She took a gander and her jaw pumped like a piston.

"Oh no!" she groaned. "It's true. A body! Here at *Read with the Chili Queens*. What are we going to do?"

If you asked me, what she was going to do was faint, and I guess Nick saw it coming, too, or maybe he was just looking for an excuse to get close to this fashionable and gorgeous woman; he raced forward, cupped the woman's arm, and braced her against his side. There was a folding chair nearby that hadn't been put away by the cleanup crew yet, so I slid it over and Nick set the woman down in it.

"Oh no. Oh no!" She fanned her face with one hand, her Texas accent as heavy as the night air. "This can't be happening. It's terrible. Think of the publicity. It's going to be awful. Our reputation is going to be ruined!"

"You work for the literacy organization?" the detective asked before I could.

The woman shook her head. "I'm Eleanor Alvarez. Our San Antonio Women's League isn't in charge of the literacy group that's getting the funds from tonight's event; we're in charge of the entire event. The whole Chili Queens week. And now . . ." She gulped. In a ladylike way, of course. "There was talk over at our tent. Someone said the police were here and that there was a body. I didn't think it could possibly be true. Oh my." She lifted one trembling hand to brush the tears from her cheeks, and the sapphire ring she wore winked at me in the glare of the lights. "It's terrible."

"Did you know the man?" Gilkenny asked her.

"Him?" Her question came out as a squeak when Eleanor

looked at the body. "I saw him earlier this evening. You know, walking around and playing his guitar. I might have . . ." She sniffled. "Yes, I think I even talked to him. You know, asked how things were going and how he was enjoying the evening. That sort of thing."

"But you don't know his name."

Eleanor shook her head. "The musicians were hired by the people from that Chili Showdown that's in town. I'm sure someone there will know him. Our organization was just in charge of logistics. You know, getting all the charities lined up, handling their mailing lists, making sure things run smoothly each night." She grimaced through a fresh cascade of tears. "Well, I guess none of that matters. I'm sorry. I'm blabbering. I can't seem to help myself. This is just so awful. And so shocking."

"You're doing fine." Since no one else seemed worried about the poor woman's mental state, I put a reassuring hand on her shoulder.

I guess maybe I shouldn't have, because it was apparently a signal to Nick that I should be officially in charge of Eleanor.

"Maxie will take you back to the main tent," he told her. "You sit down over there and get a drink of water. An officer will come by in a bit and get your contact information."

Don't think I didn't notice that this was Nick's subtle way of getting rid of me. I shot him a look he ignored and helped Eleanor out of her chair.

She didn't let me hang on to her for long. "I'm fine," she said once we'd stepped away from the crime scene. She pulled back her shoulder, lifted her head, and pulled in a breath of the air that was still as hot and humid as the inside of a dry cleaner's. "Really. I'm not usually such a blithering idiot. It was just the shock, and thinking about what's going to happen now. . . I mean, having the Women's League associated with a murder, it's just too terrible to even think about."

"Don't sweat it," I told her. "I've had the same thing happen. A couple times, in fact. As terrible as it is, murder seems to bring out more customers."

Eleanor's rusty brows dipped low over her eyes. "Really? You think we could somehow use this to our advantage? Well, we could send out an e-mail newsletter and offer our condolences and say how terrible it is and if people want to donate money in the victim's name . . ."

"Except they don't know his name," I told her. "That's why they wanted to know if you knew him."

"Me?" We stopped near the center of the plaza. Already, word had gone out about the murder, and there were a few cops there who'd established a perimeter of sorts to keep the curious at bay. We stepped around them. "Like I told that policewoman, I talked to the man earlier. But other than that . . ." As if she was waking from a bad dream, Eleanor looked around the plaza. When her gaze landed on the Consolidated Chili tent, some of the confusion washed out of her expression.

"What is it?" I asked her. "You remember something?"

She thought about it for a moment. But then, I suppose anybody who's organized enough to put on a mega-event like this one had to make sure she had her facts straight. "I did see him late in the evening," she said. "That poor man, I mean. He was over in that tent. The one that belongs to Consolidated Chili. He was talking to John Wesley Montgomery. You know who I mean; I'm sure you saw him this evening. He's the CEO of Tri-C and he's hard not to notice. Such a well-dressed man, and that amazing ten-gallon hat!"

"He's the one who left in the big black limo." As far as I'd seen, he was the only one who had, but I figured I should get my facts straight, too. After all, it was that limo that had almost run me down as I was looking for Tumbleweed and Ruth Ann.

Right before I found the body.

"That's the one," Eleanor said. "And I saw him with the victim. I was on my way to get interviewed by one of the local TV stations. You know, about the event and about the work we do in the community. And I walked right by the Consolidated Chili tent, and that's when I saw that guitarist. He and John Wesley, they were talking."

"You didn't . . ." I controlled my excitement. There was no use letting Eleanor think I had anything more than a passing interest. "You didn't happen to hear what they were talking about, did you?"

Again, she paused to think. "It was very loud around here," she said. "What with the crowd and those gorgeous young beauty queens handing out those adorable little bottle openers and talking to everyone who went by. How cute were they?"

Since I wasn't sure if she was talking about the beauty queens or the bottle openers, I figured I didn't have to answer.

"Still . . ." Eleanor cocked her head. "I did hear a bit. John Wesley, he must have asked that poor guitar player a question, because the guitar player said something about how he'd contacted her."

"Contacted who?"

"Well, I don't know," Eleanor admitted. "But that's what he said. He said, 'I contacted her. Just like you asked me to.'"

"And Mr. Montgomery, what did he say?"

"He said that was good. Because he wanted to find out everything he could about the spice. Or maybe he said the price. Ice? Advice?" She groaned. "I don't know. Like I said, it was noisy and I wasn't paying a whole lot of attention. Do you think it's important? Do you think . . ." She glanced back toward where the glow of those spotlights lit up the nighttime sky. "Do you think I should tell the police?"

"I'll tell them for you," I assured her, and I'd been at this murder investigation thing for so long, I didn't even cross my fingers when I lied. "If they have any questions, I'm sure they'll ask you when they come talk to you later."

I left her at the main tent, where she was instantly surrounded by a crowd who wanted to know what she saw and what she knew, and went looking for Tumbleweed and Ruth Ann. Just as I expected, they were worried, but I told them everything was under control (I'm pretty good at this lying thing, yes?) and said they'd better get back to the fairgrounds so they could get some sleep before the Showdown opened in the morning.

By the time I flagged down a cab for them and waved good-bye, I was all set to return to the crime scene and see what was happening. I never got that far. That's because halfway there, I met Nick coming the other way.

"So?" I asked him.

"So?" He kept walking and I fell into step at his side. Which might sound like no big deal but isn't exactly easy considering that he's tall, I'm short, and I was wearing that long black skirt. I lifted the hem of it so I could scramble and catch up.

"So what did the cops find out?"

He didn't spare me a glance. "As far as they've told me, nothing."

I figured it was only fair to give him a chance to come clean. "They don't know who the guy is?"

"Nope."

"Nobody does?"

He stopped so fast, I ended up a couple steps ahead of him and had to stumble back to him.

"Leave it alone," Nick told me.

"But Nick, he was looking for security. The dead guy. That's what I didn't tell that detective. He came over to my tent and he was—"

He started walking again, and we sidestepped the cops and continued on along the plaza. By now, there were vans from a couple of the local TV stations there along with a crowd of curious onlookers. Nick didn't say a word until we were well past all of them.

"He was what?" he asked.

"He was upset about something," I said. "He said something about a woman he called Senora Loca. And then he asked for security. And I pointed you out to him, and that man, he took one look at you, turned around, and went the other way."

At this end of the plaza the shadows were deep; his shrug was barely noticeable. "That doesn't mean anything. If the man was upset, it's only natural he'd want to find someone from security."

Since he obviously wasn't listening, I had no choice but to clamp a hand down on his arm. At my touch, his muscles bunched. "Of course it was only natural. But it wasn't as simple as that. Don't you get it? He asked for security, but when he saw you, he split. What does that tell you?"

Light and shadows played over Nick's expression, making him look as if he'd been carved from stone. "It tells me he changed his mind. Or he thought of something he had to do. Or he wanted to grab another bowl of chili. Or maybe he just decided not to talk to me because he didn't like the look of my face or the color of my tie. I can't say for sure, because I don't know. All I know for sure is I never saw that man before in my life."

CHAPTER 4

The next morning the Chili Showdown was in full swing and the sky above the fairgrounds where we were set up was filled with fat, white clouds. The gates opened exactly at ten and already, the air was so moist and heavy, it was hard to breathe.

Especially from inside the Chili Chick.

The Chick, see, is a work of art constructed from wire and mesh and heavy canvas, a gigantic red chili costume that I step into, pull up over my head, and zip up the back. The chili completely covers me all the way to down just past my hips. My arms stick out the sides. My legs in their fishnet stockings stick out the bottom. The tall stilettos I wear with those stockings are impossible to miss.

But then, so are my killer legs.

Of course, that's the whole idea. It always has been, since back in the day when Jack first thought of the Chili Chick and brought her to life through a series of Chicks who'd worn her proudly since. Sylvia's mom was once the Chick. So was my mom. The fact that Jack had fallen in love with both of them was no big surprise. Aside from being a ladies' man through and through, there is something about the Chick that makes her impossible to resist.

Kitschy.

Funny.

Funky.

In case the yellow sign above our chili pepper red food truck doesn't get customers' attention, the Chick does when she dances her fool head off and waves people in.

Dancing my fool head off, I put my face as close as possible to the red mesh at the front of the costume and sucked in a breath at the same time I managed a shuffle step and a wave to the group of people walking by. It worked. They went up to the front concession window, and Sylvia started into her spiel about All-Purpose Chili Cha-cha, Global Warming, and Thermal Conversion, our three most popular spice mixes.

This was a good thing, because while she was busy with them, I ducked around to the back of the Palace and into the shadows. Okay, so it wasn't exactly cool, but it was cooler than standing out in the beating sun. This sweltering Chili Chick leaned against the Palace, pulled in a breath of wonderfully fragrant, chili spice–filled air, and took a breather.

If only it was that easy to take a break from the thoughts of murder that swirled through my head.

Murder. A mysterious victim. And Nick.

See, I'd gotten up early that morning (and believe me when I say this is not something I am usually inclined to do), and I did a lot of thinking. But no matter how many times I went through the scene in my head, I couldn't make sense of why the victim was so desperate to find someone from security, then just as desperate to head the other way when he realized that someone was Nick.

And Nick claimed he knew nothing about the man?

To me, it just didn't add up.

"So much for that flimsy explanation, buster," I mumbled as if Nick was there to hear me and dispute the excuse he'd given me the night before.

"Curiouser and curiouser," I told myself, and really, there's only one thing to do when that kind of curiosity nibbles away at this Chili Chick's brain.

I had to do some more digging and find the answer.

A plan already spinning through my head, I poked my chili around the corner of the Palace, made sure Sylvia was still busy with those customers, and took off down the midway as fast as a chili in stilettos can move. With any luck, Tumbleweed and Ruth Ann wouldn't be in the trailer they used as the main office and mother ship of each Showdown event and I'd have a few minutes to myself to look through their files.

"Maxie, good morning!"

So much for luck. Half good, half bad by the looks of things. As soon as my chili-encased butt was up the steps and through the door, none other than Gert Wilson popped out of the chair behind the desk where Ruth Ann usually sat to take care of all the administrative details that allowed the Showdown to run like clockwork in each town we visited. Gert had her own setup at the Showdown where she sold things like chili-themed aprons and pot holders and jewelry. What she was doing in Ruth Ann's place was a mystery. At least until Gert explained.

"Ruth Ann had to step out for a minute and asked me to take her place. You know, in case anybody stopped in with questions. What can I do for you?" When I'm not wearing my Chick stilettos, Gert is a tad taller than me, but now, she needed to look up to try and see me through the mesh at the front of the costume. "Shouldn't you be outside dancing?"

"Too hot," I told her. Which wasn't exactly a lie. "I needed a break and I knew Ruth Ann would have the AC cranked." It was, and I wallowed in the glory of it. "Besides, I need a little time to myself. It's going to be busy today."

"Thank goodness!" Gert was a middle-aged woman with hair the color of a desert sunset, a wide, pleasant face, and ample hips. That day—like most days—she was wearing an ankle-length skirt. That day's choice was denim, but that day—like most days—she'd added a dozen bright beaded bracelets, a yellow shirt, and a filmy orange scarf to her outfit, just to jazz things up.

She strolled to the window that looked out over the midway and the crowds that poured in. "Ruth Ann tells me that poor Tumbleweed couldn't sleep last night from worrying. Another murder, and you know as well as I do, that can't be good for business. Thank goodness that man had the sense to get killed somewhere other than here at the Showdown!"

She slapped a hand to her mouth. "You know I didn't really mean that the way it came out," she said. "I just meant . . . well, you know, Maxie. Two Showdowns these last few weeks. Three bodies. Sooner or later, that sort of thing gives a show a bad reputation. If people stopped coming, a lot of people would lose their livelihoods. That would be a real shame. For all the Showdown folks."

"Not going to happen," I told her, stepping to her side. From outside, a man caught sight of the giant chili in the window and waved. I waved back. "The Showdown is the best chili cook-off show on the road. People are always going to want to come and taste our chili and be part of the cook-off contests and buy all the spices and the beans and the supplies our vendors sell. Real chili lovers? Not even bad news can keep them away."

"Well, at least this time, the bad news isn't just ours. Too bad for those Chili Queens people, though. That woman, the one who's in charge—"

"Eleanor Alvarez."

"Yes, Eleanor. She's the one. Ruth Ann tells me that you told her that Eleanor was plenty upset last night."

I knew this for a fact, but all wasn't doom and gloom. "Folks paid their money to get in, so the literacy organization will still collect a hefty chunk. And we took in plenty of extra tips and donations besides. Even though people were mostly only throwing in loose change and ones, Sylvia says our tent alone brought in an extra two hundred dollars."

Loose change and ones.

The words bounced around inside my head, and I

remembered what the cop at the crime scene had said the night before. The victim had seventeen dollars and seventy-five cents in his pockets. All in change and small bills.

"That's nice that people were willing to donate even more," Gert said, drawing me out of my thoughts before that idea had a chance to bounce to any sort of conclusion. "Now if only the police can figure out who killed that poor man."

"Speaking of him . . ." Although most people who know me would say it isn't possible, I can be subtle when it suits me. Subtly, I stepped toward the metal filing cabinets where all the Showdown records were kept. Well, as subtly as a giant red chili can. "We need to figure out who he was."

"We?" Gert didn't say this the way Nick might have, the word tinged with contempt and suspicion. In fact, color rushed into her cheeks. "Are you sure it's smart to investigate again?"

"It's not like I'm staking out some dive bar, waiting for the perp," I told her. "I thought I'd just do some . . . recon. Yeah, that's all I have in mind. I'm sure the cops are going to come around and question Ruth Ann and Tumbleweed. You know, about who the dead guy was, when Tumbleweed hired him, how they found him, where he lives. You know, all the usual background information."

"Just like on those police shows on TV." Gert glanced over at the file cabinets where Ruth Ann kept all the pertinent paperwork. "You'd like to get a look at the files first."

I sidled closer to the metal filing cabinets. "It can't hurt anything."

Gert looked over her shoulder toward the door. "And if Ruth Ann asks?"

"You know she'd let me look," I said, even as I pulled open the nearest file drawer. "Ruth Ann can't say no to me."

"Well . . ." Gert may have talked the talk, but I couldn't help but notice that when it came to walking the walk, she couldn't resist. She glanced over my shoulder to get a look at the files. "There's one marked *Chili Queens Event*," she said, snatching it out of the drawer and flipping open the file. "It looks like permits, and agreements with the unions who put up the lights, and notifications to the police. I bet all those details were handled by Eleanor Alvarez and her committee. The way I heard it, the only thing Tumbleweed and Ruth Ann were in charge of was . . ." Her fingers fluttered over the file folders. "Yes! Here, the entertainers."

She took the file back to Ruth Ann's desk with her. "Tumbleweed told me he did all the hiring, but none of it was done in person. I'll bet that's why he didn't recognize that poor man. You know, last night, when the police asked him to look at the body." Gert's brows dropped low over her eyes. "Poor Tumbleweed, he was pretty shaken up by the time he got back here last night." Her shoulders twitched. She slapped the folder down on the desk and flipped it open. "We've got to do whatever we can to help out Tumbleweed and Ruth Ann. They're dear people," she said. "Let's see what we can find out."

It wasn't easy reading, I mean, what with that mesh screen in front of my face and the fact that the Chick had to bend over in a pretty much not-so-bendable costume to get a gander at that file folder, but I made a valiant effort.

"Mariachi band," I said, skimming over the first employment contract Gert pulled from the file. "Guitar player." My hopes rose when I saw the second contract, then plummeted right back down when I realized that particular application had a picture of the guitarist along with it. It was the man who'd played the lovely flamenco music I'd heard wafting across the plaza during the event, not our dead strummer.

"Harpist." I remembered this musician, too, tucked away in a corner closest to the entrance to the Alamo. "Maracas player, drummer, violinist." I grumbled my way through the rest of the employment contracts. "There have to be more."

Just to be sure, Gert checked the file cabinet again.

"Not a one," she told me. "And you know Tumbleweed and Ruth Ann wouldn't misplace anything like that. They're too careful when it comes to Showdown business."

I'm not sure what we hoped to accomplish, but for a few moments, the two of us stood side by side and stared down at those employment contracts.

"What does it mean?" Gert finally asked. "Why isn't there a contract for that poor, murdered man?"

Honestly, I couldn't say. Not for sure, anyway. But . . .

"If you ask me," I told her, "it means he didn't belong there."

"You mean, he was just posing as a musician?"

"It's what I told Nick last night. Mr. Hot Guitar Player was trying to fit in, pretending that he was working there."

"But why?" Gert asked.

This, I couldn't say, either, not for certain, but it didn't take much of a leap of faith to figure it out.

"He didn't belong but he wanted to look like he did," I mumbled, mostly to get the facts straight in my own head. "To me, that means the man had some sort of secret."

"It is just like in the cop shows on TV," Gert gasped.

And maybe she was right. I couldn't say, but I sure intended to find out.

With that in mind, I told Gert I'd see her later and headed back outside. Maybe an hour of dancing in the glaring Texas sun would heat up my brain and get it working.

Or maybe I wouldn't have to wait that long.

Not far from Tumbleweed and Ruth Ann's trailer, my attention was caught by a familiar pale face.

Detective Anita Gilkenny, and she was walking toward where Nick was standing in the shade of the awning over the entrance to the spacious setup where—when she wasn't manning the desk for Ruth Ann—Gert sold her chili-themed dish towels, coffee mugs, aprons, and jewelry.

It probably goes without saying, but let me just mention here that it's a little hard to be unobtrusive when one is encased in a giant red chili.

It's no wonder I had to duck behind the nearest food truck and make my way from behind a row of vendors to where Nick and the detective chatted. I sidled between Gert's tent and Jorge LaReyo's tamale stand just in time to hear Nick's rumbling baritone when he responded to something Gilkenny said.

"You're a smart guy," Gilkenny replied. "You know this doesn't look good."

"It doesn't look like anything." With my chili butt as flat as it was able to get against Gert's tent, I couldn't see Nick, but I could well imagine the look on his face. I wondered if Detective Gilkenny would survive the icy onslaught. "It isn't anything more than I said it was last night. I didn't know the guy."

"You're sure?"

"As sure as it's possible to be. But then, by the time I got called to the scene, it was late, the light was blinding, and our victim, he wasn't exactly at his best."

There was silence for a few moments, and I pictured Gilkenny eyeing up Nick like just another perp.

I guess I was right, because I heard him growl from deep in his throat.

"What if I told you . . ." Gilkenny's voice dropped, and I inched a little closer, my head cocked so my ear was closer to the mesh panel. "What if I told you we ran the dead man's fingerprints and made an identification?"

I didn't have to see Nick. I knew him well enough. I could picture him crossing his arms over that chipped-from-granite chest. "That's your job. I'm glad you were successful."

"If I told you our victim's name, maybe that would jog your memory."

"I don't see how," Nick said. "I've never been in San Antonio before. I don't know anyone here."

"Dominic Laurentius. Unusual name, isn't it? The kind that sticks with you once you hear it."

Stony silence from Nick, and oh, how I wished I could see him. Maybe then I'd have an idea what was going on behind that gorgeous face of his.

From what I'd seen of her, I wouldn't peg Anita Gilkenny as the type who lost her cool too easily, but I guess there's a first time for everything. I heard her groan. "Come on, Falcone. You're not dumb, and neither am I. You know where this is headed. Dominic Laurentius, our victim. He was ex LA police. Just like you."

Ex LA police.

Of course, on the face of it, that didn't mean a thing. I mean, a whole bunch of people are probably ex LA police, right? And it's got to be a huge department. Not everyone knows everyone.

But not everyone knows Nick Falcone like I do, either, and I knew him well enough to read through the response he *didn't* give Gilkenny. Unfortunately, at that very moment, Tumbleweed's voice blared over the loudspeakers set up throughout the fairgrounds as he announced that the day's first judging was scheduled to start (homestyle chili—that is, chili that's made with any combination of ingredients and can include beans and pasta). Nick gave Gilkenny the "gotta work" excuse. She told him—in a no-nonsense, not friendly sort of way—that they'd for sure talk later.

That gave me some time to poke my nose further into the mysterious death of Dominic Laurentius.

With that in mind, I dragged myself back over to the Palace. Literally. When I got there, one stiletto off and in my hand, I braced my other hand against the front counter, listed to the left, and breathed so hard that not even Sylvia could fail to hear the signs of my distress from inside the Chick.

"Gotta . . ." I gulped down a breath. "Gotta sit down," I moaned. "The medic, over there at the first aid tent . . ." I glanced in the general direction. "When I fainted the first time . . . she said it's . . . heatstroke for sure. It's the costume. Too . . . too hot."

To Sylvia's credit, she didn't exactly buy into the story. I mean, it's not like she raced around to the front of the Palace, offered me an arm, and guided me to a bottle of icy cold water. But she didn't call me a liar, either. At least not to my face. Had her memory been better and had there been fewer customers waiting for service, she might have taken the time to recall a similar incident back in St. Louis years before when a cute boy wanted to take me to McDonald's for a burger and I was scheduled to work the Palace.

That time, I'd developed a sudden and terrible case of the flu.

"I'll be back after I cool off," I told her, and before she could start putting two and two together, I dragged around to the back of the Palace where she couldn't see me, then raced to our RV and got out of the Chick costume.

I knew exactly what my next move should be. Research. I needed to do some serious research and find out what Nick and this Laurentius guy might have in common. I mean other than both of them being former LAPD cops.

The trick, of course, was where to begin.

It only took me a few minutes to figure it out.

It took a little longer than that to get over to the nearest public library.

"Wasn't it all just horrible!" The woman behind the front desk waved a hand in front of her face. "I mean, it wasn't like I was there or anything, but I mean, really, a murder at a reading fund-raiser! It's all anyone here at the library can talk about today, and it's not something you can just put out of your head, is it?"

It wasn't, but I didn't bother to mention that what little sleep I'd gotten the night before was punctuated with dreams of red Sharpies and broken guitars.

"It must have been awful," the librarian went on to say. "First all the excitement of the fund-raiser and so many wonderful people who support reading. Then . . ." She'd been standing behind the desk, and she dropped into her chair. "That poor, poor man. Have the police arrested anyone?"

"They might have a suspect," I told her, all the while thinking what I didn't want to be thinking—from the way I heard Gilkenny talking back at the Showdown, I was afraid that suspect might be Nick. "That's why I need your help."

I explained my dilemma, and just as I'd hoped, the woman pitched right in. Before I knew it, she had a page open on her computer and I was standing by her side and we were both looking through old newspaper articles about Detective Dominic Laurentius.

"Seems like he was quite the hero," the librarian said, skimming an article about an armed robbery and what Laurentius had done to stop it. "What a shame that a man with that kind of reputation has to die such a violent and tragic death."

I didn't say *Whatever*, because it would have been insensitive and I was grateful for her assistance, but let's face it, none of this was very helpful. I flicked a finger at the computer monitor, urging her to get to the next article.

Honestly, I was kind of sorry when she did.

There it was. Not exactly live and in color, but in color and on the screen right in front of my nose.

The blood drained from my face and down to my toes and my stomach lurched when I looked at the photograph of handsome Detective Laurentius that had been taken three years earlier. He was sans guitar, of course, and along with his partner, he was being honored for bravery at a banquet given by some civic organization.

"Well, that picture must have been taken in happier times," Eleanor said. She pointed to the article that accompanied the photograph. "This story is about a serious altercation between Laurentius and that partner of his. It must have been really something, too, because it says here that after a department review, they both resigned from the police force. And listen to this! Laurentius, he had to give in his resignation from his hospital bed. Seems that partner of his beat him up really bad."

Yeah, that partner of his.

Again, my gaze traveled to that banquet picture taken in happier days that showed Detective Laurentius standing with his partner.

None other than the one and only Nick Falcone.

CHAPTER 5

Liar, liar, pants on fire.

Exactly what I wanted to say to Nick.

Well, maybe not in so many words. But hey, I did need to talk to him. About what I'd found out thanks to that librarian. About what the heck he thought he was up to.

About why he lied. To the police, and to me.

I was for sure going to do it, too.

As soon as I managed to locate him.

With that in mind, I scanned the crowd—again—on Alamo Plaza that Tuesday evening, but I pretty much knew it was a losing cause from the beginning. Even if Nick was standing ten feet in front of me, it would have been tough to pick him out in the huge crowd that filled the plaza. It was definitely going to be another blockbuster fund-raiser. Tonight's theme: *The Chili Queens Go to the Dogs.*

They weren't kidding.

A new tent had been added to the plaza, and it was filled with kind people and noisy dogs. Big dogs, little dogs, dogs that howled and growled and barked. All of them looking to be adopted. The dogs, not the people.

If the night before had been controlled chaos, that Tuesday was one step beyond. It was a more casual crowd, but then, I guess I should have expected that from the warm-and-fuzzy types who support these sorts of animal events. Instead of sequins, I saw lots of jeans and T-shirts with pictures of dogs on them along with sayings like *Woof If You Love a Rescue* and *I Kiss My Dog on the Lips.* If there was music, I couldn't say, because with all the barking along with the oohs and aahs coming from adoption central, I pretty much couldn't hear myself think.

"You added spices to my chili yesterday." With all the noise, Sylvia needed to stand nice and close when she sidled up and hissed the accusation. "The idea was to make a batch of chili that would be perfect for all palates. That's what I did. Not too hot. Not too mild. Perfect."

"If I made a few changes . . ."—I emphasized that first word—"then of the course the chili was perfect." I offered her a smile. For tonight's festivities, along with the black skirt and the peasant blouse (yes, I laundered it), I'd added a black wig with long braids, and I flipped a braid over my shoulder so that the end of it flicked Sylvia's nose and she was forced to take a step back. "And since I made tonight's chili, it will be perfect, too."

"I've already sampled it," she grumbled. "Too much oregano."

It wasn't true, but I had to give her credit; she had a good taster. Most people wouldn't have been able to pick out the Mexican oregano I'd added with a heavy hand, just like Jack always did. Then again, Sylvia had spent many a year writing for a food magazine in Seattle before she agreed to work the Palace with me, so culinarily speaking, she had the chops. Someday, she wanted to write a cookbook of her own. In fact, that cookbook was the reason she'd filched Jack's secret chili recipe out of one of his old notebooks. I swear, I'll get that recipe back one day. No way I'm letting her take credit for Jack's genius.

"And tequila? Really, Maxie." Sylvia shook her slender shoulders and shook me out of my thoughts at the same time. "You don't waste that kind of ingredient on this kind of crowd."

"Because, what, they'll go to the dogs?" When she didn't laugh, I elbowed her in the ribs. "Lighten up! That chili is so good, I bet we'll collect more tips in the donation jar than we did last night."

"Really?" Those baby blues of hers lit with devilish delight. "You'd really bet?"

I had to think about this for a second or two. Betting—or taking chances of any kind—was a decidedly non-Sylvia thing to do, and I wondered what she was up to. Then I remembered that I had an extra twenty tucked in the pocket of the shorts I wore under my long skirt. If, at the end of the evening, things were looking grim in the tip department, I was willing to sacrifice.

I stuck out a hand, but before we shook, I was sure to ask, "What are we betting?"

"A whole day off at the next Showdown in New Orleans," she said. "Whoever loses, that person works the Palace all of Saturday. No complaints. No backing out. And no pretending to have heatstroke so you can get out of work." Since there didn't seem to be much point, I did not rise to this bait or the very pointed look that went along with it. "The winner gets a whole day off in the Big Easy."

"Done," I said, confident that I would win. The batch of chili I'd made for that night's benefit was one of Jack's favorite recipes and included the tequila and oregano Sylvia had detected along with molasses. No tomatoes. No beans. Just a lot of meat and spices. And beer, too. A real Texas chili, and I knew it would be a crowd pleaser. Already, I fantasized about how I'd spend my day in New Orleans getting my tarot cards read in Jackson Square and sipping a couple hurricanes over on Bourbon Street.

"The line is starting to form," Sylvia told me with a look back into our tent. "We'd better get to work."

Work, we did. And I'd say *like dogs*, but that would be way too corny, even though it was true. The good news was that people raved about my chili, and by the time the first wave of visitors subsided, that stoneware bowl where we collected tips was nearly full.

"We're going to need to empty it and stash the money," Sylvia said, and when I shot her a look, she was quick to add, "I'm not going to tamper with the totals. Trust me. But there won't be any room for more if we don't do something with all this cash."

"Then just declare me the winner right now!" I knew she wouldn't go for it. She didn't. "Then how about an impartial third party to count the money?" I suggested. I glanced to the tent next to ours, and when Ginger looked our way, I waved her over.

She was resplendent that night in a figure-hugging flamenco gown the color of hot lava. It had a deep vee neckline and ruffles on the sleeves and a layered skirt that flared out just below Ginger's knees, like a mermaid's tail. I didn't know where these queens got their costumes, but they must have cost a fortune, and I had to give her credit; she wore it with sass and style. Tonight, Ginger's hair was piled atop her head, and her makeup—just like the night before—was flawless.

In the cheap costume-shop wig I'd picked up in the Halloween aisle of a local discount store, I felt second-rate.

"What can I do for you?" Ginger asked, and I explained.

"Thank goodness!" She exhaled a minty breath. "Helping you out will give me a break from Teddi." She glanced over her shoulder to where, that evening, Teddi was dressed in a knee-length, slim-fitting dress and an apron decorated with drawings of brightly colored, old-fashioned kitchen appliances. Her red lipstick matched her nail polish and her snood. "She's acting like a crazy woman! She has been all night," Ginger added. Stepping to where I motioned her, she sat down and got to work, and a few minutes later when she called me over, it was with a look that was half envy and half wow-am-I-impressed.

"You collected so much in tips!" Ginger showed me the sheet of paper where she'd added up the numbers. "More than one hundred fifty dollars so far, and the night is still young. Honey, your chili must rank up there with the best of the best. All of last night, Teddi and I only managed to bring in sixty-seven dollars."

It wasn't like I was trying to make the drag queens looks bad, but hey, I couldn't help it, could I? I scooped up the tips, put them in an envelope, and sealed it. Then Sylvia and I both signed the flap. Yeah, I know, we were being a little too obsessive, but when it came to our bet, I wasn't going to take any chances that some of that tip money would mysteriously disappear just so Sylvia could make herself look good and get that day off that I was already daydreaming about.

"So . . ." Ginger agreed to hold on to the tip envelope for us, and she tucked it under her arm. "Any word yet? About the murder? I'll tell you what, everybody who walks into our tent is buzzing about it. Has there been an arrest?"

Automatically, I scanned the plaza again.

Still no sign of Nick.

"I sure hope not," I told Ginger. I didn't bother to explain and she was too much of a lady to ask what I was talking about.

"Well, it gives me the heebie-jeebies just thinking about it." A shiver ran across her shoulders and twitched those ruffles on her sleeves. "The police came around when we were setting up and talked to us, and just thinking that there was a murder so close to where we're standing, well, I just about fainted."

Ginger was pretty tall, and I had to duck to one side to

look past her and toward the tent where she and Teddi were working. "What about her?" I asked. "Is that how Teddi feels, too?"

"You'd think she wouldn't. You know, when she's not Teddi, she's Teo and Teo works down at the Bexar County Medical Examiner's Office. Not doing autopsies or anything." Another shudder danced over those broad shoulders that looked so perfect with Ginger's narrow waist and rounded-just-enough hips. "When he's there, he's one of the people who counsels grieving families. I don't know about you, but that tells me when she's here as Teddi, well, you'd think she'd be plenty used to death."

"And she's not?"

"Like I said, she's been a crazy woman all night! Jumping at every little sound. Looking like she's about to burst into tears at any moment. You know, we do these sorts of charity events because we love to dress up and mingle and do some good for the community. We work for weeks on our costumes, and Teddi's usually so proud of how she looks. And tonight . . . ?" Once again, her gaze slid to the nearby tent. "Housedress? Really? What was she thinking? I'm afraid Teddi is about to have some sort of breakdown."

"You want me to talk to her?"

"Would you?" Ginger pressed a hand to my arm. "That's so sweet. Maybe she'll tell you what's going on, because when I ask, she clams right up."

It was the least I could do for the person who was going to make sure I had that day off in New Orleans.

I slipped out of our tent and over to the one next door

where Teddi was scooping a batch of chili into the slow cooker where it would stay hot until it was served.

"Hey, Teddi, what's up?"

The ladle she was using clattered to the table, and, one hand pressed to her heart, Teddi jumped back and her gaze shot to mine. "Oh, it's you." Her apron was polka-dotted with chili, and she reached for a rag and dabbed at it. "I didn't see you. You startled me."

"Ginger tells me that's been happening all evening."

"Ginger!" Teddi was not as carefully made up as she had been the night before. I swear, I could see the faint trace of a five o'clock shadow on her thin face. "What else has Ginger told you?"

"That she's worried about you. She says you're not acting like yourself."

"Well, I'm obviously not myself, am I?" she shot back. "I'm Teddi tonight. The way I always am at these sort of events."

"Ginger knows that."

"Ginger needs to mind her own business."

"She cares about you."

Teddi chewed the lipstick off her lower lip at the same time she bit back her anger. "That's nice. Really." She grabbed the ladle and starting filling the pot again. "But there's nothing wrong. I'm just a little moody, is all. Now, I've got work to do and I bet so do you. You'd be better off worrying about your chili than about people you don't know anything about."

All rightee then.

I backed out of the drag queens' tent, gave Ginger a

shrug when I went by that pretty much said *Don't ask me what's the matter with her!,* and would have gotten right back to work if something near the entrance to the Alamo didn't catch my eye.

Charcoal gray suit.

White shirt.

Red tie.

Did the man never see a weather report?

I gave Sylvia a flimsy excuse about needing to find a ladies' room, lifted my long skirt, and took off before Nick could slip from my sight.

"You're not in jail!" It wasn't what I meant to say when I finally caught up with him, but honestly, I was so relieved, I couldn't help myself.

Nick jerked away from the hand I automatically clamped on his arm. "Jail? Why would I be in jail?"

All that running and I was winded. I sucked in a breath of tropical air and pressed a hand to my heart. "This is how we're going to handle the problem?" Good thing all that barking and woofing was going on at the fund-raiser or everyone there would have heard me when my voice rose to the night sky. "You're going to act like you don't know what I'm talking about?"

"I don't know what you're talking about."

Nick stepped away.

I stepped in front of him.

"Let me refresh your memory," I said. "Back in LA, you beat up Dominic Laurentius and put him in the hospital. Before that, he was your partner on the police force. After that, you were both forced to resign."

For a moment, he was so still and quiet, I thought maybe he didn't hear me. Then I saw a muscle jump at the base of his jaw. "I didn't kill him," he said.

"But you did beat him up really bad."

Nick's gaze flickered to mine, then moved away just as quickly. "You did your homework. Yeah, I beat up Dom. Two years ago. And believe me, I paid the price. I resigned from my job, gave up my career, sacrificed my pension."

I knew the answer to my next question would tell me a lot, so I paid close attention to Nick's expression when I asked, "Was it worth it?"

Of course he didn't give me the satisfaction of a flinch. Or a grimace. Or even a groan.

"What exactly are you trying to prove here, Maxie?" he shot back.

My temper snapped. "Oh, I dunno. Maybe it would be nice to prove that you're not the one who smashed ol' Dominic's guitar, then wrapped the strings around his neck and pulled them tight enough to slice through his windpipe. But then, I guess I'm the glass-half-full type. Always looking for the bright side of a situation."

"Maybe you should just mind your own business instead."

"Really?" I propped my fists on my hips. "What were you thinking, Nick? You lied to me. Heck, you lied to the police. You said you didn't know Dominic. You think they don't already know what I know?"

"They know." Nick ran a hand through hair the color of Vermont maple syrup, and though he did his best to hide the reaction, I noticed that just a little bit of the starch went out of his shoulders. "I went into the station this morning and saw Gilkenny. I told her everything."

"And she said . . . ?"

"They already knew most of it. Of course they already knew." He puffed out a breath of annoyance. "I used to interview suspects and wonder how they could sit there and tell bald-faced lies, then when it came to be my turn . . ." There was something about a helpless shrug from a macho guy like Nick that was especially pathetic. "I don't know what I was thinking. It was stupid. I told Gilkenny it was stupid."

"And she told you she agreed."

One corner of his mouth pulled tight. "She did, and she was right. We've cleared the air. She knows everything now."

"Great. So now she knows you once beat up your partner so bad, you put him in the hospital. How do you think that makes you look?"

"It doesn't matter how I look. It happened, and I can't change it. That doesn't mean I killed the guy."

"It looks like it does."

Those intense blue eyes of his snapped to my plain brown ones. "You think I killed Dom?"

"Does it matter what I think?"

"I had no idea he was in San Antonio. Not until you called me last night and I came back here and saw the body."

"Except . . ." I'd almost forgotten! I sucked in a breath. "When he saw you last night, he hightailed it in the other direction. He recognized you right away."

"Obviously. And he didn't want to see me any more than I would have wanted to see him."

"I didn't tell the cops about that because I wanted to talk to you about it first."

"Not to worry, I told them. And I told them I had no idea Dom was here in town."

That didn't make me feel much better. "You told them that Laurentius came looking for you? You're making it look worse and worse for yourself."

"What do you want from me, Maxie? First you tell me I should have told the police the truth; now you say it should only be part of the truth."

"But you're digging yourself a bigger hole!"

"I didn't kill Dom." Nick's voice snapped with authority. "You can believe me or not. The police can believe me or not. But it's true. I never saw him last night, not until he was already dead."

"All right then." I balled my hands into fists and pressed them to my sides, the better to contain the desperation and anger that built inside me like steam in a teakettle. "If you didn't do it, then we need to figure out who did."

"No, we don't need to figure out anything. You don't need to figure out anything. I'll take care of it."

"But I can help. Really, Nick. You know I can. Look what I've already found out. I found out who the victim was and how he used to be your partner and how you put him in the hospital. And now the cops know all that, too, and you know they're going to glom on to you as a suspect and they're not going to look any further. If the two of us are working our own angle—"

"I don't need to work an angle; not when I didn't do it."

"Okay, not an angle then. That's not what I meant,

anyway. I mean if the two of us talk to some people and see what we can find out, we've got a better chance at uncovering the truth. And with two of us, it will go faster."

The way his brows dropped low over his eyes, I knew he was trying to find a way to dispute this, but in the end, he really couldn't. He puffed out a breath of surrender. "I've already done some digging," he said. "But so far, I haven't come up with much."

"Teddi's worried about something," I told him. "You know, the drag queen. We need to figure out if she knew Dominic. She's jumpy and nervous and she wore a housedress tonight."

When Nick shot me a look, I figured it was easier just to keep going rather than to explain. "And I saw one of the beauty queens give Laurentius a bowl of chili last night. Too bad he wasn't poisoned, huh? That would make things nice and easy. I saw him talking to Eleanor Alvarez, too. You know, the woman in charge of the whole shebang. She says they were just chatting, but I'll tell you what, whatever they were talking about, she didn't look happy."

"That's all good." Nick nodded, confirming this to himself.

"But really, Nick, I think the first thing we need to do is figure out what Dominic was doing in San Antonio in the first place."

"I did some digging of my own, and I've already got that covered," he said. "Dom was working security. For Consolidated Chili."

CHAPTER 6

Lucky for me, Nick got a call just then. Something about some drunk guy over near the entrance to the fund-raiser who was trying to get in and rescue all those dogs he heard barking. Thank you, drunk guy. I didn't have Nick tagging along when I made my way over to the Consolidated Chili tent.

I got there just in time to see the butt of the guy in the very nice suit and the very big ten-gallon cowboy hat when he got into the back of that sleek black limo of his.

"That's John Wesley Montgomery, right?" I asked a woman standing nearby. "He's some big shot, huh?"

"The biggest," she told me. "There's a lot of money in canned chili."

And a lot of sodium, too, I suspected, along with a

long list of chemicals and other ingredients that were never intended to be consumed by man or beast.

John Wesley Montgomery couldn't see me, but I made a face at the limo, anyway, as a way of showing my solidarity with real chili lovers everywhere.

Then I got down to business.

I looked over the crowd of jeans-clad animal huggers enjoying heaping bowls of Consolidated Chili's products and dodged a couple beauty queens who were insistent (in a very nice and toothy way, of course) about shoving hokey souvenirs at me. It wasn't until after I was the proud owner of four cardboard coasters, two bottle openers, and one of those rubbery jar openers that was shaped like a can and had the word *Consolidated* emblazoned across it that I found the beauty queen I was looking for, the one I'd seen giving Dominic Laurentius a bowl of chili the night before. I made a beeline for her.

This particular night, she wasn't looking so beautiful. Oh, she had on a very short, very tight black dress. Just like she had the night before. And she still wore that corny sparkling tiara and the satin banner across her chest that proclaimed her *Miss Texas Chili Pepper.* And that big hair? It was just as blond and just as big, and every single hair of her amazing shoulder-length flip was exactly in place. How it stayed that way when the humidity pressed around us like a smothering pillow, I can't say.

No matter. She looked as perfect as a beauty queen could.

But I knew the telltale signs when I saw them—Miss Texas Chili Pepper had been crying. The tip of her nose was just the teensiest bit red. So were her eyes. Me? Jump to conclusions? All the time! I jumped for all I was worth.

"Hey, too bad about that murder that happened here last night, huh?"

Whatever she was expecting from the woman in the cheap wig and the long black skirt, it wasn't this. She actually flinched before she could hand me a red pen that said *Consolidated Chili* on it in bright yellow lettering.

I tucked my hands behind my back, the better to send the message that I could not be bought with Consolidated's pieces of silver. "You knew him?" I asked her.

"Him?" Nobody does I-don't-know-what-you're-talking-about quite as well as a beauty queen. Not that I knew that many beauty queens, of course, but they aren't all that different from those oh-so-cool girls back in high school who had all of Daddy's money, Mommy's credit cards to use at the mall, and every boy in school after them because there's no guy in the world who can resist a conquest, especially when it comes along with perky breasts, a perfect smile, and a don't-touch attitude.

Phony eyelashes batting, Miss Texas Chili Pepper mustered up all the attitude she was able. "Who on earth are you talking about?"

"The guy who was murdered about fifty yards from here last night? Over near the porta-potties? Don't tell me you don't know about it, because if you don't, you're the only one in San Antonio who hasn't heard the news. It's all anybody around here can talk about."

Right hand to cheek. "Oh, that man."

Like she thought that lame gesture was enough to

distract me? News flash: that sort of tactic didn't work on an old pro like me; I'd used it myself plenty of times.

I kept my eyes on her face to better gauge her reaction. "You were talking to him here in your tent last night. You handed him a sample of chili."

She had green eyes, like a cat's, and she rolled them ever so innocently, her Texas drawl suddenly as heavy as the muggy night air. "I talked to a whole lot of folks last night. It's my job. My duty. You know, as Miss Texas Chili Pepper."

"How did you know him?"

"A dead person?" Her eyes went wide. "I didn't. I mean, I may have spoken to him. After all—"

"It's your duty. Yeah. Whatever. So some guy you didn't know but talked to once got killed and you've spent the day crying?"

Her shake of the head might have been more convincing if she didn't sniffle at the same time. "I don't know what you're talking about."

"Your image, for one thing. What are people going to think if they see Miss Texas Chili Pepper has a red nose?"

"Is it? Red?" Don't asked me where she stashed anything in a dress that formfitting, but she reached into a pocket, pulled out a compact, and took at gander at herself in the little mirror. She winced, set the compact down on the nearest table, and bent closer so she could peer into the mirror at the same time she powdered her nose.

"I'm allergic," she said once she was done. "You know, to cats and dogs and such. And with so many animals here tonight . . . well, what's a poor girl going to do?"

"Not attend animal fund-raisers?"

Her smile was tight. Oh, how she pitied me! "We all have a duty to our world and the poor, innocent creatures that inhabit it," she said. "Even if it's sometimes painful. Allergies or no allergies, my own needs aren't as important as those of the poor animals that suffer out on the streets of cities all across this great country. They need to be housed and fed. They need medicine, and most importantly, they need plenty of love. I can't help deliver that message if I'm home and avoiding my duty."

"Looks to me like all you're delivering is pens with the Consolidated Chili name on them."

"Would you like one?" When she held out a pen to me, her smile was as wide as the dome of stars above our heads.

"I'll pass," I told her. "Besides, rather than a pen, I'd like the truth."

"The truth?" That lifted chin, those thrown-back shoulders . . . it all might have been more convincing if not for the fact that her bottom lip quivered. "The truth is that I don't know what you're talking about. Now if you'll excuse me, I have people to greet."

She glided away, reaching into the sparkling bag she had hung over one shoulder for the booty, and handing out pens left and right.

"Jar opener?"

The question brought me spinning around, and I found myself nose to jar opener with a very tall woman with inky hair. She, too, was in a formfitting dress and was wearing the requisite tiara and sash. It said she was *Miss Texas Triangle*.

"No thanks," I told her. "You already gave me one."

"Oh, come on, take another one." She shoved the rubbery opener into my hands. "We've got oodles of them, and you can always use a jar opener."

"What I could really use is the lowdown," I said.

"About Consolidated Chili? Why, it's the largest manufactured chili company in the world! Did you know that? I did not, not until that wonderful Mr. John Wesley Montgomery talked to us all before last night's event. The largest in the world. I'll tell you what, that just impressed me no end. Doesn't it impress you no end?"

"No end," I assured her. "But what I'd really like is the lowdown on her." Since I had my eyes on Miss Texas Chili Pepper, Miss Texas Triangle couldn't miss who I was talking about.

"She's upset," I said.

"Has been all the while we've been here tonight," Miss TT told me.

"She says the sniffling and the red eyes, it's because she's allergic to dogs."

"Is that what she said?" The tiny smile that played around the woman's very red lips told me that gossip was second nature. "Well, that may very well be true. But only if dogs play the guitar."

"Aha! I thought so." I spun away from watching Miss Texas Chili Pepper, who wasn't doing much of anything interesting, anyway, and looked up at the woman. The way she'd positioned herself under the lights, the rhinestones in that crown of hers winked down at me. "She knew the victim?"

"Let's see, what did those people on the news say his name was?" Honestly, I don't think Miss Texas Triangle needed to think about it, but she pretended she did. "Dominic Laurentius. Yes, that's it. Did she know him? We all knew Dom. He worked for Consolidated Chili."

"Security, right?"

"That's what Dominic always said." She twitched her shoulders. "Personally—and I don't mean to speak ill of the dead, believe me when I tell you this—but personally, I wasn't sure I could always believe Dominic. Oh, he talked a good game. And if you saw him at all yesterday, you might have noticed he had dreamy eyes."

And dreamy shoulders, and a luscious mouth, and a strong jaw, and . . .

I batted the thoughts away.

"But you . . ." I looked around, taking in all the beauty queens with one look. "How did you know the victim? You don't work for Consolidated Chili."

"Heavens, no!" Like Miss Texas Chili Pepper, she'd perfected the art of hand to cheek and she used it with wild abandon. "That would be a conflict of interest, wouldn't it? Me, working for the company and vying for the title of Miss Consolidated Chili this coming weekend? I just knew him from events like this. When I appear in public . . . well, I don't mean to sound too full of myself, but you understand." She glanced down and gave me the quickest once-over in the history of mankind, her gaze lingering on the wig.

"Well, maybe you don't," she conceded. "But ever since the seven of us here were named finalists for the Miss Consolidated Chili crown, we've been appearing in public together. Dominic, he provided security on behalf of the company."

Like I was actually impressed, I smiled. "And is that how Miss Texas Chili Pepper knew Dominic Laurentius?"

"How she knew that man was in a way that a woman isn't supposed to know a man. Not until they're married, anyway. I mean . . ." Eyelashes flapping. "I may be a little old-fashioned, but that is what I believe. It's how my mother raised me."

"So Miss Texas Chili Pepper . . ." I paused to let her fill in the blank.

"Tiffany. Tiffany Jo Baxter. And I . . ." She extended a hand. "I'm Bindi Monroe."

She wouldn't let me get back to business until I shook, so as soon as that was taken care of, I asked, "So Tiffany and Dominic, they were an item?"

"If that's what you want to call it."

I let my gaze wander over the crowd, but there was no sign of Ms. Baxter. "Well, no wonder she's so upset."

When Miss Texas Triangle realized she let out a screech of laughter, she pressed one perfectly manicured hand to her equally perfectly bowed lips and glanced around to make sure she hadn't made a scene. It was so loud there in the midst of the crowd what with the chatting and the oohing and the barking, she hadn't, and she breathed a sigh of relief.

"She didn't start that crying just last night when she heard the news," Miss TT told me. "Tiffany, she's been crying and moaning for more than a week."

"Because . . . ?"

"Because Dominic, he broke up with her, of course. A little over a week ago. Walked right over to her before the Fall Festival Parade over in Figueroa. Right before we were all set to get on the Texas Beauties float. Imagine, a man being as heartless as that, dumping that sort of news on her when she needed to look her best."

"Did he say why?"

"Why he broke up with her?" Miss TT needed to consider this. Or at least she needed to pretend like she had to. "Well, it's not like I was eavesdropping or anything. I mean, a lady wouldn't do a thing like that, would she?" She didn't give me a chance to answer, but then, maybe she knew I wasn't much of a lady. "He said something about moving on. About how it was fun while it lasted, but . . ." She shrugged. "Well, something tells me a woman like you, you've heard all the same things yourself a time or two."

Or three or four or a dozen.

I did not admit this and give Miss TT the satisfaction of pegging me just right. Instead, I stepped a bit nearer to her.

"Was she mad?" I asked her.

"Tiffany?" She wrinkled up her nose. "Well, not at first. But then like I said, Dom, he caught her off guard. But by the next day . . ." Just thinking about it made Miss TT's dark eyes pop open wide. "I saw Tiffany the next day. You know, on account of how we're both going to be in the Miss Consolidated Chili pageant this coming weekend at that Chili Showdown over at the fairgrounds. And the winner, the winner is going to be the Consolidated Chili spokeswoman! I can't tell you how exciting just the very thought is. I have nothing but admiration for the Consolidated Chili folks."

"And Tiffany?"

"Tiffany, well, she claims she's a huge fan of Tri-C chili, but truth be told . . ." She leaned in close to share the secret with me. "Tri-C served us dinner before we got out here tonight, and Tiffany, she passed on the chili. She had a salad instead."

"I don't really care what she eats. What about Tiffany and Dom?"

"Oh. Well, next time I saw her, I mean after the day Dominic dropped that news on her like a load of bricks, well, the way she stomped into our first walk-through rehearsal, I thought the heels of her shoes would just poke right through the floor. She was that mad."

"At Dom?"

"At the world! At cruel, cruel fate. But yeah, mostly at Dom. What that woman said she'd do to him if she ever got her hands on him was positively—"

Just when things were starting to get really interesting, the realization of all she was telling me dawned on Miss Texas Triangle, and she clamped her lips shut.

I smiled to make it look like I didn't care nearly as much as I did. "Been there," I assured her, and she didn't have to know it was true. "And let me tell you, I had plenty of nasty plans for my ex." Also true. "I'm sure there was a time or two that I said I'd like to kill him. And it's not like anyone could blame Tiffany, is it? After all, she was dumped. Of course she said she'd like to kill Dominic. Right?"

"I've known Tiffany for years and years," Miss TT told me, and she was sure to add, "You know, she's older than me. Nearly twenty-five."

"So you probably know her better than a lot of people do."

"I do. And I know that no matter what she might have said—"

"So she did say she wanted to kill Dominic."

"That doesn't mean she meant it."

"But she was still mad yesterday. Even though he dumped her over a week ago."

She nibbled on her lower lip. "Well, I hadn't seen her in a while. And yesterday when I got here, I asked how she was doing."

"And she said . . . ?"

Miss TT threw me a quick glance. Maybe she was trying to decide if she could trust me or not. "She said if she bumped into Dom, she was going to grab a knife and push it straight through his stone-cold heart." She gave a nervous little laugh. "But you understand, she couldn't have been serious. She was just acting like a crazy lady."

A crazy lady.

Senora Loca.

Could Tiffany have been the one Dominic was referring to? Was that the reason he'd come frantically looking for Nick?

"Did you see them together after that?" I asked Miss TT.

"They were talking. Once. But it's not like they were arguing or anything. It was just a chat. Tiffany gave him a sample of our chili."

"Was it a friendly chat?"

"Tiffany's face was a little red."

"And Dominic's?"

"Well, you didn't know Dom, did you? The man wasn't bothered by a thing. I mean, really. To that man, everything was like water rolling off a duck's back."

"Including how he made Tiffany feel when he dumped her."

Her top lip curled. "Just watching from the outside, I could tell he didn't give a d—" She cleared her throat and looked around to make sure no one had overheard what was apparently a no-no word for beauty queens. "Dom didn't care. Not one little bit. He broke Tiffany's heart, and he acted like it didn't matter. It's no wonder the poor girl was angry."

"Angry enough to kill?"

"Tiffany is Miss Texas Chili Pepper. She'd never do a thing like that. Of course . . ." Miss TT's attention was distracted when Tiffany strolled by about twenty feet from us. She had an odd way of holding herself, her right hand out to offer pens to the people around her, her left arm close to her side. No doubt it was how beauty queens were trained. After all, it took a special girl to hang on to her composure and her bouquet of flowers once that sparkly crown was placed on her head.

"Tiffany's got a following. In the pageant world, I mean," Miss TT said, almost to herself. "And that Miss Consolidated Chili pageant is coming up. It's not that I have one little ounce of doubt that I'm going to win and become the company spokeswoman, but if something happened and she couldn't be there . . ."

I could just about see the wheels turning inside her head.

"You wouldn't say anything that wasn't true, would you?" I asked, because let's face it, I might want to get to the bottom of our little murder mystery, but having Ms. TT lie and send me heading off down that road would get me nowhere fast.

"I'm Miss Texas Triangle, and after this weekend, I'm going to be Miss Consolidated Chili." Her shoulders shot back. "And if there's one thing I've learned from John Wesley Montgomery, it's that his business is based on quality and integrity. Of course I'd never lie. I haven't lied. I told you, Tiffany said she'd like to kill Dominic."

"And do you think she could have done it?"

When Tiffany sashayed by with a string of adoring fans behind her, Miss TT's eyes narrowed.

"Oh yes," she said. "I know it for a fact. Tiffany was as mad as a whole box of hornets. She hated Dom Laurentius. Oh yes, she very well could have killed him."

CHAPTER 7

It should come as no surprise that I am something of a night owl.

I blame this habit on years of growing up with a mother who tended bar in our Wicker Park neighborhood in Chicago and whose hours were erratic at best. Sure, there were babysitters. They all pretty much gave up after staying with me one time, and after enough of them waved the white flag, Mom surrendered, too. She took me to work with her, and I camped out in the bar owner's office. In theory, I was supposed to be doing my homework and catching up on my sleep. The reality looked something more like me sneaking out of the office to play pinball, hustle the clientele who didn't think a little girl could play pool (they were oh, so wrong!), and bugging Big Sal, the cook, for burgers and chicken soup and her chili, too, until I realized my own chili was way better and took over the chili cookin' duties.

By that time, my own personal time clock was set, and I kept the crazy schedule, feeling more energetic once the sun went down than I ever did when it was shining in my eyes.

Still, nights of working the fund-raisers over at Alamo Plaza and days at the fairground for the Showdown were taking their toll.

The next day when I was dressed as the Chili Chick and supposed to be dancing up a storm in front of the Palace, I was instead leaning against the RV, tuckered out and dying for a nap.

And it was only a little past noon.

I yawned and stretched and reminded myself that it wasn't fair to leave Sylvia out there handling customers on her own.

That was right before I told myself that it was Wednesday and the Showdown wasn't anywhere near as busy that day as it would be on the weekend. For all I knew, Sylvia was getting in a little nap herself behind the display she'd created on our front counter, orderly pyramids constructed out of jars of our most popular chili spices. The weekend, that's when the real crowds would arrive, along with the beauty queens vying for the title of Miss Consolidated Chili.

"Miss Consolidated Chili." There was no one around to hear me, but I snorted anyway, because it was the right thing to do. "What was Tumbleweed thinking to let them have a contest for a canned chili maker at the Showdown?"

No matter that there was no one around to answer my question; I already knew the answer. Tumbleweed was thinking about what Tumbleweed was always thinking about—the vendors who traveled the country with the Showdown. He knew that the pageant meant publicity and that publicity meant customers and that customers meant sales. I got it. Really, I did. But I wasn't about to swallow my pride and cozy up to Tri-C, and there was no way I was going to attend the pageant.

Unless, of course, it was to see Tiffany Jo Baxter, Miss Texas Chili Pepper, led away in handcuffs for the murder of Dominic Laurentius.

Tiffany, see, wasn't just my best suspect. She was my only suspect.

And it was driving me crazy.

"Too easy," I grumbled. "Guy dumps girl. Girl kills guy." As much as I got it (and believe me, after being played for a sucker by Edik back in Chicago, I got it), I just couldn't wrap my head around the reality. It wasn't that I didn't think a beauty queen could be nasty enough to kill; it was just that I wasn't sure Tiffany was smart enough.

Not like, say, Nick was.

Had anyone been hanging around behind the scenes, they would have heard a sigh whoosh out from behind the mesh at the front of the Chick costume. This was not the usual sigh I sighed when sighing about Nick. That one was all about plain ol' unadulterated lust, and this one . . .

I thought about what Nick had said, about how he wasn't the one who killed Dom.

And then I thought about how he'd once beat up Dom so bad, Dom ended up in a hospital.

And I wondered if I was being played for a fool again.

Another sigh, and I knew all this thinking and sighing was getting me nowhere. It was time to get to work. I pushed off from the RV and headed out front.

Or at least I tried.

Before I made it even as far as the back door of the Palace, two strong arms went around my chili and held me in place.

"Hey!" I yelled and squirmed. I gasped and strained to take a look out of the mesh and over my shoulder to see who had hold of me, but let's face it, in a giant chili constructed of canvas and wire, that was nearly impossible.

And what was really annoying was that something told me that the person hanging on to me knew it, too.

Those two strong arms tightened around the Chick, and before I could scream or call out for help, my feet were off the ground. That's when my attacker braced me against a muscular chest and started spinning.

The scenery beyond the mesh whirled in front of my eyes.

The side of the RV.

The back of the Palace.

The tires of the RV parked next to ours.

The side of the RV.

The back of the Palace.

I gulped and tried my best to remember the spotting technique I'd learned in a long-ago dance class. Stare at one place. Find it again. Keep from getting dizzy.

It didn't work for me then, and it sure didn't work now. My stomach swooped, and I was pretty sure I was going to upchuck the Twinkies that had been my breakfast.

Around and around, my head spun along with the slice of scenery I saw when I dared to look beyond the mesh.

I flapped my arms and tried to elbow my attacker in the stomach, but I missed by a mile and ended up stabbing nothing but air.

As quickly as it started, the spinning stopped.

"Mind your own business," a gravelly voice that definitely belonged to a man growled close to my ear.

And just like that, my assailant loosened his hold.

My stilettos slammed back down to the ground, but by then, my legs were rubber. I crumpled face-first in a heap of canvas and wire and mesh and nausea, my knees bloodied from where I landed in the gravel. I managed to brace my hands in the grit and push myself up, but looking around was another thing altogether.

I grunted and spun and landed on my chili butt. I cursed and rolled and managed to get to my side.

By that time, my attacker was gone and I was all alone.

Moaning, I flopped down on my back, my legs spread out, my arms flung out to the sides, and my breath coming in gulps that burned my lungs and heated up the inside of the Chick.

I couldn't move, and after a minute or two of struggling, I didn't even try. I lay there like a chili lump, staring up at the cloudless Texas sky and wondering what the heck just happened and who the heck had just threatened me.

That's exactly where Sylvia found me.

She bent over far enough to peer beyond the mesh at me. From my vantage point, all I could see were her big blue eyes.

"I'm up front working my fingers to the bone," she grumbled. "And here you are, taking a nap. Honestly, Maxie, don't you ever do anything useful?"

Call me superstitious.

Go ahead, see if I care.

When I finally hoisted myself up off the ground and dragged into the RV, I peeled out of the Chick costume and refused to put it on again that day.

No way was I going to take the chance of being bushwhacked again.

Sans costume and wearing denim shorts and a chili pepper red shirt with Jack's face embroidered above the heart, I stayed busy and worked the Palace the rest of that day. Yes, Sylvia was suspicious about my sudden burst of diligence, and honestly, I can't say I blame her. Even when I tried to explain what had happened there behind the Palace earlier in the day, she didn't quite get it.

"Well, I can see why some people would want you to mind your own business," she said. We were restocking shelves, and she handed me a box that contained individual packages of dried peppers and reminded me to be sure I put them out alphabetically. "But I can't think of anything you've done lately that would make someone threaten you." She gave me a piercing look. "Or have you done something?"

"Scouts honor." I held up a hand, three fingers folded down and two extended, as if to prove it. "I'm hardly investigating at all."

"Investigating!" She combined a sniff and a harrumph

into a new and altogether demeaning sort of sound. "You know better than to stick your nose where it doesn't belong."

"I know if I didn't, you'd still be in jail back in Taos," I reminded her.

Big points for Sylvia; she didn't dispute this. Instead, she propped the cardboard box she was holding against one hip and, thinking, pursed her lips. "So if someone told you to mind your own business, maybe you're minding their business."

This was an observation convoluted enough to be worthy of me, and Sylvia must have known it because she made a face. "What I mean is, someone must want you to back off. Because maybe you're getting too close to the truth."

Of course I'd come to this same conclusion sometime between when I landed on my chili butt on the ground behind the Palace and when Sylvia had been gracious enough to offer me a hand to help me to my feet. "The only person I was looking at as a serious suspect was a woman," I told her. "And the person who grabbed me . . ." I relived the scene. "Definitely a man."

"And you don't have any men in mind?" Her eyes were the same color as the Texas skies above us, and she rolled them for all she was worth. "You know what I mean. I mean, I know you always have men in mind and they're always the wrong kind of men and obviously a murderer would definitely be the wrong kind of man. So are any of your suspects men?"

I debated about telling her what I was thinking, but in the end, talking out my worries seemed a better plan than keeping them all hidden inside, nibbling away at my brain.

"Nick knew Dom," I said.

"The victim." Sylvia nodded. "Did Nick know him well enough to hate him?"

I thought about how they were former partners and about how Dom ended up in the hospital. "Yes."

"Do you think Nick killed him?"

"Why do you have his number on speed dial, anyway?"

Honestly, those were not the words I planned to have come out of my mouth, and just listening to them, I cringed. The last thing I needed to do with Sylvia was show any kind of weakness. If I did, it would be the hungry lion and the injured wildebeest scenario. I'd just revealed myself as a limping wildebeest, and I waited for her to pounce and devour me.

Instead, she finished stacking a fresh row of Thermal Conversion, flattened the box the jars had come out of, and set it in the pile of cardboard we'd take to Tumbleweed's trailer for recycling.

"It's not what you think," she said.

"You don't know what I think."

A tiny smile played its way around her mouth. "Give me some credit, Maxie. I've known you nearly thirty years. Of course I know what you think. You think Nick and I—"

"Do you?"

"Have a thing going? With Nick?" There was another box of spice jars sitting on the floor of the Palace waiting to be unpacked and put out on display, but she didn't bend to retrieve it. Instead, she cocked her head and studied me. "You like him."

This was not something I was going to discuss. Not when Sylvia might be about to reveal what I thought she was about to reveal.

I chewed on my lower lip.

Sylvia picked up the box of spice jars and slit it open with a box cutter. "He's a good man," she said. "Not that I know him very well or anything, but you can tell that sort of thing, you know?" Apparently, she remembered who she was talking to, because she added, "Well, maybe you don't know. You've never been very good at figuring out who the good guys were and who the stinkers were. Nick . . . well, I can tell, he's one of the good ones."

This wasn't news to me. Tell that to the chunk of ice that suddenly formed in the pit of my stomach.

"You and Nick . . ." I did my best to make it sound like it didn't matter, like this was good news and I was happy for her. To tell the truth, maybe I was. If Nick and Sylvia had a relationship, that meant I could put him out of my mind once and for all.

Of course that didn't explain the sudden hollow feeling that settled itself somewhere between my heart and my stomach.

"You and Nick, you're—"

When Sylvia squealed with laughter, I didn't get a chance to finish the sentence.

"Come on, Maxie. You know me better than that!" She smiled in the way she often did when she was doing her best to be understanding and I was doing my best to pretend I didn't notice. "He's not my type," she said.

"So you're not—"

"In a relationship? I don't need some bang-bang, shoot-'em-up type. You know that, Maxie. I like people and relationships and situations that are—"

"Boring?" I ventured.

She didn't hold this against me. At least not too much. "I was thinking more like stable," Sylvia said. "Nick's not my type."

Since I couldn't exactly explain the funny little splurt of hope that tangled around my heart, I tried not to be too obvious when I said, "So you're not—"

"We're not," Sylvia assured me. "Not now, not ever."

"Then why—"

"Is his number on speed dial on my phone?" She set down the box of spice jars so she could fold her arms over her chest and give me one of those big-sister looks of hers that she'd been practicing on me for years. Maybe she was finally wearing me down. As far as I could remember, it was the first time I didn't resent it. "I figured I'd better keep Nick's number handy," she said. "You know, in case you get in trouble."

Arguing with her was second nature. Only this time, I couldn't think of anything to say.

In most towns we visit, we start our Chili Showdown on Thursday night and go all the way through the weekend, but because of the fund-raisers on Alamo Plaza all week,

Tumbleweed had decided on a different schedule here in San Antonio. I wasn't complaining. A few more days of cook-off fun is always good by me.

But the new schedule presented a new set of problems, namely, how to bring in customers who were used to this sort of an event on weekends, not Wednesday afternoons.

Leave it to Tumbleweed to come up with an answer.

That afternoon, we'd be holding the cook-off contest for chili verde.

By the time Sylvia and I finished stocking the Palace shelves, the fairgrounds was already teeming with eager contestants and verde fans. Verde, see, has a following all its own, its proponents as fanatical as the chili lovers who favor more conventional chili.

In the world of chili cook-offs, chili verde—sometimes called Colorado Green Chili—can be made with any meat and green chili peppers, but absolutely no beans or pasta. My own favorite version was an old recipe of Jack's that I'd kicked up a notch by adding Anaheim peppers instead of poblanos to the heavenly mixture of pork, fresh tomatillos, cumin, and heaping portions of our own Thermal Conversion spice, but I'd seen dozens of cooks around the country add their own touches, from shredded cheese to cornmeal, lard to limes. There's nothing ordinary about verde, and nothing I enjoy more than watching the competition unfold.

With that in mind, I was all set to head over to the main fairgrounds building where the judging was about to begin when a very weird thing happened.

Well, come to think of it, it was two very weird things.

Martha and Rosa strolled by.

"Is that . . . ?" Sylvia was setting out a new load of brown paper shopping bags with Jack's picture on them, and she stopped and stared. "What are they doing here?"

A nugget of information dislodged itself from the logjam of my mind, and I remembered something I'd seen on the flyers Tumbleweed had sent out to advertise the event. "Martha and Rosa . . . !" In a move worthy of a beauty queen, I slapped a hand to my cheek. "I never put it together. Not until right now. They're judging chili verde."

"Together?" Sylvia leaned to her left so she could look around me to where the two women walked down the midway side by side.

Together we watched them stop at Gert Wilson's setup and admire a set of yellow dish towels with tiny red chilies on them.

Martha said something to Rosa.

Rosa laughed and picked up a gigantic coffee cup with the words *Everything's Bigger in Texas* written across the front of it.

I sucked in a breath. "She's going to clunk her," I told Sylvia. "Rosa's going to use that coffee cup as a weapon."

"Or not," Sylvia told me, watching Rosa set down the cup and go on to examine Gert's display of chili earrings, chili pepper–shaped evening bags, and funny T-shirts with things on them like peppers wearing sombreros, or the words *Capsaicin Junkie*, or my own personal favorite, the one with a picture of a fire-breathing dragon and the words *Monster Hot.*

Now that I knew Sylvia didn't have her eye on him,

maybe I'd wear that one the next time I saw Nick and see if he got the message.

Unless he was in jail, where the message might not have been all that appropriate, anyway.

I batted the thought away just in time to see Rosa bend close and say something to Martha. Martha's laughter streamed across the midway.

"Weren't they the ones who were at each other's throats the other night at the plaza?" Sylvia asked me.

"You got that right." I watched Tumbleweed greet the two women and escort them to the main building for the judging. "And if you ask me, the fact that they're suddenly getting along is more than just a little suspicious."

CHAPTER 8

That night on Alamo Plaza I did my best to keep an eye on Martha and Rosa, and anyone with half a brain could see why. They were cordial—practically chummy—at the Showdown that afternoon. In fact, at the chili verde judging, they chatted like longtime friends, voted for the same winning chili, and left the fairgrounds arm in arm.

After what I'd seen of the two of them on the night of Dom's murder, this struck me as mighty strange. Strange in a murderous sort of way? That remained to be seen. I only knew that at this stage of the game, anything that deflected suspicion away from Nick was a good thing. What is it psychologists call something like that? Transference? I was transferring to beat the band, and the suddenly palsy-walsy Martha and Rosa were as good a place as any to start.

It would have been easier to keep the two Queens descendants in my sights if the night wasn't devoted to raising money for a local food bank and if the place wasn't packed. Apparently, word had gone around about the quality of the chili at the Texas Jack food tent (hurray!), and the line for our chili samples snaked over to the Consolidated Chili tent and looped back around to where Ginger and Teddi were set up. This was a good thing, I told myself, wiping my forehead with the back of one hand. Word was getting out, and plenty of people who tasted the chili verde I'd made in honor of the day's cook-off back at the Showdown said they'd stop in for spices and chili advice that weekend when the Showdown was in full swing.

But the crowd, it was a bad thing, too. Every time I tried to see what was going on with Martha and Rosa . . . and I tried right then and there, standing on my tiptoes and craning my neck and pretty much getting a glimpse of nothing at all but the heads and shoulders of the people who crowded around . . . I got stymied by all those chili lovers. Martha and Rosa could have very well been killing each other—or someone else—and I never would have known it.

"You girls are just amazing!" I guess Ginger's tent wasn't nearly as busy as ours, because she had the time to sidle over and watch me ladle samples into bowls that Sylvia then handed to attendees along with a thank-you for their contribution, a reminder that if they left a tip, the food bank would get even more out of the night, and one of her sunshiny smiles. "I can't believe how busy you are tonight." She gave me a playful poke with one elbow. Just for the record, it was encased (as was her other elbow) in a satin glove that went almost all the way up to her armpit. At the same time I wondered how anyone could keep satin gloves and an emerald green gown studded with rhinestones clean at an event devoted to chili, I marveled at Ginger's sense of style.

"You won the contest, you know," she said with a smile. "I did a final count on your tips from last night before I dropped them off with Eleanor over at the main tent. A day off in New Orleans! You lucky dog! Sylvia's pea green with envy. Not that she'd ever show it." Ginger studied my half sister with something very much like admiration in her eyes before she added, "She's got class."

"And me?" I shot her a sidelong look and did my best to pretend that I wouldn't be offended by anything she said. "I've got—"

"Sass!" Ginger laughed. "And if you ask me, honey, that's way more important!"

I agreed, and laughed, too. My smile was still firmly in place when Ginger's melted right away.

"I need your help," she confided.

I scraped out the remains of one of the pots of chili and moved on to the next, filling bowl after bowl, and as long as Ginger was standing there, she helped, handing one bowl after another to Sylvia.

"What kind of help?" I asked.

She shot a look over at the tent next door. "When I was counting your tips from last night . . . well, it got me thinking. About our tips. You did so much better than we did!"

Even though I knew I didn't have to apologize, I felt a little guilty, and apparently, Ginger knew it. Between bowls, she put an arm around my shoulders for a quick hug, and the warm floral scent of Calvin Klein Euphoria enveloped me.

"Believe me, I'm not taking it personally," she assured me. "But I am curious." Again, her gaze strayed over to the next tent where Teddi was handing out chili samples, stone-faced and unsmiling. "And worried."

"About Teddi?"

"It's just not like her," Ginger confessed. "She loves dressing up. She loves showing off. And look at her." We did. "Last night a housedress. Tonight . . ." She looked over Teddi's outfit—a pair of '80s-inspired acid wash jeans, an off-the-shoulder shirt, leg warmers, and transparent jelly shoes, all in Pepto-Bismol pink. "She didn't even try to look like a Chili Queen tonight."

"You're worried Teddi's losing interest in the fund-raisers?"

Ginger sighed. "I'm worried . . ." She took a breath for courage and threw back those wonderfully wide shoulders of hers. "I counted your tips last night, Maxie. And I know your tent has been a little busier than ours, but really, that doesn't explain why we're taking in so very little. I'm worried . . ." She shot another look at Teddi and lowered her voice. "I'm worried that Teddi is dipping into the till."

"Stealing the tips?" I gasped out the words. "Why?"

"Who can say! Believe me, I've never seen her do anything like this before. I've never even thought it was possible. But it's like I said last night; I think she's gone a little crazy. You've got the perfect vantage point from over here. I thought if you had a chance . . . I mean, don't worry about it when you're busy or anything . . . but I thought when you had a chance and if you think of it, if you could just look over to our tent once in a while. Our tip jar . . . well, you can see it perfectly from here. I thought maybe if you noticed anything fishy going on . . ."

She didn't say what she wanted me to do if that happened, and that was okay. If I saw something fishy going on, I'd worry about it then.

"No problem," I assured Ginger.

"And no progress with finding the murderer, right?"

She didn't wait for me to answer, but then, I guess the way I grumbled, she pretty much knew my answer.

"I wish I could help," she said.

"I wish you could, too. I wish someone could. People say they saw Dom on Monday night. A couple of them admit talking to him. But there's only one who has any real motive."

This, of course, was not precisely true since, transference or not, I knew there was someone else. Even if he didn't want to come clean and tell me what his I-hate-Dom feelings were all about.

"You should talk to her again," Ginger told me. "That beauty queen. That is who you're talking about, right? Word is out all around here, and everybody knows that the victim dumped her. Obviously, she's got motive galore. Besides, I didn't trust her from the moment I saw her. Imagine wearing cappuccino-colored lipstick with her pale complexion!"

"You're talking about that murder, right?"

Apparently, not quietly enough. That's why the guy

who came to empty the trash cans butted in on my conversation with Ginger.

"Some story, huh?" The name embroidered on the man's gray shirt said he was Serge, and ol' Serge stepped right up as if we were at a cocktail party and just looking for someone new to join the conversation. "I saw the pictures in the paper," he said. "You know, of that guy that got killed. And I keep wondering if I saw him around here on Monday night. And I can't remember."

"You probably did," I informed him. "He had a guitar."

"That guitar guy!" Thinking about it, Serge pursed his lips. "That's the one who was sick all night, right? You know, I don't usually pay much attention to that kind of stuff. I mean, people coming and going and all—it's always too busy at something like this to notice any one person. But this guy, this guy with the guitar, I saw him a bunch of times. He was always heading toward those porta-potties over on the other side of the plaza. After five or six times, I couldn't help myself. I asked him if everything was all right."

"And what did he say?" I asked Serge.

"Told me he must have gotten a bad batch of chili somewhere. And the way he looked, I believed him. All pale and shaky. You know, like he had the flu or something. Imagine that, a bad batch of chili! At a Chili Queens event. Hey, speaking of chili . . ." Serge eyed the nearest pot, and I loaded up a bowl for him.

After all, I owed him. Thanks to Serge, I knew something more about Dominic Laurentius.

A bad bowl of chili? Did it mean anything?

I couldn't say, but I did know that when I saw him talking to Miss Texas Chili Pepper on Monday night, she just so happened to be handing him a bowl of chili.

I chewed over this new nugget of information and bided my time, scooping and handing out chili while I kept an eye on Ginger and Teddi's tent—and Ginger and Teddi's tip jar. I filled Sylvia in on what Ginger had told me about the missing tips, and she kept her eyes peeled, too. Truth be told, I think we were both relieved when we didn't notice anything even vaguely sketchy going on. For one thing, I wouldn't want to be the one to inform Ginger that she'd been right about Teddi's thieving ways, and for another, I liked Ginger and Teddi, in spite of the fact that their makeup was far more professionally applied than my own and their outfits (even Teddi's '80s apparel) looked better than the black skirt I'd paired up that night with a shirt I'd found at a small shop over near the fairgrounds, a sleeveless red peasant top embroidered with lots of flowers. Shamed by Ginger and Teddi's sense of style, I'd left the wig with the long black braids back at the RV.

Thinking and sweating and wondering what Dom being sick might have to do with how a big guy like him could have been overpowered and what Tiffany handing him a bowl of chili might (or might not) have had to do with the whole thing, I waited for a lull in the crowd, swallowed my disgust at even looking like I was supporting the canned-chili crowd, and headed over to the Consolidated tent in search of Miss Texas Chili Pepper.

"Not here," a woman told me. She was dressed in black pants and a yellow T-shirt with CCC emblazoned on it in alligator green letters. Since the color scheme reminded me of the sign above the Palace, I couldn't help but bristle. Leave it to scumbags like Tri-C to not only co-opt chili and stick it in a can, but to try and copy the most iconic sign in chili-dom.

"She was here not too long ago." The woman glanced around. "She was handing out bottle openers just a little while ago. Would you like one?"

I ignored her offering.

"Do you know when she'll be back?" I asked.

"She's probably just on break. You know, over in the motor home where we go to cool off. Whew!" She fanned her face with one hand. "I sure could use it tonight. Aren't you just dying, honey, in that long skirt of yours?"

I was, but rather than admit it, I scampered off in the vague direction she indicated. It didn't take me long to find the Tri-C motor home. But then, it was chili pepper red and had the words *Consolidated Chili* painted on it in letters taller than me.

I knocked and waited until I heard a "Come in" before I went inside, and when I did . . . well, I am not an especially shallow person, or envious, either. At least I don't like to think so. But it was a little hard not to get jealous when I looked around and found myself thinking about the RV Sylvia and I used to pull the Palace and travel around the country.

About the tile floor in our RV that was the same color as the faux-maple cabinets.

About the table bolted to that floor directly behind the driver's seat, and the green vinyl bench on either side of it.

About how small our RV is and how cramped, and how it hasn't been updated since . . . well, I couldn't remember when our RV didn't look exactly like our RV looked now. And I'd been traveling in that RV all my life.

Stepping into the Tri-C motor home (let's face it, it was far too grand to be called an RV), I felt like Dorothy stumbling into a Technicolor Oz.

We're talkin' hardwood floors, cherry cabinetry, a couch bigger than my bed, even a bar and an industrial-sized cappuccino maker. Need I mention the giant flat-screen and the wine cooler and the AC that was cranked and set blessedly low?

If I ever doubted it before, I knew for sure now—there is money in canned chili.

Big money.

"What do you want?"

There is not, however, anything that says a beauty queen who wants to represent a canned chili company needs to be polite when she is out of sight of her fawning fans.

Tiffany had been reclining on the couch with her feet up and a bottle of fizzy water in her right hand. When she saw me, she sat up and swung her bare feet down on the floor. "Why are you bothering me again?" she asked.

"Am I? Bothering you?" Of course I was, but I wasn't about to admit it. Instead, I sashayed across the wonderfully clean and slick floor so I could stand nearer to Miss Texas Chili Pepper. "This is where you guys relax, huh?"

"If by *you guys* you mean the pageant winners who are

vying for the title of Miss Consolidated Chili, yes." Tiffany took a sip of water. "What we do is very hard work. We always have to be at our best and look our best. We need a place where we can rest and relax. You know, before we face our adoring fans again."

"And hand out crappy souvenirs." I strolled a little farther into the cavernous motor home to check out the stairs that led up to a second level, and while I was at it, I checked out the makeup cases that sat in a straight, soldierly line nearby. Black, purple, leopard print. All pretty standard, and each one was knee-high and had a telescoping handle and wheels, and all but one was marked not by the name of its owner but by her title.

Miss Chili's Cookin'.

Miss Texas Spice.

Miss Hotter than a Chili Pepper.

I took a moment to look over the case next to that one. No title on it, but then, there wasn't a lot of room. The entire case was covered with old photos—teenagers playing neon green and blue instruments in a garage band, a shot of a blue ocean and a sweep of beach, Bindi Monroe with a smile on her face and a tiara on her head.

I guess I knew who that case belonged to. I moved on to the next.

Miss Texas Chili Pepper.

I glanced over my shoulder from the shiny, purple case to the Miss it belonged to.

"You haul around an awful lot of makeup."

She stood at the same time she clicked her tongue. "You wouldn't understand."

"Not even about Dom and the bad batch of chili he got?"

Don't think I didn't notice that she hesitated just for an instant.

Don't think she didn't notice that I noticed.

Which was precisely why Tiffany acted like that momentary hitch in our conversation was no big deal.

"I told you. I didn't know that man who got killed. And I certainly don't know anything about bad chili. Consolidated is the largest chili manufacturer in the world. It comes in ten different varieties and—"

"Not really interested in the party line," I told her. "Though it sounds like you're all set for the pageant on Sunday. What I really wanted to talk about was you and Dom."

"Dom, you mean the man I don't know?"

"I mean the man who broke up with you in Figueroa."

She was caught and she knew it, though I have to say, maybe all that beauty pageant training was good for something. Tiffany didn't waste any time disavowing herself from the story.

"Well, it looks like you know all sorts of interesting things," she said. "And Dom was sick on Monday evening? I'm not especially sorry to hear that. If it's true. But I don't see how that concerns me. Since you've apparently been spending your time gossiping about me, you already know, at the time of his unfortunate demise, Dominic and I were no longer seeing each other."

"Because he broke up with you."

"Is that what you heard?" There was a slide-out drawer built into the nearest kitchen cabinet, and Tiffany put her water bottle on the countertop, opened the drawer, then tossed her bottle inside in a recycling container. "The fact is," she told me, sliding the drawer closed, "I'm the one who told Dom I didn't want to see him anymore. As you might imagine, it broke his heart."

"Would that have been right before that parade in Figueroa? Because the way I heard it—"

"The way you heard it obviously isn't the way it happened." In a motor home the size of Delaware, there was plenty of room for Tiffany to get by, but she knocked into me when she sauntered toward the stairs. "Now if you'll excuse me, I need to freshen up and get back outside. You can show yourself out."

I assured her I would.

But I never said how fast.

I stood at the bottom of the stairs and waited until I heard Tiffany's footsteps overhead, then made a move for her makeup case.

Don't ask me what I thought I'd find. I mean, besides a wide variety of lipsticks in that cappuccino shade Ginger didn't like.

But hey, I figured it was worth a try.

I flipped open the case and pulled out the accordion-style foldout trays and did a quick inventory of the contents.

Just like Ginger said, there was plenty of lipstick in the same funny brown shade Tiffany was wearing that day. There was also mascara and fake eyelashes and blemish concealer, and any number of products I never even knew existed. Seaweed soak and skin brightening mask made from tomatoes? I'd stick with soap and water, thanks.

While it was all mildly interesting in a who-has-time-for-this-nonsense sort of way, none of it proved that Tiffany had tried to off Dominic with poisoned chili.

When I heard a door close upstairs and Tiffany's footsteps directly overhead, I moved quickly, sliding those expanding drawers together, and lifted out the top tray of the case so I could take a quick look into the bottom compartment.

The corner of a blue and white box caught my eye, and a distant memory flashed in my brain.

I'd been visiting my grandmother—my mom's mom—and I was bored and looking to get into trouble. I dug through the medicine cabinet in her bathroom and—

With something very much like hope blossoming in my heart, I grabbed the blue and white box and realized it was empty. Fine by me; that made it easy for me to wave it in front of Tiffany's face the moment she was down the steps.

"Laxatives!" I stopped just short of adding a triumphant *aha*. That would have been corny, and besides, the way Tiffany's mouth dropped open told me I didn't need that little bit of drama, anyway. "And don't tell me you're trying to keep your weight down, Tiffany. The box is empty. And the night he died, Dom spent the night running to the bathroom. You tried to poison him with laxatives!"

"Poison?" It would be nice to imagine that Tiffany spit out this single word in a wicked-witch, I'm-the-evil-bad-guy sort of way. Truth be told, she laughed so hard, I thought she was going to keel right over. "Oh, honey, if I wanted to poison Dom, I wouldn't have bothered with laxatives. Don't you read mystery novels? There's cyanide and strychnine and rat poison and—"

Just rolling off the names made her twinkle like . . . er . . . a beauty queen, and I stopped her because it was weirding me out.

"You weren't trying to poison him?"

She puffed out a breath of frustration. Or maybe she was just annoyed. "Of course I wasn't trying to poison him!" Tiffany threw her right hand in the air. "What kind of person do you think I am?"

"But I saw you give him a bowl of chili, and Dom was sick, and—"

"And don't you get it? Haven't you ever had your heart ripped in two?" Tiffany knew she'd opened mouth and inserted foot; her face went ashen. But by then, it was too late, and she knew that, too. She pulled in breath after breath, and when that didn't work to calm her nerves or settle her emotions, she brushed a tear off her cheek.

"You're right, okay? Is that what you wanted me to admit? You're right. Dom dumped me. There. Now you can gloat about it. Or laugh. Or whatever it is you want to do. Now you know that just because I'm beautiful and graceful and talented . . . well, that doesn't mean that my life is perfect. Dom dumped me and he broke my heart and sure, I was plenty mad. I was so mad . . ." Reliving the memory, her eyes narrowed and her shoulders hunched.

"I knew I had to get even," Tiffany said from between perfectly even, blindingly white clenched teeth. "I knew I had to pay him back for the way he hurt me. And I knew he'd be here at the Chili Queens festival. So yes, I bought the laxatives." She tore the empty package out of my hands. "And I took some with me to the Tri-C tent. And I put some in a bowl of chili. And you know what I did?" Her smile was as sleek as the one she'd no doubt offered Dom that night. "I told that low-down, no-good Dom that we needed to let bygones be bygones. That I was willing to get on with my life and forget him, and I wanted him to know that so he didn't have to feel guilty about the way he treated me."

"Did he? Feel guilty?"

Tiffany snorted in a very un-beauty-queen-like way. "Dom never felt guilty about a thing in his life. Surely not about the way he treated women. But the point wasn't to make him feel better about himself, was it?"

Even though an answer wasn't necessary, I answered anyway. "The point was to get him to eat the chili laced with the laxatives."

"Exactly!" Tiffany grinned. "And that's exactly what he did. Gobbled that big ol' bowl of chili right down. And now you're telling me he really was sick the rest of the night?" She hooted with delight. "There is justice in this world. You remember that. There is justice, and scumbags like Dom, they're made to pay the price."

"So a person who can lace chili with laxatives, that person must be coldhearted."

Tiffany's face went hard. "So I put laxatives in Dom's chili. So what? It doesn't prove anything. He was a creep and he deserved what he got. I did it. I admit it. But that doesn't mean I killed him."

CHAPTER 9

The twinkling eyes.

The sunny smile.

The honest-to-gosh goodness.

No, not Sylvia! I'm talking about Tiffany.

About that darned perfect little personality of hers, and about how she could wring her perfectly manicured little hands all she wanted and bat those perfectly fake eyelashes until the cows came home and I still wouldn't believe a word she said.

After all, I'd been done wrong by a guy once, too, and I knew that a little laxative in chili might be fun in a perverse sort of way, but no way did it qualify as revenge.

See, I was convinced that behind the twinkle and the

sparkle and the smile and the style, Tiffany was out for revenge.

But then, I never did trust a blonde.

Blame that on Sylvia.

Yeah, yeah, I know . . . I'd been grabbed, spun around, and told to mind my own business by a guy. But I didn't let even that pertinent fact change my mind. I convinced myself that Tiffany had a minion with strong arms, a flat chest, and a deep voice and went right on believing in the soundness of my theory. In fact, I spent the next day at the Showdown dancing in the Chick costume and hatching up scheme after scheme about how I'd trap Tiffany into making a confession. How hard could it be? The girl was a beauty queen, right?

It helped that on that Thursday afternoon, all the women who were working their beauty queen tushies off over at Alamo Plaza would be packing all their beauty and all their talent and their sparkle and their shine into the Showdown for a rehearsal for Sunday's big Miss Consolidated Chili pageant. I could expose (figuratively speaking, of course) Tiffany onstage in front of everyone! I could make her admit that she'd smashed Dom's guitar and taken the strings and yanked them so tight around his neck that she cut into his windpipe and cut off his air supply!

I could prove once and for all and to everyone—including myself—that Nick was innocent. Then maybe he'd finally realize there was more to me than just some woman who donned stilettos and a chili costume and danced like a fool, all in the name of selling spices and dried peppers.

The thought snuck up and sucker punched me, and I froze, mid–shuffle step with my left leg raised and bent, and ignored the Showdown patrons who stared at me, wondering what had gotten into the Chili Chick and why she was suddenly as still as a statue.

I wondered what had gotten into the Chili Chick, too, and reminded myself in no uncertain terms to get a grip.

Me? Worried about what Nick or any man thought of me?

If that mesh wasn't over my face, the patrons who surrounded me would have heard me grumble.

"This has nothing to do with Nick," I reminded myself. But, of course, it did. Especially if I couldn't prove that Tiffany was our killer.

I danced and planned and plotted until I couldn't move another step or think another thought, and then the Chick dragged through the back door of the Palace for a little shade and a nice, cold bottle of water.

"Work the counter for a while if you need to cool off," Sylvia suggested, and though I refused to come right out and say that was a good idea, I took her up on it. I peeled out of the Chick costume, moved behind the front counter, and spent the next few hours blissfully talking about chili and not thinking about murder.

At least until it was time for the pageant rehearsal.

That's when I told Sylvia I was ducking out for a late lunch and hightailed it toward the building where the rehearsal had already begun.

"Ladies, you've got to remember, you're the best of the best!" I stepped inside just as things were getting started, and I guess I wasn't all that surprised to see Eleanor Alvarez at the center of it all. Eleanor and her Women's League were one of the sponsors of the pageant, because I guess it's only natural that something as crass and commercial as canned chili needs the sort of validation that comes from the Women's League. In fact, the League's special charity—a shelter for abused women—would benefit from the concessions and the take at the gate on the day of the pageant.

The closer I got to the stage, the more I could feel the nervous energy that buzzed around the seven contestants. And there was Miss Texas Chili Pepper in the heart of it all. In skinny jeans and a loose top the color of cherries—and sans crown—Tiffany looked younger than she had back at the Tri-C tent. Younger and more vulnerable.

But don't think that made me change my mind about her murderous heart.

My gaze trained on her, my concentration complete, I watched Tiffany take her place between a petite dark-haired woman and a dazzling redhead as the women were herded into a neat, soldierly row.

Speaking of redheads, Eleanor looked mighty swanky herself that day in a sleeveless dress with a slightly flared skirt. She waved a hand, and the overhead lights caught the honkin' big sapphire ring on her left hand. The ginormous gem was the same color as her silk dress.

"Before we get started," Eleanor said, "let's have some fun. Let's start by shaking out the jitters!"

Like she'd had too many cups of coffee (if there is such a thing), Eleanor jiggled her arms and shook her legs, and that sapphire winked and blinked at me in the glare of the lights. Once they were over their surprise at seeing elegant Eleanor acting like a darned jumping jack, the beauty queens joined in. They shook, rattled, and rolled, and pretty soon, the auditorium was filled with the sounds of their laughter.

"That's a good beginning," Eleanor told them when she finally stopped gyrating. She put a hand to her heart and hauled in a breath. "Now let's do a little practicing. What are you going to do . . . ?" She let her gaze roam slowly over the assembled beauty queens. "What are you going to do when the girl next to you wins?"

A couple of the queens gasped. Somebody called out, "I'm going to cry, that's what I'm going to do."

Somebody else said, "Demand a recount!" and everyone laughed.

I, of course, was more interested in Tiffany's part in all this than in anything else. I sidled into the row of theater seats in front of the stage, picked one that would allow me to keep Tiffany in my sights, and plunked down.

"What you're going to do is what you always do," Eleanor told them. "Not just in beauty pageants, but in life. Because I know, ladies, that you have it all. You're young. You're gorgeous. You've all accomplished something difficult and special, or y'all wouldn't be standing here today vying for the job of Tri-C spokeswoman. But I've got to tell you, life isn't always easy. I know this from experience. Oh, sure, plenty of people look at me and they see the glamour and that famous Alvarez fortune!" She didn't so much laugh as she smiled knowingly.

"From the outside, my life looks ideal, but it came with a price. My dear husband, Jacob . . ." Eleanor turned away from the girls just long enough to compose herself. "Yes,

I've got it all. But I've also lost a great deal. Like my poor, dear Jacob. He was a wonderful man, and yes, I know what you've heard—he was older and I was just a starry-eyed twenty-year-old. He taught me so much! Jacob cared about this city and the institutions that make it great. When he met me, I was just a girl from a Podunk town who didn't know just how wonderful and satisfying it is to give back to my community. Then one day, he was gone." She breathed in deep, a hand pressed to her heart.

"That might not be the kind of sadness you ever experience in your life. In fact, I hope it's not. But one of these days, you're also going to find out that no matter how beautiful you are, no matter how talented you are, and no matter how you never have a bad hair day . . ." More laughter, but this time, it sounded a little uncomfortable, like the queens couldn't believe that was actually a possibility.

"No matter," Eleanor drawled in that wonderfully cultured Texas accent of hers. "Someday things aren't going to go your way. The sun isn't going to shine and you . . ." She pointed to one of the girls. "And you and you and you and you . . ." She went down the line, indicating each of the girls in turn. "There's going to be a time when you're not going to win. Oh, it might not be a title. It might be a man you think you love." There were a couple grumbles in response. "Or it might be a job you want. Or it might be something as small as a smile from a person you'd wish would notice you. It's going to happen, ladies. I can tell you this from experience. Life isn't always a bowl of cherries, and there will come the time when you're going to feel like the pits."

As crazy as this seems, I think this was news to many of the women up there onstage. A couple of them actually looked like they might burst into tears. Tiffany, it should be noted, was not one of them. Her chin was high, her shoulders were steady in a brave-little-soldier pose, and I wondered if she was trying to convince Eleanor, or herself.

"So what are you going to do?" Eleanor asked no one in particular. "You're going to be gracious, that's what you're going to do. You're going to be grateful, too. You are all winners and you know it. And you're going to act like winners. No matter what. Now, let me see you be winners. What are you going to do when that girl standing right there next to you is named Miss Consolidated Chili?"

Miss Hotter than a Chili Pepper down at the end of the row clapped. It was a slow, tentative sort of sound that picked up steam when one beauty queen after another joined in.

From my vantage point, I watched smiles that started out just as tentative blossom on every single face as the women put their hands together and applauded for all they were worth.

Well, except for Tiffany.

Eyes narrowed, I studied the odd way Miss Texas Chili Pepper applauded. She didn't bring both her hands above her waist the way everyone else did. She kept her left arm at her side and brought her right hand to it down near her hip.

If anyone else noticed or if anyone else cared, no one pointed it out. I wasn't sure I cared, either, but I did think it was a little odd.

Odd got odder when Eleanor had the girls do the next role-playing exercise.

"Now," she said, "let's see what y'all are going to do if you win!"

A couple of the women squealed. One put a hand to her forehead like she was going to faint. Another one jumped up and down.

Eleanor shook her head. "Well, that's all well and good, but it's going to be mighty distracting for the people down in the seats," she said. "So watch me, and do what I do."

Eleanor stepped back, sucked in a breath like she was plenty surprised, and put her hands on either side of her open mouth.

The beauty queens followed suit.

Except for Tiffany, who brought only her right hand to her face.

The pieces fell into place, and my mouth fell open, too, but not because I was surprised or because I'd been named Miss Consolidated Chili.

More like I'd just realized how stupid I'd been.

"Darn!"

I plunked back in the plush theater seat and gave myself a figurative kick in the pants.

I'd been blind and oh, so wrong about the one person I wanted to be oh, so right about.

The rehearsal lasted another hour and a half, but believe me when I say I didn't pay a whole lot of attention. Walk this way. Move this way. Next will come the talent competition.

I heard all the instructions that came from the middle-aged women who took over for Eleanor and whose job it was to direct the logistics of the show; I just didn't care.

My one and only theory of the crime had been shot down in flames, and I was a little busy stewing.

And trying to figure out how I could prove if I was right. Even though I knew I was. And didn't want to prove it.

By the time the beauty queens cleared the stage so they could freshen up before their evening duties back at Alamo Plaza, I knew what I had to do. I trailed backstage, keeping an eye out for Tiffany when I cruised past the dressing rooms where female chatter oozed from every nook and cranny.

She didn't leave with the first group of queens.

Or the second.

Fine by me. That gave me a chance to look around. The main auditorium of the fairgrounds is used for concerts and shows of all kinds, and like most theaters, there were things lying around backstage like ropes and ladders and miles of wires. There were a couple beanbag-sized sandbags anchoring the ropes near the red velvet curtains, and I grabbed one and hefted it in one hand.

Perfect!

I stepped back in the shadows and waited.

Lucky for me, Tiffany was the last one out of the dressing room, and she was all alone when she walked out with her right hand looped around the handle of that rolling purple makeup case of hers. I had plenty of elbow room to step forward, call out her name, and lob the sandbag at Miss Texas Chili Pepper.

It hit her in the left side and plunked on the floor.

"Darn!" I stomped one sneaker-clad foot. "Darn, darn, darn!"

Maybe Tiffany wasn't as dopey as I thought she was, because she looked at the sandbag on the floor and went as pale as a ghost. "What are you doing?" she demanded. That is, right before she looked around to make sure there wasn't anyone near to overhear us, and then hurried over so she could hiss at me. "What's wrong with you? What are you trying to prove?"

I retrieved the little sandbag and tossed it back where I found it. "I should have seen it right from the start," I told her. "I can't believe how stupid I've been."

She swallowed hard, and now that she had a couple seconds to think about it, she lifted her chin and sucked in her bottom lip. "I don't know what you're talking about."

"I'm talking about the way you hand out crappy souvenirs. I'm talking about the way you threw your water bottle into the recycling bin in the motor home yesterday. You set the bottle down on the counter, Tiffany." A pretend bottle in my hand, I demonstrated. "Then you slid the drawer open, dropped the bottle in and shut the drawer."

"We all need to be more environmentally conscious," she said. "We owe it to Mother Nature, and to the generations of children who—"

"Yeah. Right. Whatever." I stepped back, my weight against one foot, and looked her over. "What does the environment have to do with the way you . . ." I let my mouth drop open and slapped my hands to my face in one big, exaggerated, I've-won-the-pageant move.

"You can't tell me the way you only put one hand to

your face has anything to do with how much of a tree hugger you are."

Tiffany's shoulders shot back. "I have my own style."

"You have a left arm you can't use."

She tried to counter my accusation—her eyes squinched and her jaw worked up and down in silent protest. I nearly felt sorry for her. And when she realized there was no story she could make up that would satisfy little ol' me, Tiffany's eyes filled with tears.

"What do you want? Do you want money? Is that why you're doing this to me? Do you want money not to tell?"

Honestly, at that point, I wished I was really as hard-hearted as some people think I am. It would have been fun to toss out a figure—say, five hundred a month—and watch Tiffany squirm. But hey, in spite of what Sylvia might say, I'm not anywhere near that heartless. Well, not most of the time, anyway.

I glanced at Tiffany's left arm. "What happened?"

Automatically, her right hand went to her left arm in a protective little move. "A riding accident. When I was thirteen. I was already involved in pageants, and my mother and I, we didn't see any reason not to continue. I mean, why shouldn't I? I'm still just as beautiful as I ever was, right? I'm still just as talented. And I'm pretty good at covering up. I can compensate. You know? But if anyone finds out . . ." Again, Tiffany looked all around and peered into the backstage shadows, just to make sure we were alone.

"I can't let anybody find out," she burbled. "Then they'd know . . ." A single tear slipped down her cheek. "They'd know I'm not perfect!"

For me, the road less traveled is the high road. Since I'd already chosen it, I kept my feet firmly in place. "Your secret is safe with me," I told her. "But as it turns out, this is really good news for you."

She sniffled. "It is? How can it be?"

"Don't you get it? Dom, he was sick the night he died thanks to your chili practical joke. That meant he was weak and shaky and that whoever killed him wouldn't have had too hard of a time sneaking up on him and overpowering him. But it still took two hands to wrap those guitar strings around his neck."

Tiffany pouted. "I told you I didn't do it."

"And I finally believe you. But darn . . ." I kicked at the nearest coil of heavy black wires. "You know what this means, don't you? You were my best bet, and since there's no way you could have killed Dominic, I have to start my investigation all over again."

CHAPTER 10

"I need your help."

This was not something I was used to hearing from Nick, so I guess I could be excused when I spun around from the table where I was dishing up chili and gave him an openmouthed look worthy of a beauty pageant winner.

"What?" he asked.

I shook myself out of my temporary paralysis. Or at least I tried. See, this was the first time I'd seen Nick since the day before, when Sylvia admitted that she didn't have any designs on him. And even if she did, it wasn't like I was going to back off just because Sylvia wanted to get up close and personal with Nick. I mean, really, there was a time when if I found that out, I would have dated him whether I liked him or not, just to get her goat.

Still, somehow, knowing my half sister had left the door wide open for me to swoop in and make my move on Nick bushwhacked me. It was crazy and pretty ridiculous. It was downright nuts that I suddenly felt nervous and self-conscious and just a little shy with a guy I'd known a couple months and had never been skittish around before.

Or maybe my sudden case of the jitters had something to do with the fact that my best murder suspect had washed down the drain and I might at that very moment be looking into the (really nice blue) eyes of a killer.

"What?" Nick asked again, and who could blame him, since I was gawking at him like he'd grown another head. "What's wrong with you? Why are you staring at me?"

I shook myself out of my stupor. Thinking of Nick as a murderer was as unworthy of me as thinking of myself as some sort of shrinking violet. Never going to happen. On both counts.

"You? Want my help?" It was so far out of the realm of possibility, I didn't even consider it. Instead, I grabbed a couple more bowls and filled them with the traditional, not-too-spicy, just-meaty-enough, forget-the-beans chili I'd made to tempt the taste buds of the crowd that was there that Thursday evening to raise money for the San Antonio Symphony. "Whatever kind of joke you're playing, I'm not interested."

"I'm serious."

"And I'm Mother Teresa."

"Hardly. Though in that outfit . . ."

I had decided I was sick of the long black skirt, and that night, I was wearing a white pencil skirt that went down past my knees and a sky blue blouse. It might not have been exactly true to the Chili Queens and the late 1930s, but it wasn't exactly Calcutta, either.

I gave Nick a narrow-eyed glare. "What's wrong with my outfit?"

"Nothing."

"But I look like Mother Teresa."

"You don't look like Mother Teresa. You'll never have a halo. It's just that these long skirts you keep wearing . . ." He looked me up and down. "I guess I'm just used to seeing you as the Chili Chick. You know, the costume and the stockings and the heels."

A couple days earlier I would have pounced right on this and asked if he liked what he saw when he looked at the Chili Chick. That night, the words were smothered by the sand that suddenly filled my mouth. To cover, I filled a few more bowls of chili.

"I'm not kidding about the help," Nick said, taking a bowl out of my hand and passing it over to Sylvia, who then handed it to an elderly man in a tux. "I talked to Sylvia, and she said—"

"I don't need Sylvia's permission to do anything," I reminded him.

"Which is why I didn't ask her permission. I just told her I'd like to borrow you for a while."

"It's not a problem." Sylvia was apparently paying more attention to the conversation than I realized, because she joined right in. "Ginger and Teddi aren't all that busy tonight." She glanced around at the mostly elderly people in their diamonds and their tuxes and their gowns. "This isn't the kind of crowd that patronizes drag queens. Ginger's going to come over here and help while Teddi keeps an eye on things over at their tent. You can go." Sylvia made a little shooing motion. "You'll only think of some excuse to go off on your own and leave me here with all the work, anyway, so you might as well go with Nick."

I crossed my arms over my chest. "I might as well go where with Nick?"

He put a hand on my shoulder "We'll talk about it once we leave here."

When he gave me a little nudge, I locked my knees. "I might as well go where with Nick?"

He puffed out a breath of annoyance and moved in close. This was a good thing, because it allowed me to breathe in the heady scent of his aftershave. Woodsy with hints of leather, but believe it or not, it wasn't the divine aroma or even the heat of his breath tickling my ear that distracted me. It was what he whispered.

"We're going to Dom's apartment."

I knew if I moved, his lips would be dangerously close to mine. I dared to turn my head, anyway, so I could look him in the eye when I asked, "Are we supposed to be there?"

"Nope."

"Do the cops know we're going?"

"Nope."

"Are we going to have to break in?"

"You'll see when we get there."

"Why?" I asked him.

"Why are we going there? It's a chance for us to look around and see what we can find out. I'm sure the cops have already checked out his apartment, but I knew Dom pretty well. I might spot something they've missed."

"Not that why. Why me? Why are you asking me to go along? Are you finally ready to admit that I'm a pretty darned good investigator?"

Nick put a hand to the small of my back and prodded me out of the tent. "Actually, I want a witness," he said. "You know, so if word gets out that I was there, somebody's got my back who can say that I didn't tamper with anything."

Okay, so it wasn't much of a compliment, and not the best reason for inviting me to tag along on this foray to Dom's apartment, and it sure wasn't the most romantic invitation a girl had ever gotten to leave a fund-raiser long before the event was over with a guy who was the guy she'd been dreaming about.

But hey, the idea of breaking and entering at a murder victim's apartment . . .

There wasn't a chance I could resist, and Nick knew it.

I settled into the passenger seat of his black Audi and waited until he pulled out in traffic before I said anything. The plan, see, was to catch him off guard.

"So did the cops ever tell you how long Dom was dead before I found his body?"

He took my question at face value, and I couldn't fault him for that. I can look pretty innocent when I put my mind to it. "From what I heard, it wasn't too long. Maybe thirty minutes or so."

I thought back to Monday night, from the time *Read*

with the Chili Queens wrapped up until Sylvia and I were done with cleaning up our tent and I took that walk to look for Tumbleweed and Ruth Ann. As near as I could tell, that would have been somewhere around eleven.

"So where were you at ten thirty that night?" I asked Nick.

He shot me a look that might have been longer and more lethal if the idiot in front of us wasn't driving twenty miles an hour because he was texting and if Nick didn't have to do some pretty quick maneuvering to get around him. "You're kidding me, right?"

"Just covering my bases."

"And you think I'm one of your bases."

"I think you're one of the suspects. The cops do, too. Otherwise that Detective What's-Her-Name wouldn't keep hanging around. Unless she's hanging around for other reasons?"

I gave him time to tell me I was wrong—about either scenario—and when he didn't, I decided to nudge the subject slightly in another direction.

"You never finished telling me why you beat up Dom back in Los Angeles."

"Not technically true." Nick's expression might have been mistaken for a smile if his teeth weren't clenched so tightly together. "I didn't finish telling you the story because I never started telling you the story."

"So maybe you should."

"It's a pretty boring story."

"I doubt that. Nothing that ends in hospitalization and resignation can be all that boring. Besides, here we are, stuck in a car together. I'm not doing anything else. And you're not doing anything but driving. You might as well talk, and I might as well listen."

"It's not going to prove I killed Dom. That is what you're looking for, isn't it? Proof that I killed him?"

I swear, if he wasn't driving, I would have punched him right in the nose. Since that violent avenue wasn't available, I slapped the leather armrest instead. "Are you that dense? Really? I'm not trying to prove you killed Dom; I'm trying to prove you didn't kill Dom! Why else would I have wasted so much time this week on Tiffany the beauty queen?"

"The girl who couldn't have done it because of her bad arm?"

I grumbled my opinion of the fact that Nick had picked up on this pertinent bit of information and never shared. "I want to believe you, Nick," I told him. "But if I don't know all the facts—"

"The fact is that Dom and I were partners on the LA force for three years," he said. "We worked well together. We were tough, but fair. I thought he was my friend."

"Friends don't beat up friends."

"Friends don't steal friend's wives."

It took a couple seconds for the sense of this to sink in. When it did, I turned as much as I was able in the confines of my seat belt so that I could see Nick better. "You were married?"

"For like a second and a half."

"And Dom . . ."

"Dom and Nichole—"

"Wait!" Yes, we were talking about a serious subject, but really? I couldn't help but chuckle. "Nick and Nichole? You're kidding, right?"

"It gets worse. Her family called us Nicky and Nicki."

"Sweet."

"Too."

"What was she like?"

Since we were stopped at a red light, he had a chance to give me a sour look. "That's not what we're talking about."

"We're talking about Dom and how he stole your wife and—" I didn't like it one bit, but I couldn't deny it; my stomach soured. "Wife or ex-wife?" I asked Nick.

"Definitely ex."

I hoped he didn't notice when I let out a breath of relief. "So you and Dom were partners. And you and Nicki were married and she was . . . ?"

"Cheating on me."

"Which wasn't what I was going to ask. Not yet, anyway. I need some background so that I can understand the whole thing better. What was she like?"

He slapped the steering wheel in frustration. "She was like the woman I thought I wanted to spend the rest of my life with!" he said.

"What does she do for a living?"

"Really?" Nick rolled his eyes. "I got in the car with the Chili Chick and now I'm sitting with Dr. Phil?"

"I'm curious."

"You're nosy. And none of this matters. Nicki is the office manager for a cosmetic surgeon. There, you satisfied?"

"What does she look like?"

"She's a blonde."

"You like blondes." I hoped my disappointment didn't ring as loud in Nick's ears as it did in my own.

"She's tall."

And I'm a shrimp.

"She's smart."

I wasn't willing to go there so instead I said, "But not smart enough to resist those dreamy eyes of Dom's."

Nick made a face. "Did he have dreamy eyes?"

"You were partners for three years and you never saw that his eyes were dreamy? What kind of cop were you?"

"Not that kind of cop."

"Well, he did have dreamy eyes. But dang, what was that Nichole chick thinking? You have dreamy eyes, too."

For the first time since we'd started the conversation, the barest of smiles relieved Nick's thunderous expression. "Do I?"

I pretended that smile didn't sizzle through the space that separated us and heat me inside and out, and kept my voice light when I told him, "I suppose some people might think so."

"Well, Nichole was one of those people, but obviously, she has a pretty short attention span."

I didn't even know Nichole and I thought she was crazy. I'd met Dom, and while his eyes were plenty dreamy, he didn't even begin to compare with Nick. Especially if he was the kind of sleazebag who would fool around with his partner's wife.

"I guess I can see why you were mad at Dom," I said.

"I was. Mad enough to request a transfer out of homicide. I couldn't partner with him anymore."

This, I understood. "You know all that only makes you look guiltier."

"I know."

"And you've told the cops?"

"I've told them."

"And that detective . . ." I didn't need to remind myself that she was a blonde. "What does she say?"

"She says the same thing I say. If I was going to kill Dom, I would have done it back when I walked in from work early one day and found him in bed with Nichole. I wouldn't have waited this long. And I couldn't possibly have known he was here in San Antonio. After I left the police force, I never heard another word about Dom. Not until Monday night, anyway."

"Unless even after all that time you were still mad. Or jealous. Or if you still care about your wife."

"My ex-wife, and believe me when I tell you that after what she put me through, I no longer care."

This, too, I understood, because I'd had the same sort of reaction when I found out what Edik did to me. Sure, it hurt like hell, but that wasn't because I wanted to get back together with him. After what happened, my hurt was all about betrayal. Just like Nick's must have been.

Still, I understood that there was a huge gulf between that sensible little voice in your head that tells you you're better off and that hollow feeling in the pit of your gut, the one that tells you that it's going to be a long, long time before you meet someone who can hug you so tight, it will put all your broken pieces back together again.

"Do you miss her?" I asked Nick.

"Not anymore."

"Do you miss the police force?"

"Like hell."

"Are you sorry you beat up Dom?"

Nick barked out a laugh. "Not even a little. And speaking of Dom . . ." He slowed at the entrance to an apartment complex and turned down a driveway lined with blooming roses. "We're here."

Just thinking about what we were up to caused a crazy beat to start up inside my rib cage. I sat up and looked around.

The apartment complex that Dom had once called home was a series of four-story, light-colored stone buildings. Each unit included a balcony. Nick pulled up and parked outside the clubhouse. I couldn't help but notice that he kept far away from the nearest streetlight.

"Dom lived in the clubhouse?"

"It wouldn't make a whole lot of sense for us to park right in front of his building, would it?" He locked the car, and instead of starting off down the sidewalk, he grabbed my hand and pulled me behind the building.

"We're staying in the shadows," I said.

"Let's just say that we don't want to be too obvious."

"And how exactly are we going to break in without being too obvious?"

He didn't have an answer to this. In fact, he didn't say

another word until we'd walked all the way to the last building in the complex.

"Third floor," Nick said.

I glanced up. It wasn't late, and light shone through the windows of most of the apartments.

"We're not climbing the balconies, are we?" I asked him.

"Don't have to." Nick reached into his pocket and pulled out a key.

"Let me guess. Detective Gilkenny."

For this brilliant bit of observation, I got a sour look. "Don't be ridiculous. I told you, the cops don't know we're here." He stuck the key in the front door and we went inside.

"Then how—"

Nick pocketed the key and hit the call button on the elevator.

"Nichole," he said.

"She lives here?"

He shook his head. "She's visited a time or two. She and Dom were trying to reconcile."

We stepped into the elevator, and I tried to make sense of this. "So they were together and then . . ."

"And then they broke up," Nick said. "And just recently, they were thinking about getting back together again. Nichole came to visit a couple times."

"You know this because . . ."

"Because someone had to tell Nichole that Dom was dead."

The elevator stopped at the third floor, and we got off.

"How did she take the news?" I asked.

Nick didn't so much shrug as he twitched his shoulders. "Like I said, they were trying to reconcile. A stupid move on Nichole's part, if you ask me. But she didn't ask me."

"She didn't kill him, did she?"

He shot me a look. "She was in LA."

"And you know this . . . how?"

"I actually checked." His brow furrowed; he hated admitting this. "On Tuesday morning, I called the doctor's office where she works. I told them I'd misplaced her phone number and needed to talk to her. She was at work that day."

"And the day before?"

"Thank you for the suggestion, Sherlock. I do have some experience. I thought of this, too, and I asked. She was at work the day before. All day and into the evening. No way she could have gotten to San Antonio on Monday night then back to LA for work on Tuesday morning."

"But she did send you a key."

Nick took the key out of his pocket and stuck it in the lock on the front door of apartment 316. "She said I had to do whatever I could to find Dom's killer."

"So we're not breaking and entering?"

He pushed the front door open, looked around quickly to make sure no one was nearby, and ushered me inside. "No," he said, "we're not."

I was actually kind of disappointed.

CHAPTER 11

"Nice!" I crooned, when Nick arced the beam of a flashlight against a black leather couch and chair, sleek stainless and glass tables, understated artwork, and a wet bar along the far wall of the living room. "Dom had good taste. I mean, in apartments," I added quickly, just so Nick didn't get some sort of idea that I was referring to Nichole.

"Dom was a no-good lowlife." Maybe he did think I was referring to his ex, but even if he did, Nick didn't take it personally. With a practiced eye, he glanced around. There was a wall of windows to our right and a balcony outside that overlooked a garden where there were benches set along a brick walk. Two buildings over and to our left, I could see just a smidgen of the swimming pool that belonged to the apartment complex and the couple dozen people in it splashing around.

Following the beam of the flashlight, I sidled toward the dining room on our left and into the galley kitchen with its stainless appliances and Corian counters in a shade that, in the dim light, reminded me of buttered rum.

"So what are we looking for?" I asked Nick, careful to keep my voice down when I followed him along a hallway and into a bedroom.

"Anything." Since the bed had been left unmade, it didn't make much difference when Nick threw back the blankets. He looked under the mattress, too, and since he was the one with the flashlight, there wasn't much I could do. Just like in the living room, there were floor-to-ceiling windows on one wall. Curious, I peeked around the vertical blinds and saw that outside, the balcony continued around from the living room. There was a small table and chairs set up there, and I thought about what it must be like to roll out of bed and have a morning cup of coffee on the balcony. While I was at it, I dreamed about that big ol' swimming pool I could see from there, too, and how a dip on a hot evening sounded like heaven on earth.

"You do the dresser."

Nick's command snapped me out of my thoughts. He was done with the bed and the nightstand next to it, and he flashed the light toward the opposite wall and a chest of drawers. The light glanced against a photo in a frame, and I picked it up and studied a smiling Dom who had his arm around a blonde with big dark eyes, a killer figure that was shown to perfection in a tight-fitting red sundress, and an ear-to-ear grin.

"Told you they were attempting a reconciliation." Nick took the picture out of my hands and set it back where it came from.

"That's Nichole."

He barely spared the photo a look. "Yes, that's Nichole."

"She's gorgeous."

As if he'd forgotten, he glanced at the photograph. "I suppose."

In my mind, I pictured Nick instead of Dom in the picture standing beside Nichole. They must have been a beautiful couple.

I am not usually sappy, but dang, I just couldn't help myself. A ball of emotion clogged my throat. "Do you miss her?" I still somehow managed to ask.

"You asked me that before. And I told you, not anymore."

"But you did miss her."

"I was married to her."

The way Nick held the flashlight, I was pretty sure he couldn't see my face, but I screwed up my mouth and crossed my eyes, anyway, when I looked at Nichole. "Well, I don't like her," I said.

He barked out a laugh. "Something tells me your opinion wouldn't faze her."

"I mean it." I crossed my arms over my chest. "Any woman who could do that to a guy like you who—"

Who what?

The words bounced around inside my head, just daring me to complete the sentence.

What had I just been about to say?

A guy like you who is so nice?

That definitely did not apply to Nick.

Then what about, *A guy like you who I have no doubt was loyal to a fault and who must have felt like he'd had a ton of bricks dropped on him when he realized what was going on between Dom and Nichole?*

Yeah, that was more like it, and thinking it through, I liked Nichole even less than I had before. And I didn't like her very much to begin with.

But even dislike didn't explain why just thinking about the whole Nick and Nichole thing left me feeling like I'd been kicked in the gut.

Just like Nick must have felt when it happened.

It was stupid. And useless. And way too mushy, too, and since I am usually anything but, I pushed the sensation away and got to work.

"The dresser," I said, and pointed toward the top drawer so Nick could aim his light that way.

"Underwear and socks," I said, after a brief (no pun intended) look. Not that I needed to tell Nick what was in the drawer. In order for me to see what I was doing, he had to come stand behind me and slant the light down to where I rummaged through the top drawer of the dresser.

"Ties in this drawer," I said, starting in on the next. "And in this bottom one . . ." I pulled out a stack of T-shirts. "Not much. Except . . ." There was something that looked like paper at the bottom of the drawer. I moved aside another stack of T-shirts, grabbed for it, and instead of coming out with one piece of paper, I found two.

"Menus." I held them closer to the light so that both Nick and I could see them. "One from a place called El Restaurante del Rosa and the other from La Cocina de Martha. Rosa and Martha!" I glanced over my shoulder at Nick to make sure he caught the significance of this, but I shouldn't have bothered. Of course he had. He was Nick, and Nick didn't miss a thing. Well, except maybe the thing his wife was having with his partner.

I shook away the thought. "What do you suppose it means?" I asked him, but I didn't wait for him to answer. Instead, I scooted over to the bed and sat down so that I could take a better look at the menus.

Rosa's menu was the prettier of the two, oversized and decorated with flowers and foliage in lush, vibrant shades of red, green, and yellow. The flowers twined around the lettering on the front and framed a grainy, old-fashioned photograph of a woman who was dressed kind of like I was, in a skirt that went down past her knees and a sleeveless blouse. She had an apron around her neck and a ladle in one hand.

"Rosa Garcia," the caption said. "San Antonio Chili Queen."

Inside the menu . . .

I flipped it open.

"Look at this." I pointed. "Dom has a couple of the menu items circled. Hey, and check out the names of the chilies on the list! Rosa's got *Leve*; that means mild," I told Nick. "And *Picante*, which is spicy, and *Caliente*, which means hot, and *Hirviendo*—"

"Is boiling hot. I know that much Spanish."

"Well, Dom must have been keeping track of what he thought of each of the chili dishes on Rosa's menu. He's got notes in the margin, too. And awfully cramped handwriting." I bent closer for a better look. "This one next to *Hirviendo* says, 'No way!' and the one next to *Caliente* says, 'Too spicy for most tastes.'"

"And *Picante*?" Nick asked.

Since there was a listing of margarita flavors and prices right next to the chili selection, Dom didn't have much room to write. There was an arrow drawn from *Picante* up to the top of the menu, where he'd written, "Spicy enough to satisfy most chili lovers but doesn't have a burn." I looked over my shoulder at Nick. "Do you think he wanted to be a food critic or something?"

Nick grabbed for the menu from Martha's restaurant. It was smaller than Rosa's menu, and the front of it featured a drawing of the Alamo along with cameo portraits of four men.

Davy Crockett, Jim Bowie, and William Travis.

I remembered the names I'd heard Martha and Rosa tossing around on the first night of the fund-raiser and wondered if the fourth man—a guy with a big nose and a droopy mustache—was that ancestor Martha was so proud of.

"Dom was more of a basic meat and potatoes kind of guy than a foodie," Nick said, studying the menu. "At least back when I knew him. I suppose a person's tastes can change."

"Did he make notes in that one, too?" I asked Nick when he flipped open Martha's menu, and when he didn't answer right away, I stood up and sidled closer so I could read what he was reading.

"More notes next to chili entrees," I said, even though Nick could see that. "'Too hot' next to that one." I pointed. "'Just right' next to this one, the one for Chili ala Martha." I sat back down on the bed. "What does it mean?"

"I guess it means he couldn't remember which chili he liked and which he didn't like. He wanted to be sure of what to order next time he went to one of the restaurants."

"Really?" I plucked Martha's menu out of Nick's hand. "That's the dumbest theory ever. Who doesn't remember which chili they like? You know you like your chili hot or you like your chili mild. With beans or without. Everybody knows stuff like that. You know if you like the smokiness of poblanos or the three-alarm of ghost peppers or—"

"Not everyone lives and breathes chili," he snapped.

"Well, they should." I hoped my smile was especially dazzling in the icy LED light. "The world would be a better place. Besides," I added, "even if you did keep notes about what you ate and what you liked at various restaurants, you're not going to bring along the menu the next time you go to that restaurant. So why keep the menus? And why hide them under your T-shirts?"

"All right." I was shocked that he admitted there was any merit in my argument, but the way Nick crossed his arms over his chipped-from-granite chest told me he didn't like it. "So what's your theory?"

"Maybe he wanted to make his own chili and, you know, have it taste like his favorites. So he wrote down what he thought and—"

"And not any of the ingredients. Which aren't listed on the menus, anyway."

He was right, and like him, I didn't especially like it. "Whatever!" I said with a wave of one hand. "Since we can't ask Dom, I guess we'll never know."

"I wish we could ask him who killed him," Nick grumbled. He raked the beam of the flashlight around the room one more time, then pointed it toward the doorway. "Let's see what else we can find."

Dom had used a second bedroom as an office, and seeing a desk covered with papers and a laptop computer, Nick cheered right up. "See if you can find an appointment book," he said.

"Yeah." I headed to the desk. "Maybe Dom was scheduled to meet the killer after the fund-raiser."

"That would be a little too easy, wouldn't it?" There was a gooseneck lamp on the desk, and after he'd crossed the room and closed the mini blinds, Nick flicked it on.

"Told you he had good taste." I fingered the sheet of paper on the desk closest to where I stood. It had been printed out from a website and was an ad from a Porsche dealership. "One hundred forty-five thousand? For a car?" The words stuck in my throat. "Who has that kind of money?"

"Let me see that." Nick plucked the paper out of my hand and put it closer to the light for a better look.

"Here's another one," I said, sliding another printed Porsche ad closer. "This one's only one thirty. A deal, huh?"

"Interesting."

Since Nick mumbled the word, I'm pretty sure he wasn't talking to me, but that didn't stop me. I leaned closer for a better look at the ad. "Why?" I asked him.

He set the ad down exactly where it had come from.

"Because I did a little digging. And I happen to know what kind of money Dom made over at Consolidated. No way he could afford a car that expensive."

"So maybe he was saving up," I suggested. "Or maybe he was just dreaming."

"Maybe."

Nick moved on, but since Dom's emails and personal files on the computer were password protected, he got nowhere there.

I didn't have much better luck looking through the desk drawers. I found the usual utility bills and credit card receipts, but nothing that would help us figure out who killed Dom, or why. In fact, the only even mildly interesting thing I found was a single DVR case at the bottom of a drawer.

"What do you think?" I asked Nick, waving the case in front of his nose. "Maybe there's something juicy on it."

"Maybe not," he reminded me, but he grabbed for the case, anyway, opened it, and stuck the DVR in the drive of the laptop. I moved to stand next to Nick so I could see the screen.

"Wow!" When the DVD started up, I couldn't help myself. The video was of a hulking gorgeous guy with dark hair and flashing eyes who wasn't wearing anything at all.

"Stand back a little farther from the camera," a muffled voice said from out of the frame. "Turn left. Now turn right."

The guy did exactly as he was told, and believe me when I say I watched every move.

"He's cute," I told Nick, who did not have a chance to reply because a flash like sunlight glinting against a glacier filled the screen and the picture flickered off, then came on again.

This time, there was another good-looking guy on screen. This one was slimmer than the first, and his golden tresses caressed shoulders as bare as the rest of him.

"He's cute, too," I said, though truth be told, I wasn't exactly looking at his face. "Do you think Dom was gay?"

With a grumble, Nick ejected the DVR from the computer, and there was acid in his voice when he asked, "You do remember the story about Dom and Nichole, right?"

I did. "But then why—"

The words stopped dead in my throat when I heard a sound from the living room. One that told me we weren't alone.

"The front door," Nick mumbled. "Somebody just walked in."

"Somebody . . ." My heart beat double time, and my feet were flash frozen to the spot. I glanced toward the door and swallowed hard.

Nick turned off the desk lamp. "Come on," he whispered, and he handed me the DVD and its case so I could put it back where I found it.

"Come . . . on?" I couldn't help myself. I kept staring at the doorway, waiting for a police officer—or a whole darned SWAT team—to come charging through. "Come on, where?"

"Shhh!" He grabbed my hand, slipped his fingers

through mine, and tugged me toward the doorway. He paused there for a moment, hardly breathing, listening. Over the noise of my pounding heart, I heard footsteps. They were moving our way.

Keeping a tight hold on me, Nick dashed out of the office and took me along with him into the bedroom.

"What are you doing?" I rasped.

Nick didn't answer. But then, he was busy over at the window. A second later, he slid open the door that led onto the balcony and tugged me outside with him.

"Over the side," he said.

I looked from the railing that ran around the edge of the balcony to Nick, then back to the railing. "You're kidding."

"I don't have time to kid." He threw one leg over the side of the balcony. "I'll drop down to the balcony one floor below, then I'll help you down."

"But, Nick, I—" There was no use arguing; he was already gone. I heard a thump when he landed, and a grunt. I glanced over my shoulder toward the bedroom. Like us, the person who'd just come into the apartment had brought a flashlight, and I saw its beam rake the wall out in the hallway.

"Come on!" Nick called up to me softly. "Get a move on!"

I swallowed hard and pivoted, my back to the scenery and the garden and that slim bit of swimming pool I could see from up there. After one deep breath for courage and another because hey, it might be my last and I might as well get all the air I could, I put one leg over the railing, found my footing, and dragged my other leg over the side.

My hands were so tight against the railing, my knuckles were white. But when I saw the beam of the flashlight again just outside the bedroom door, I dropped.

Just like he promised, Nick was on the balcony below to break my fall.

I *ooph*ed into him and knocked him backward just as we heard the sliding door in Dom's apartment open, and he wrapped his arms around me and dragged me closer to the building and farther from the edge of the balcony.

Above us, we heard the sounds of footsteps, as the person who'd come into the apartment after us paced the balcony.

I held my breath. Which actually wasn't all that hard, considering that Nick's arms were around me and he was just about squeezing the life out of me. I squirmed and he lost his footing. Together, we plopped back against the window of the second-floor apartment.

A light flashed on in the bedroom, and Nick didn't waste a second. He didn't so much point to the railing as he hauled me to it, and again, he dropped over the side and urged me to do the same.

The sliding door of the second-floor apartment whooshed open just as I dropped down on the ground-level patio.

I barely had time to catch my breath before we were off and running. Forget the brick walkway! We crashed through a bed of roses, and I yelped when thorns dragged against my bare legs. We zipped around a park bench or two, zigzagged around a burbling fountain, and made our way to the back of the building next door. It wasn't until we were safely behind it that Nick stopped. Good thing, since I was pretty sure my lungs were about to burst.

I pressed my back against the building and drew in a dozen breaths of the humid night air, waiting for my heart to explode. When it didn't—when it finally settled down from a headlong race to a bumpety canter—I dared to peek around the corner of the building toward Dom's.

It was already dark and nearly impossible to see, but in the glow of the light that flowed from the bedroom of that second-floor apartment, I knew one thing: there was a person on the third-floor balcony outside of Dom's bedroom.

I could feel his eyes on me.

CHAPTER 12

"What have you two been up to?" Sylvia's gaze assessed my skirt—ripped at the hem from where it had gotten snagged on a rosebush—and Nick's tie—stained with some unnameable something and the knot hanging loose—and her eyes lit. "When you said you needed to borrow Maxie for a while, Nick, I thought it had something to do with working on the murder investigation. I didn't know you two would be—"

"No way!" I blurted out.

"We didn't!" Nick said at the same time.

And why both of us got red-faced was anybody's guess.

"Right." Sylvia's smile was angelic and her words were

singsongy. "I guess what happens in San Antonio stays in San Antonio."

"Unless nothing happens in San Antonio," I told her.

"Right." She crooned the word one more time before she moved over to the table where four slow cookers simmered with my mild-enough-for-the-symphony-crowd chili. "You can tell me all about it," she said, as if I ever actually would if something really happened. Which it didn't. "Over here."

Sylvia didn't so much motion me closer as she screwed up her face and tipped her head in a weird sort of gesture designed to make me leave Nick's side and go over to where she was standing.

"Nothing happened," I told her again.

"So why don't you come over here . . ." There was that weird look again. When Sylvia scrunched up her eyes like that, she reminded me of a gnome. Okay, yes, a pretty blonde gnome, but a gnome nonetheless. "And tell me all about it."

"All about nothing?"

"Over *here*."

I rolled my eyes and grumbled my opinion of this nonsense right before I told Nick I'd see him later.

All in all, that was far superior to discussing what hadn't happened between us.

Even though Sylvia was pretty sure it had.

"You're way off base," I told her once Nick was gone. "Nick and I didn't—"

Her squeal of laughter cut me off. "Of course you didn't! If you did, you wouldn't have come back. I mean, come on, Maxie, I know you well enough to know that if you and Nick were . . ." Her cheeks turned a color that matched her summery pink dress. "Well, let's just say that I'm pretty sure you'd take advantage of the situation and the last thing you'd be thinking about was work. You'd be gone all night. And you'd leave me here to do all the heavy lifting. Just like usual. But that's not what matters!" Her words vibrated with excitement, and she sidestepped closer.

"That's not what I need to talk to you about," Sylvia said in a stage whisper.

For this, I was grateful. I mean, about how she didn't want to talk about the nothing that had happened, not about how there was nothing to talk about to begin with, though come to think of it, maybe I was grateful for that, too. Anyone who knows me knows I have no small measure of self-esteem, but something told me I didn't want to get into any situation that would make Nick draw comparisons between me and the beautiful and vivacious Nichole. It was the same something that told me I could never measure up.

I twitched the thought away. "What's up?" I asked Sylvia.

Her gaze slid to the tent next door. "I didn't want Nick to hear. Not until we decide what to do. It's . . . *Teddi*." She mouthed the name more than said it. "I've been keeping my eye on him . . . er . . . I mean her. Ginger was right."

My heart dropped down to my stomach. "About the tips? About Teddi stealing them? Dang! I hate when I find out bad things about people I thought were good." I glanced over my shoulder toward Ginger and Teddi's tent. Right now, they were both busy dishing up chili, and from where I stood, I could see that their tip jar was about one third full.

I checked out our crockery bowl. It overflowed with tips.

"What did you see?" I asked Sylvia.

"Exactly what Ginger thought I'd see. Ginger . . . he . . . she was busy talking up some of the patrons over there toward the front of their tent. That's when Teddi came up behind the table and . . . well, there's no getting around it. I saw her with her hand in the tip jar. She scooped out a bunch of bills and a bunch of change and stuck it all in her pocket."

"A bunch of bills and a bunch of change . . ." Once again, my mind traveled back to Monday night and the scene of Dom's murder. He'd had a bunch of bills and a bunch of change on him at the time he was killed.

"It's almost like Dom had his fingers in the tip jar, too," I said, not particularly to Sylvia, but because talking about the puzzle made it seem more manageable. I shook away the thought to concentrate on an even more pressing matter. "Have you told Ginger yet?"

Sylvia put a hand on my shoulder. She likes to do that when she's about to tell me she's doing something for my own good, and she proved my theory once again when she said, "You know Ginger better than I do, and you're better at this sort of thing, anyway, and it will be a good way for you and Ginger to bond. You do like Ginger, don't you? That's why I thought I'd leave it up to you to break the news. Go on. Go over there and talk to her." Her nudge had a little too much oomph in it.

My feet dragging, I headed to the tent next door.

"What on earth happened to you?" When she looked me

over, Teddi's mouth twisted into what was clearly a critique of my ripped skirt. "You look like what the cat dragged in."

I guess it was better than looking like Mother Teresa.

Rather than point this out, I looked over Teddi's outfit—the same dress she'd worn on Tuesday night covered by the same apron decorated with drawings of kitchen appliances—and I had to defend my honor. "Look who's talking," I said, and though I tried, I just couldn't help myself. I thought about what Sylvia had just told me, about the tip jar and Teddi stealing from it. I thought about what the news was sure to do to Ginger. And I couldn't keep the acid out of my voice. "That's the same outfit you wore the other night. You and Ginger, I thought you were all about style and fashion. You look so yesterday!"

Her lips puckered. "Not for long," she crooned. "You just wait and see."

Before I could ask her what she meant, a customer showed up for chili, and I left Teddi to it and cornered Ginger. There was no way to soften the blow, so I didn't even try.

"You were right," I told her.

It took a second for her to make sense of what I said, and as soon as she did, her dark eyes filled with tears. "I didn't want to be."

"I didn't want you to be."

Her lashes were long and luxurious, and when she darted a look at Teddi, they brushed her tear-stained cheeks. "She's probably been doing it all week. That would explain why we haven't taken in nearly as much as you and Sylvia. Not that you don't deserve it for working as hard as you are," she assured me, a hand on my arm. "But you know what I mean."

I did, and she didn't need to apologize. "What are you going to do?"

Ginger pulled in a shaky breath. "I don't know. I'll talk to her. But not here. We don't need a scene. My goodness, we've had enough drama around here already this week, haven't we? It's such a shame." She swiped a hand across her cheek. "We've always gotten along so well, and we've raised a lot of money at events like this for worthy causes. Now here I am wondering if Teddi's been skimming off the top for years. I hate to think that we'll end up bickering like Rosa and Martha."

Rosa and Martha.

I remembered the menus we'd found at Dom's and the way some of the dishes were circled.

And then I remembered that the last time I saw Rosa and Martha, they weren't bickering at all.

In fact, they were fast friends.

I wished Ginger luck and told her if she needed reinforcements when she talked to Teddi, I'd be around, then since Sylvia was busy and couldn't see me, and she thought I was over at Teddi and Ginger's tent handling the dirty work, anyway, I zipped across the plaza to Rosa and Martha's tent.

"You." Martha barely spared me a glance. "You come to cause more trouble?"

"Me?" I gave Martha a careful look, sizing her up and wondering if she could have been the shadowy figure I'd seen on Dom's balcony. "All I did the other day was show up to try your chili. And to hear your stories, of course. You know, about the Alamo and your ancestors."

The starch went out of her shoulders, and a tiny smile played around her full lips. "They were heroes."

"So were the Chili Queens. In their own way, I mean. They got an entire town eating chili, talking about chili, and now all these years later, we're still celebrating chili. Just like you do over at La Cocina de Martha. I'm thinking about stopping in one of these days. Just so I can try your different dishes. What do you recommend?"

"All of them, of course." Martha handed a bowl of chili to a dowager type in a sparkling gown before she wiped her hands against her white apron. "We don't serve anything at the restaurant that isn't first class."

"Maybe not, but there have to be some dishes that appeal to people and others that don't. Chili ala Martha, I hear that's one of the favorites."

Something told me that it was no coincidence that the smile dissolved on Martha's face the moment the words were past my lips.

And no wonder that I was more curious than ever.

"How about Rosa's place?" I asked, raising my voice a bit so Rosa could hear me from where she was going from table to table beneath the tent, collecting the used bowls and tossing them in the trash. "I've heard *Caliente* is plenty good, but nothing compares to *Picante*."

Who would have thought that an old woman could move so fast?

Rosa was up in my face in a matter of seconds.

"What do you know about my *Picante*?" she asked.

"And why are you asking about it? How dare you just come barging over here and—"

"Rosa." Martha stood next to her and slipped an arm around her waist. "Rosa, you probably don't want to talk about this. Not here. Not now."

"Or maybe I do." Rosa pulled away from Martha. "Because I want to know what this little girl is talking about. What do you know?" She reached back to the serving table, and when she swung back around, she had a knife in her hands. It was maybe a foot long, and the pointed blade flashed in the gleam of the overhead lights. She didn't point the knife right at me, but that didn't stop me from knowing exactly what she'd like to do with it. And me.

I managed to hold my ground, even when Rosa gave me a narrow-eyed look. "You tell me right now," she demanded. "Or I'll—"

"You'll what? Do what you did to Dom?" Okay, so it wasn't the smartest thing in the world to accuse a woman holding a knife of a murder, but something told me the moment would not present itself again so perfectly. Rosa was irritated, and if I had to guess, I'd say she was afraid of something, too. Otherwise she wouldn't have gone off like a bottle rocket. It was the perfect combination. At least when it came to getting her to spill the beans.

It was not so perfect if she planned on actually using that knife.

I crossed my arms over my chest and refused to look at the glittering blade of that knife. Courageous? Tell that to the crazy drum-line rhythm my heart was pounding out inside my rib cage. I swallowed hard and raised my chin.

"You want to tell me about it, Rosa? Because you were the one who killed him, right? And Martha, you knew about it. You were part of it. That would explain why you two are so chummy all of a sudden. You were in it together!"

The sounds that came out of Rosa started out small. Like the squeaks of a chipmunk. After a couple seconds, the squeaks blended together into one long screech, Rosa's mouth fell open, and she let out a laugh that practically knocked her off her feet.

I missed the joke, but Martha did not. She started laughing, too, the sound more of a bray to Rosa's guffaw. Martha threw back her head and laughed loud enough to shake the lights that hung in twinkling arcs above our heads.

"This little girl, she's hilarious!" Pressing one hand to her heart, Rosa tossed the knife down on the nearest table and fought to catch her breath. "You think I killed that no-good Dominic? You know what?" She leaned in nice and close. She smelled like garlic and oregano and guajillo, those peppers so often used in mole sauces. "I wish I had. Oh, how I wish I had! Instead . . ." She reached behind her and whisked the knife off the table, and the blade sparkled. "All I did was scare the living daylights out of that rattlesnake. Just like this. All I did was wave this knife in his face. Oh yeah, that was enough to scare the bejabbers out of him!"

I thought back to the night of the murder and how Dom had run into my tent looking for security and talking about—

"Senora Loca!" I pointed at Rosa. "The crazy lady. That was you!"

"You bet it was." When she laughed, Rosa's breasts

jiggled and she wheezed. She plunked herself down in the nearest chair. "Oh, that was fun what I did to that Dom, let me tell you. I pulled out my little knife and I waved it under his nose and that no-good son of a gun, he went running away like a scared little *conejo*. You know, a little bunny rabbit."

"I told her not to mess with him." Martha took the seat next to Rosa, and though she was apparently trying to prove that when it came to scaring Dom, she was the sensible one, she couldn't hide the smile that went ear to ear. "But she wouldn't listen, and really, I couldn't blame her. That scumbag, he deserved it. Put a little scare in him. He deserved it after what he did to us."

At the same time I tried to take it all in and make some sense of it while I was at it, I looked from one woman to the other. "So you didn't kill Dom?"

Martha tsked. "Wish I would have."

"Wish I helped," Rosa added.

"And that's why you're friends now? Because you wished you'd planned a murder together?"

Martha shook her head. "Well, it didn't hurt," she admitted. "But what made us realize we had a lot in common . . ." She looked to Rosa.

"It was Dom," Rosa said. "See, when we were here Monday night, first I took a break—"

"No, no," Martha butted in. "I took my break first."

"Did you?" I could just about see the argument form on Rosa's lips, but instead of allowing that to happen—like the Rosa I met on Monday night would have—she laughed. "No matter. What matters is we each took a break, and when we did, what else could we do? We walked around the plaza."

"And tasted some of the chili available in the other tents," Martha said. "Those society ladies . . ." She looked to the nearby tent where I saw Eleanor with a small circle of well-dressed people around her, laughing (ever so politely, of course) at some story she told. "And of course, your chili, it's good. Believe it or not, so is theirs." She didn't so much look at Ginger and Teddi like she didn't like them. It was more like she just didn't get them. "But it was when I stopped over there . . ." Her gaze went over to the Consolidated Chili tent and her top lip curled.

"We each tasted some of the samples of their new chilies." Rosa took over the telling of the story, and the look she shot at the Tri-C tent was hotter than a ghost pepper. "They're doing testing. You know." Thinking, she scrunched up her nose. "They're doing what-do-you-call-it."

"Test marketing." Martha filled in the blank. "They were handing out tastes of their newest chilies, you know, the new flavors that they're going to can and bring to market within the next few months."

More canned chili. Exactly what the universe did not need.

I shivered at the very thought.

"I tasted the first new flavor," Rosa told me, "and it was good." She glanced at Martha. "In fact, it was very good. Then I tasted the second flavor, the one Tri-C is calling Texas Favorite. I took a bite and . . ." Reliving the moment, she sat up like a shot, and maybe Texas Favorite is especially spicy, because Rosa's face turned as red as a Fresno pepper. "It was wonderful. And . . . and so familiar. So like the recipe I call *Picante*."

"The same thing happened to me," Martha added. "I tried Texas Favorite first. And it was very good. But when I tasted what Tri-C calls its Southwest Glory chili . . . well, I . . ." She fanned her face with one hand. "I couldn't believe it. I would know those flavors anywhere. I should. My mother made that chili, and my grandmother, and her mother before her. It was my Chili ala Martha!"

"*Picante* and Chili ala Martha." I chewed this over (figuratively, of course) and just about heard the pieces thunk into place inside my head. "Those were two of the items Dom had circled on your menus. And Dom worked for Tri-C. Did he . . ." The thought hit with all the subtlety of a punch to the solar plexus, and I grunted. "Your recipes? For Tri-C's canned chili? How?"

"That's what we didn't understand," Martha said. "Because we talked about it, of course. We both felt like we'd been sucker punched, and we put our heads together and we talked about it."

"And then . . ." As if it was happening right there before our eyes, Rosa pointed a finger out to the plaza. "We saw that lowlife Dominic walk by with that stupid guitar around his neck."

"I said he looked familiar," Martha told me.

"And I said he looked like someone who used to work at my restaurant as a chef," Rosa said.

"And that's when I realized he worked as a chef at my restaurant, too," Martha added.

I'd heard of it before—industrial espionage—I just

didn't think it could possibly happen. Not in the fine and spicy world of chili.

"He worked for each of you at the same time he was employed by Consolidated Chili. And when he worked for you, he—"

"Stole our recipes," Martha said.

Rosa grunted. "And now those low-down rattlesnakes over at Tri-C are canning our chili."

"Canned." A tear slipped down Martha's cheek. "My ancestors are turning in their graves."

"And mine." Rosa patted Martha's hand. "That's why I went after him with a knife," she admitted. "Not that I ever really would have hurt him." She pouted. "I wish I would have had the nerve to gut him. He deserved it."

"And after you found out what Dom had done to both of you, that's when you realized that arguing all the time was silly. That's when you became friends."

"Well, yes." Martha smoothed a hand over her apron. "Something like that."

"It was the wake-up call we needed," Rosa added. "It helped us see the light."

"And the folks at Consolidated Chili?" I asked. "Have you talked to them? What do they say?"

Rosa sniffed. "Said those recipes have been in production for a couple years. That's how long it takes, you know, for a new food to be introduced to the market."

"That Mr. Montgomery, he said he'd look into it," Martha added. " We haven't heard back from him yet."

"But that doesn't change what Dom did to either of you." I could imagine their outrage, because I felt it deep inside my bones. Chili is more than just a food; it's a philosophy of living. Like yoga, only without the deep breathing and with a whole lot more oomph. It boiled my blood to think someone could be despicable enough to do what Dom and Tri-C had done to both these ladies.

It did something else, too, and as I scurried back across the plaza to take my place beside Sylvia in our tent, I wondered if Rosa and Martha even realized it.

Knowing that Dom had stolen their recipes . . . that made the two once-warring Chili Queens look guiltier than ever.

CHAPTER 13

In spite of what some people—Sylvia, for instance—might say, I do actually have a conscience. I knew we'd be busy at the Showdown on Friday, and rather than make my half sister do all the work all day long, I got up brighter and earlier than I think is civilized and headed to downtown San Antonio.

Yes, I would be back in the same part of town for that night's fund-raising event, but that wouldn't do me any good. Not for what I had in mind. I needed to be there during business hours.

An Internet search, a scramble for enough cash to pay the fare, and a cab ride later, I was standing outside a twenty-six-story glass and steel monstrosity of a building with a wide plaza out front. There was a fountain gurgling away at its center, and for a couple cool and glorious moments, I let the spray splash over me. Sure, it was early, but already, the sun baked the plaza and my skin. The sprinkle off the fountain was heavenly, and I tipped my head back and enjoyed it. That is, until I realized the gleaming stainless steel sculpture that rose from the center of the fountain like Godzilla out of Tokyo Bay was actually a can of chili.

Talk about putting a damper on the mood!

Shaking off the bad vibes and the tiny drops of water that touched my face and my shoulders and the semi-professional-looking white blouse I'd worn with a black skirt and sensible black flats I didn't own and had to "borrow" from Sylvia (hey, she was still asleep when I left the RV and she'd never know), I headed into the building.

As I have noted before, there must be big money in canned chili, and nothing proved it like the lobby of the world headquarters of Consolidated Chili.

Marble floor polished to a sheen.

Bank of elevators that whisked away groups of conservatively dressed people who talked in hushed tones and carried leather briefcases and Coach bags and their lunches in cute insulated sacks that had apparently been a handout at some corporate event because they were all alike—yellow with a picture of a can of chili on it and the word *Consolidated* arched over it in alligator green letters.

Somehow it wouldn't surprise me to find out that it was against company rules to use a plain ol' brown paper bag.

Chili cans that matched the gigantic sculpture out in the fountain dangled from the ceiling of the atrium at the center of the lobby on invisible wires. The cans looked as if they were floating, flying, ready to swoop down on unsuspecting diners and snatch them up into the great big nothingness of taste that was canned chili.

Behind the massive desk where four receptionists fielded phone calls and handled visitors, the entire wall was lined with real cans of chili. As if they were stars and all the world was a stage designed for singing the praises of mass-produced, tasteless, soulless chili, a bright spotlight shone on them, accentuating their familiar red labels and the names I'd grown up hearing touted on TV commercials that always gave me the willies.

North, south, east, and west,
Consolidated Chili is the best!

Nothing proved the alluring nature of advertising better than the fact that I couldn't get the words and the tune of the perky Tri-C jingle out of my head. No matter how hard I tried.

Of course a guard in a dark uniform, his expression as stiff as the collar of his white shirt, stopped me.

I explained that I had an appointment with John Wesley Montgomery, which wasn't true but was better than telling the guard that I had to talk to his big, big boss because Montgomery might be mixed up in a murder. After all, it was Montgomery's company that was producing Southwest Glory and Texas Favorite, using the recipes that had been stolen from Rosa and Martha by Dom, who'd gone undercover as a chef in both their restaurants.

Rosa and Martha—and who could blame them?—were about to blow the whistle on the whole dirty scheme, and Montgomery knew it, because they'd talked to him about how Tri-C's newest concoctions tasted awfully familiar.

But wait!

Didn't I think that Rosa or Martha might have killed Dom because one (or both) of them was mad about the stolen recipes?

Well, I did. But I had to hedge my bets.

Rosa and Martha weren't the only ones with motive.

See, if John Wesley Montgomery knew that Dom could finger him in the recipe-rustling scheme, he might want to keep Dom permanently quiet.

And don't forget, I had seen that trail of Tri-C handouts on my way to finding Dom's body.

And as I followed that trail, I had been nearly run down by the sleek black limo that belonged to Tri-C's president.

I had also been grabbed by a man at the Showdown, remember, who had warned me to mind my own business.

As for that figure on Dom's balcony . . .

I puffed out a breath of annoyance. I wished I could have seen better. Shadowy figures aren't much help. Not when it comes to a murder investigation.

Of course, I couldn't tell the security guard any of that, so with a wide smile and a ring of confidence in my voice, I assured him that I had an appointment and that Mr. Montgomery was—even as we spoke—waiting for me. And when that guard went over to the reception desk so one of the women there could call upstairs and check it out? That's when I hightailed it into the nearest elevator.

I rode up to the top floor and wasn't the least bit surprised when I stepped out of the elevator and onto a plush Oriental rug in muted shades of tabasco and jalapeño. The fresh flowers in vases all around the outer office were a nice touch, as were the mahogany desks of the three assistants outside a closed doorway with a brass plaque on it that told me I had found what I was looking for. In fact, the only thing that seemed out of place was the giant inflatable red chili next to John Wesley Montgomery's door. It reminded me of the Chick, and I went over and gave it a pat.

"Can I help you?"

The voice that came from behind me was as chilly as the AC that poured out of a vent just above my head.

I turned and found myself face to sneer with a woman in a black suit and pearls. Her dark hair brushed her shoulders. Her glasses gleamed in the early morning sunlight that flowed in from the windows on the far wall.

"Great chili," I said, looking back at the inflatable. "Just what this place needs, a little bit of fun!"

My guess is that she didn't agree with me, because the woman's blank expression never changed. "Can I help you?" she asked again.

I poked a thumb over my shoulder toward Montgomery's closed door. "Appointment," I said. "He's waiting for me."

Her perfectly plucked eyebrows rose a fraction of an inch at the same time her gaze fell to the tips of my shoes then slid up to the top of my head. Her lips pinched. "Oh?"

"Yeah. And really . . ." I fished in my gigantic denim hobo bag and pulled out my phone to check the time. "I hate to keep him waiting, and I'm already a minute late."

"Oh?" This time, she didn't wait for me to respond. The woman slipped behind the nearest desk and tapped on her computer keyboard.

"I don't see that Mr. Montgomery has any appointments scheduled for this morning," she said.

I waved away this bit of news as inconsequential. "He probably just forgot to tell you to put it on his calendar. We talked. Last night at the fund-raiser. You know, over at Alamo Plaza. And he asked me to stop by this morning and—"

When she picked up the phone, I nearly breathed a sigh of relief. She was buying my story!

Or at least I thought so until I heard her say, "Yes, Security? We have an unauthorized person here in the executive suite."

"Oh, come on!" When she hung up the phone, I tried to reason with her. "All I want to do is talk to the guy."

"That's unfortunate because *the guy* . . ." Her tongue twisted over the words. "Mr. Montgomery isn't in this morning."

"He must have forgotten our appointment," I assured her.

To which she did nothing but give me a knowing little smile.

A second later, a couple beefy security guards showed up, and I threw my hands in the air by way of telling them they wouldn't get a fight out of me. "Going," I said and scurried toward the elevator. The two guards fell into step beside me, and the woman with the pearls brought up the rear of our little procession. "But I'll tell you what, when Mr. Montgomery finds out how you treated me, he's not going to be happy."

"Mr. Montgomery is always happy," she replied, and I can't say for certain, because I'd already stepped into the elevator between those two burly guards, but I could have sworn before the doors slipped shut, her lips pursed and she mumbled, "That's one of the things I can't stand about him."

By the time I got back to the fairgrounds, the Showdown was in full swing. That day's cook-off contest was for the traditional red category—that is, chili made with any meat and red chili peppers but with no beans or pasta added—and we anticipated a bigger-than-usual crowd. Texans are famous for liking their chili bean-less, and the contest that day would provide an opportunity for many of the state's best to vie for the top prize.

When I got to the Palace, Sylvia was busy with customers.

But not too busy to notice my shoes.

Her lips pinched. "The least you can do is put them back where you found them," she said.

I did when I went into the RV to change into the Chili Chick costume. Then, back out in front of the Palace, I finished forty-five minutes of hot and sweaty dancing before there was a lull in the crowd.

We were doing well that day; even this early, Sylvia needed to restock the jars of Thermal Conversion on the front counter. Since the overhang at the front of the Palace offered a minimal amount of shade, I offered to help.

"So?" Unlike so many of our patrons, Sylvia knew exactly where to look to see into the mesh at the front of the Chick. "What did you find out? You were out investigating, weren't you?" she added when I didn't answer either of those first two questions fast enough. "That's the only reason I can imagine you'd get out of bed early. Where were you? And what did you find out?"

It was a couple minutes before I could tell her, but that was because a big man in a big cowboy hat and big, big boots sauntered over. Like everything else in Texas, the fairgrounds was massive, and there was a rodeo going on for the weekend at the other end of it. From the look of the dust—and other stuff—on his boots, I guessed he was part of it.

"Lookin' for the hottest peppers you have," he said, and unlike Sylvia, he didn't try to see into the mesh. He was too busy checking out my legs. "Although from the looks of things," he drawled, "I think I'm already seein' the hottest thing to come around these parts in a long, long time."

"The peppers are over there." I waved toward the counter and the display set up just behind it where we had bags of dried peppers arranged alphabetically (guess whose idea that was).

With thumb and forefinger, the cowboy knocked his hat a little farther back on his head. "All right, then, I can take a hint. You're all business and no fun, hey, little pepper?"

Since I was not technically a little pepper, I figured I could ignore this.

"If you're looking for heat, you might want to try Scotch bonnet peppers," I told him.

He scratched a hand along his jawline. "Those are for sissies. I'm looking for something that packs a little more punch."

"Three hundred fifty thousand Scoville Heat Units." I jiggled a bag of Scotch bonnets in front of his nose. "That's plenty of punch. A bell pepper is—"

"A bell pepper is zero. A banana pepper is somewhere around one hundred. You're not dealing with an amateur here, little pepper. I know how Scoville Heat Units are used to figure the spiciness of a pepper. And three hundred fifty thousand . . ." His smile inched up a face that was as craggy as some of the desert we'd driven through on our way from Las Vegas to San Antonio. "Here in Texas, we can handle our heat."

"Then how about Red 7-Pot?" We didn't keep a lot of these around, and I needed to rummage through the display for the right bag. "They're from Trinidad, and there, they say one pepper is enough to spice seven pots of chili."

His eyebrows rose a fraction of an inch. "SHUs?"

"Seven hundred eighty thousand," I told him.

"Gol darn!" He screwed up his face. "That's girlie stuff!"

It was a shame he couldn't see the sour look I shot him. "Then how about this?" I slapped another bag of peppers on the counter. "Moruga Scorpion. Two million SHUs."

He rubbed his hands together. "Now you're talkin'! Anything else? Anything more?"

There was. One more pepper. That last fiery step of the descent into spicy hell from which there was no escape. I sized him up. He wasn't a kid, and that, at least, was in his favor. Young guys often think that how much heat they can take is a sign of their manhood. But we were in blistering territory here, and I didn't like to think what kind of pain might result if some crazy cook decided that his manhood depended on the size of his SHUs. This guy was middle-aged. Old enough to be careful. At least I hoped so.

I put one more bag on the counter. "Carolina Reaper," I said. "Starts out sweet. Right before it demolishes your taste buds. It's a little hotter than the Moruga Scorpion."

"I'll take it!"

He reached for the bag.

I held it just far enough away so he couldn't get it. "You'll be careful?"

The man threw back his head and laughed. "Oh, honey! This is Texas. Careful ain't in our vocabulary!"

It was all the advice I could offer, and he wasn't going to listen, anyway. I turned him over to Sylvia and let her ring up the sale.

Once he was gone, Sylvia slipped out of the Palace to stand at my side. "So? Where were you this morning? And what did you find out?"

"Not much of anything." I hated to admit it. "I tried to talk to John Wesley Montgomery, but his secretary claimed he wasn't in this morning. Yeah, like I believe that!"

Sylvia tipped her head. "Montgomery? That canned chili guy? He's the one who's been at the fund-raisers, right? The one who gets chauffeured around in that big black limo with the Tri-C plates?"

I nodded, then remembered she couldn't see me. "Yeah. Dom worked for him, and he stole some recipes from Rosa and Martha and Tri-C is making the chili and putting it in cans."

Sylvia, of course, did not understand the significance of this. Or feel the outrage that boiled through me at the very thought.

She turned to scan the fairgrounds, and I didn't know what she was looking for. At least not until she clamped a hand on my arm tight enough to cut off my circulation.

"Well, of course his secretary told you Montgomery wasn't in," she said, pointing with her free hand. "It's true. He couldn't have been in his office. See! See, over there! That's the fourth time I've seen it today. You do see it, right?"

I did see, and my heart thudded at the same time my brain whirled over the possibilities.

It was Montgomery's black limo, and it was slowly cruising the perimeter of the fairgrounds.

Was Montgomery hanging around in the hopes of snaffling up a few more chili recipes?

Or was there an even more sinister reason for his visit to the Showdown?

This I did not know, but believe me, the thoughts twirled through my head until later that afternoon when, out of the Chick costume, I walked by the whitewashed fairgrounds building with the word *Security* written in red letters on the side of it. Until I talked to Montgomery, I couldn't even begin to try to figure out what he was up to, and with that in mind, I made a vow to corner him at that night's fund-raiser. He was bound to be there. Maybe if I made like a beauty queen, he'd actually give me the time of day!

For reasons I can't explain, this struck me as especially funny, and that would explain why Nick thought I was smiling at him when he walked out of the security builidng.

"Promised I'd get Ruth Ann a cotton candy," I said, showing off the five-dollar bill Ruth had given me to pay and pointing with it in the direction of the carnival midway that stood between the Showdown on one side of the fairgrounds and the rodeo on the other. "You want some?"

He made a face and stepped closer. "You okay?" he asked. "I mean, after last night and having to climb down the balcony to get out of Dom's apartment?"

"Piece of cake!" I waved away his concern, but speaking of concerns . . .

"You know, Nick . . ." Something had been bothering me, and I knew I couldn't let it go. Not until I got it straight with him. "About the murder . . ."

He puffed out a breath. "Now what? You think I killed Dom and I was also the person who walked in on us at the apartment? I'm good, Maxie, but I'm not good enough to be two people. There's no way I'm the one who was watching us when we ran last night."

"You saw him, too, huh?" I was wearing black shorts and a Texas Jack Pierce T-shirt in habanero red, and I crossed my arms over my chest. "Obviously it wasn't you, because you were with me. But I keep thinking about the night of the murder. Dom must have been killed soon after the fund-raiser ended that night. We need to get everyone's timeline straight. Like, for instance, where were you?"

His eyebrows rose just enough to make it loud and clear that my question was as unexpected as it was nervy. "Are you asking me if I have an alibi?"

"I've already asked you if you have an alibi. You dodged the question. That means I have to ask it again. Do you?"

"Do you?"

"I don't need an alibi. I'm not the one who was partners with a murdered guy who stole my wife."

He grumbled a word he shouldn't have used in public. But then, I didn't hold that against him, since I used the word plenty myself.

"You're impossible." Nick turned away.

"And you're ignoring my question." I stepped in front of him. "Where were you when Dom was killed?"

"I was—" He clamped his mouth shut for a moment before he muttered, "I was busy."

"Busy killing Dom?"

"Don't be ridiculous."

"Then what were you busy doing?"

"Busy being busy, all right? That's what I was doing."

And before I could tell him that it wasn't nearly the explanation I needed, Nick stalked away.

"Busy being busy," I grumbled and spun the other way; the five-dollar bill Ruth gave me for her cotton candy—and one for myself, too, she told me, if I wanted it—was in my palm, and I squeezed it so hard, I swear Abraham Lincoln had tears in his eyes.

I was still grumbling when I got over near the midway and found myself at the back of a crowd of folks watching a juggling act. My mind was already plenty mixed up; the last thing I needed to see was juggling. I scooted around the crowd, darted between the Ferris wheel and a shooting gallery where folks could win giant teddy bears, and ducked behind the vendors who sold everything from corn dogs on a stick to ice cream cones that wouldn't last two minutes in the afternoon heat, sniffing the air and hoping the aroma of cotton candy would let me know when I was at the right spot.

It was a smart move; there was no one back there among the wires and whirring generators, and I could move far quicker than I could out in the crowd.

And it was a dumb move.

Because when someone came up behind me and threw a pillowcase over my head, there was no one there to see.

Just like there was no one around when that same someone zapped me with a stun gun and I dropped to the ground.

I have no idea how long I was out. A minute or two? Longer? I only know that when I opened my eyes again, the world in front of me tipped and whirled. I was still down in the dirt, but I couldn't hear the generators anymore. My head felt like it had been filled with those fluffy cotton balls that Sylvia used to remove her makeup every night. Since the pillow case was no longer over my head, I dared to look around.

"No generators." My voice sounded as if it came from a million miles away. It was as heavy as my eyelids, my words as slurred as if I'd guzzled a dozen margaritas.

Margaritas!

My mouth felt as if it was filled with sand, and I ran my dry tongue over even drier lips and checked out the area.

It was no wonder I couldn't hear the generators; I wasn't where I'd been when I was waylaid. I was in some sort of fenced enclosure that was maybe twenty feet wide and just as long, and I was all alone. The ground beneath me was gritty, and somewhere in the deep, dark recesses of my head, I knew I should get up or I'd end up covered with dirt. Too bad I didn't have the energy to stand, or even to drag myself over to the tall fence where I could prop myself until I figured out what was going on. Instead, I tried to make sense of what had happened and stared at the sort of pen in front of me. There was a gate in the center of it, and even as I watched, something moved behind it.

Something big.

Warning bells went off inside my head. At least I think they did. I was too woozy to listen, and too punch-drunk to care.

That is, until that gate popped open and the ground shook. Instinctively, I got to my knees. I was still trying to steady myself when a two-thousand-pound brown rodeo bull emerged from the shadows, dipped its head, and charged.

CHAPTER 14

As if it were all happening in slow motion, I watched that gigantic bull rumble closer, its dark, beady eyes on me. He lowered his enormous head and came straight at me.

I was paralyzed, and it wasn't until I was looking right into those big brown eyes and felt the heat of his breath that something kick-started me into action.

I dropped and rolled and squeezed my eyes shut, waiting to feel those hooves and all that muscle trample me like I was a rag doll.

Lucky for me my timing was right and my roll was perfect. I skidded to a stop in the dust just as the bull ran by, kicking up a storm of dirt a foot or so away from me. Realizing how lucky I was and how little time I had until I'd have to try my luck again, I scrambled to my knees, pulled myself to my feet, and lurched over to that gate that the bull had come out of.

It was closed. And locked.

From the other side.

"Hey!" I jiggled the gate and called out, and even to my own ears, my words sounded like they came from inside a thick coating of Bubble Wrap. "Hey!" I joggled the gate again, even though it hardly moved the first time, and I guess I would have gone right on trying to open it if I didn't feel the ground tremble and hear that bull grunt right before it headed back in my direction.

"Nice bull! Good bull!" My words bumped along with my breath when I zigzagged around him and over to the far side of the pen. The wooden fence around the enclosure was taller than me, and because the slats were so close together, it was impossible to see through. Was there someone nearby on the other side? Someone who could get me out of there?

"Help!" I called out just in case there was anyone around. "I'm in here. Help!"

"Maxie?"

I was so relieved to hear the voice call out my name from the other side of the fence, I nearly cried. As it was, I didn't exactly have the time, since that bull made another charge at me and I took off like a shot to the other side of the enclosure.

"I'm in here!" I yelled, though with all the noise of thundering hooves and bellowing bull, I wasn't sure anyone could hear me. I pounded on the wooden fence with my fists and ended up with a splinter. "Help!"

"Maxie?"

Across the enclosure, something appeared just above the top of the fence, then disappeared again.

"Is that you?" the voice asked. "What are you doing in there?"

Again, the something appeared, then vanished, and I was left with a quick impression: hair the color of brandy. Collar of a white shirt. Knot of a killer (bad choice of words) blue tie. Like his eyes.

"Nick!" This time, I did allow myself the luxury of a few tears, and hey, who could blame me? Right before I took off again to get away from the frenzied bull, I caught another glimpse of Nick just as he jumped to try and see over the wooden enclosure.

"Is there a bull in there? Maxie, why are you messing around with a rodeo bull? Don't you know that's dangerous?"

I pressed my back to the enclosure and imagined that where I stood, Nick must be right on the other side of the fence. Good, then he wouldn't have an excuse not to hear me when I screamed, "Are you crazy? You think I'm in here because I want to be here? Get me out of here, Nick! This bull, he's—"

He's what, I didn't have the chance to say, because the bull charged again, I took off running again, and I was too freakin' scared to get another word out of my mouth.

This time, I ran toward the gate where the bull had come in. When I saw Nick on the other side of it, I would have sighed with relief if I had any breath left.

"Get me out of here!"

Both hands wrapped around the metal gate, he wiggled

it and jiggled it just like I had. "Well, if there was a key, it isn't here now. This gate is locked."

"Really? Gosh, I never thought to check that."

He gave me a sour look which I was fully justified in returning in equal tart measure.

"Here's what we're going to do . . ." Nick eyed the bull, the height of the gate (well above both our heads), and me. "I'm going to start climbing from this side. You're going to start climbing from that side. When I get to the top, I can reach over and help you to the other side. Got that?"

I eyed the gate. The whole thing was made of chain link, like fencing, and every eight inches or so, a heavy metal bar went side to side across it. It looked plenty sturdy. No doubt it had to be to contain the beast. I looked over my shoulder and saw that even now, he was eyeing me up and snorting.

"Maxie! Maxie!"

When Nick called out to me, I swung around from the bull back to the gate.

"That's better." His voice was firm and encouraging. His expression was as hard as stone. I wondered if he was trying to convince me—or himself—that it was actually possible to get me out of that enclosure in one piece.

"Don't worry about the bull," Nick instructed. "Just keep your eyes on me. Okay, see what I'm doing?" He started up his side of the fence, bracing first one foot, then the other, on those heavy metal crossbars. They were narrow and he was wearing dress shoes. His foot slipped, and he slammed against the gate, righted himself, and started the climb again.

"I'm going all the way to the top," he said, and he made his way up another couple feet. "And you're going to do the same thing. And when you get close enough, I'm going to grab your hands and help you the rest of the way. You got that?"

I did, and it was a mighty fine plan. Or at least it would have been if not for the fact that the bull made another charge. I climbed as fast as I could, and I had sneakers on, so my footing was better than Nick's. But with that bull coming at me full speed with murder in its beefy heart, I knew I wasn't fast enough. I panicked. Okay, I admit it. I lost my cool and then my footing and then my nerve, and even though I wasn't quite close enough for either of us to be balanced, I grabbed hold of both Nick's hands before he had a chance to brace himself.

The bull did a U-turn right at my heels, and, feeling his wet breath on the back of my legs, I screamed.

What with all the scrambling and the squealing and with me holding on to him for dear life, Nick lost his balance. He tumbled and hit the dirt on my side of the gate at the same time I let go and slithered to the ground beside him.

"Are you all right?" I asked him.

He didn't answer. Instead, he jumped to his feet and snatched me up just as the bull got over to the other side of the pen, turned, and pawed the ground, ready to make another run at us.

Nick pressed me toward the fence. "Climb!"

"But Nick, I—"

"Climb!" He lifted me off my feet and set me up on

the second crossbar from the bottom, and I wrapped my fingers through the wire fencing.

Nick poked me in the back. "Make it fast! Because I'm going to be right behind you!"

Climb I did, and it was a good thing I spent all those hours dancing as the Chili Chick and was in good shape. When I got to the top of the gate, I raised my left leg like I was doing a high kick and swung it over the top crossbar, then pulled myself up to straddle the gate. From this altitude, that bull didn't look so big anymore. But he still looked like he wanted to take somebody's head off, and right about then, the nearest somebody was Nick.

"Hurry!" I urged him, and I didn't need to tell him twice. When I dropped to the ground on the other side—the safe side—of the gate, Nick was right behind me. We both landed on our feet a second before that bull slammed into the gate. The entire enclosure shivered and shook like we were on a fault line in the middle of a quake. The vibration hit me like a wave and shuddered through my bones. It knocked me back against Nick, who lost his footing, and we ended up in a heap in the chute carpeted with straw and decorated with bull droppings.

With a grunt, Nick sat up, set me aside, and looked at what had been a gorgeous gray suit. He grabbed a handful of clean straw to scrape the muck off his sleeve, and I realized I wasn't the only one who was out of breath when he asked, "Are you okay?"

Was I?

It took me a couple seconds to do a quick inventory. No

broken bones. At least none I could feel. No blood except for the thin stream of it that welled up around the sliver in my hand. If I had any other injuries, I honestly couldn't say. But then, my head gyrated and my stomach lurched and the adrenaline pumped through my body so hard and so fast, it felt like the front of my skull was going to explode.

"I'm . . ." I dared to take a look past the gate and into the pen and was just in time to see the bull huff out his opinion of us and turn to trot into a pool of sunshine at the far end of the enclosure.

I picked straw—and other stuff—out of my hair. "I was on my way to get Ruth Ann's cotton candy and—"

"Yeah. That's what I thought." Nick pulled a five-dollar bill out of his pocket. "I came looking for you and found this on the ground. It seemed strange to me, since I just saw you with a five."

"You came looking for me?"

He got to his feet and offered me a hand up. My knees were rubber, so nobody could blame me when, even after I was standing, I held on tight to him.

"Why?" I asked.

"Why were you in there with that bull? That's what I'd like you to tell me."

If I had the energy, I would have screamed. I pressed a hand to my heart. Yeah, like that would do anything to help the pounding. "Why were you looking for me? The last time I saw you, you were busy dodging about an alibi for the night of the murder."

"I did. I was." He looked down at his tie, saw that it was smeared with goo, and, grumbling, untied it and tossed it aside. "I thought about it, and I decided I had to tell you the truth. I was going to tell you the truth. But then I found that five and what looked like the tracks of a golf cart right nearby, and it just seemed off to me. I don't know why."

I had little memory of any of it, but it made perfect sense. I passed a hand over my eyes. "Somebody . . ." I gulped and swayed on my feet. Shock? Or was the smell on my skin and clothes getting to me? "Somebody put something over my head. Like a bag or a pillowcase or something. And then . . ." I flinched at the memory. "I think I got hit with a stun gun."

He backed up just enough so he could look me over, and I guess he didn't see anything broken or any blood, either, otherwise he would have started bellowing like that bull and insisting on a trip to the hospital. Right about then, a shower sounded way more appealing than the ER.

"And then you got dumped in here?" he asked.

I nodded. "I guess I must have been out of it for a little while, and then I came to and . . ." I looked back at the enclosure and the two-thousand-pound killing machine inside it and gulped.

Nick reached down into the straw and came up holding a cattle prod. "Well, that explains why he was not in a good mood," he said with a look back at the bull. "This was no accident." He said what I was thinking.

"And it wasn't meant just to scare me." I said what he didn't put into words. "Someone wanted me dead. And I would have been dead, Nick. If not for you."

He shrugged off the praise. "You would have thought of climbing the fence yourself."

"Maybe. Yeah. Eventually. But I was so out of it and so

scared . . ." When I went to wipe a tear off my cheek, I realized my hands were trembling, and rather than let Nick think that I was wimpy, I dropped my hands and held my arms tight against my sides. "I couldn't think straight."

"That's perfectly natural when something like this happens, something life-threatening."

Rather than think about it, I looked past him down the chute the bull had come out of. "And you didn't see anyone? When you got here, there was no one around?"

"Not a soul. Except for you." He slipped an arm around my shoulders. "Let's get you back to the RV so you can get cleaned up."

I wasn't about to argue.

But let's face it, I wasn't about to forget, either.

"What were you going to tell me?" I asked him once we were safely away from the enclosure. "You said you came looking for me so you could tell me something. You said you were going to explain. You know, about your alibi for Monday night."

He breathed in deep, then thought better of it and made a face. It's not like I could blame him. We both smelled like we'd just gone one-on-one with a rodeo animal, and even the sickly sweet smell of the kettle corn cooking nearby couldn't mask that.

"It's like this." Nick scratched a hand along the back of his neck. "I do have an alibi."

"Yeah, you said that. And now you're going to tell me what it is."

"I am. Sure."

If I didn't know better—and I did, I knew that Nick

doesn't get rattled and he doesn't get embarrassed and he isn't self-conscious at all—I would have said that he was rattled and embarrassed and self-conscious as hell. But then, his cheeks flushed a dusky red that reminded me of a Dundicut pepper.

"I was . . ." A muscle jumped at the base of Nick's jaw. "I was with Ginger."

It took a moment for what he said to sink in, and another second for me to put two and two together. It took even longer for me to close my flapping jaw. "Ginger? Our Ginger? Ginger with the great wardrobe? The drag queen from the plaza?"

I guess I said all this kind of loud, because Nick looked at the people who crowded around the nearby midway food trucks and clamped a hand on my arm to drag me away.

"Yes, Ginger the drag queen," he said from between clenched teeth. "Do you have to tell the world? And before you ask, yes, the cops know. I told them. Ginger told them. They know exactly where I was."

It is not often that I am at a loss for words, but at that moment, I couldn't get even one past the sudden lump that blocked my throat. What was the emotion that robbed me of my voice? Was it surprise I was feeling? Or outrage?

Was it jealousy?

We were near the center of the fairgrounds midway, and the Ferris wheel whirled on one side of us, the merry-go-round on the other. I locked my legs and refused to move another step, and I realized that the crazy emotion that slammed me like a professional wrestler (or a two-thousand-pound rodeo bull) was jealousy, all right. Like every other jealous woman, anytime, anywhere, I was not about to wait even another minute to hear the whole story.

I untangled myself from Nick's iron grip so I could throw both my hands in the air. "First I saw that DVD of all those cute guys over at Dom's place and I thought he was gay. And now . . ." I could barely believe it. "You? Why didn't you tell me, Nick? Because I'll tell you what, I would have been just fine with the whole friendship thing, and I wouldn't have wasted my time and a whole lot of really good fantasies on you, either."

His eyes lit. "You fantasize? About me?"

I guess throwing my hands in the air once didn't dispel all the nervous energy that had built inside me because I did it again. "Not anymore, that's for sure. You should have told me. You should have told me you were gay!"

Suddenly, I felt like I was looking at Nick in a fun house mirror. His expression froze into a mask of astonishment, then melted into what was almost a smile. That lasted maybe a second. Then again, he scooped me into his arms so fast, I didn't have time to see. Exactly one half of a nanosecond after he clamped his mouth over mine, I didn't care.

The kiss was long and luxurious. It was slow and wet, but not in that slobbery sort of way some guys kiss. Nick, he knew what he was doing, and when my knees buckled and I leaned against him, I didn't even care that he smelled as bad as I did, like straw and beast and bull droppings.

"There." He stopped as quickly as he started, and with

his hands on my shoulders, he set me back on my feet, but he didn't give me time to catch my breath. "Now you want to tell me who's gay?"

I touched a hand to my lips. Yes, I know it's cliché and all, but I swear they were burning. "Not you." I stepped forward, all set for another kiss in spite of the crowds that drifted by and their oohing and aahing and the one guy who called out, "Get a room!" My own curiosity stopped me in my tracks.

"Then what were you doing out on a date with Ginger?" I demanded.

"Did I say I was on a date?" Nick, it seemed, was not as comfortable with public displays of affection as I was. He took my hand and hauled me through the crowd and over to the Showdown side of the fairgrounds.

"I wasn't on a date with Ginger," he said once we got there. "I was doing Ginger a favor."

"Helping her pick out a new gown?"

Nick was in no mood for jokes. He stopped under the awning in front of Jorge LaReyo's tamale stand, but Jorge took one whiff and told us we'd better move on or someone would think he was cooking with month-old meat. I knew we wouldn't get even that nice of a reception from Sylvia, so when we got back to the Palace, I led the way around back where we stood in a strip of shade.

"Ginger, she . . . he . . ." Nick crinkled up his nose, and it wasn't because of how we smelled. "That whole cross-dressing scene, it's not exactly my thing. I'm never even sure what to call them."

"Ginger's a she. At least when she's in costume. And

she . . ." I leaned forward, urging him to fill in all the blanks that left my mind reeling.

"She was performing at a club on Monday night after the fund-raiser. She does this Dolly Parton thing. You know, with the wigs and the dresses and the . . ."

He didn't explain any more. He didn't have to.

Ginger as Dolly. Just thinking about it made me grin, and I wished we were going to be in San Antonio long enough for me to attend one of her shows.

"Is she any good?" I asked.

I guess Nick never considered this. He nodded, shook his head, shrugged. "Like I said, not exactly my thing. Besides, I wasn't paying all that much attention to Ginger's performance. See, she does a show at this club every Monday, Wednesday, and Friday. Late. And there's this guy who's been hanging around. You know, a real stalker type. He's been making Ginger really nervous. She talked to me about it earlier in the evening and asked my advice, and she was so upset, I told her I'd stop over at the club and see what I could do."

"Was he there?"

"Yeah, and as soon as I saw him, I got why he made Ginger uncomfortable. He was one of those guys who has a real bad vibe coming off him. I should have told you right away where I was. I just felt—"

"Embarrassed?"

Deep color stained his cheeks. "Yeah. Not that I care or anything. Those guys, they can do whatever they want. With whoever they want. It's just not my thing."

"And you told Detective Gilkenny?"

"She never batted an eye. But then, after a few years on the force, I'm sure she's heard it all. Just like I had when I was on the job."

"And when you told her, she didn't think you were gay?"

"I'm not sure if she did or if she didn't. I don't think she cares if I am or I'm not."

"And you're not." I thought back to the kiss and to the way the touch of Nick's lips made my head spin like the Ferris wheel and my body feel as if I'd stood in the Texas sun too long. "You're not."

"I'm not. But I knew you'd think I was, and that's why I didn't want to get into it with you."

"Except you did." Believe me, I wasn't talking about getting into a discussion about gender or wardrobe or Nick's choice in entertainment. I was talking about the kiss.

I guess Nick knew this, because the tiniest smile touched his lips. "I did. We did."

"And we didn't get into it just because we had this near-death experience and you were feeling relieved and glad to be alive and you wanted to celebrate with the first woman you could find?"

"There are plenty of other women around," he said.

I inched closer and grinned.

He stepped nearer and made a face. "You smell awful!"

"There's one way to a woman's heart! And you're no treat yourself, by the way."

"So I'm going to change." He backed away a step. "And I'll catch up with you later."

It wasn't what either of us wanted—not right then, not

right there—but I could see his point. Landing in the sack when I smelled like I smelled with a guy who smelled like Nick smelled . . . talk about a buzz kill!

"Except, Nick!" I stopped him before he could walk away. "What happened?"

He gave me a blank look and I elaborated. "What happened with Ginger? And the stalker?"

Nick brushed a hand through his hair. "I took him outside the club and had a little . . . er . . . talk with him. He won't be bothering Ginger again."

"Because you told him if he did, he was going to get arrested?"

Nick smiled. "Because I told him I was Ginger's boyfriend and if he ever came near her again, I was going to break both his legs."

CHAPTER 15

After all the excitement (not to mention a much-needed shower and a quick change of clothes), the last thing I felt like doing was working the Showdown for the rest of the afternoon. Lucky for me, I didn't have to. Tumbleweed was looking for someone to get over to Alamo Plaza early with the paperwork for that night's event—*The Chili Queens Help the Homeless*—and I was happy to volunteer. Rest and relaxation. That's what I needed. And to me, the plaza sounded like a better place to find it than the fairgrounds, where I'd been wrangled and almost mangled.

It was also where I'd been kissed.

In spite of the little voice inside me that told me to play it cool when it came to Nick, I found myself smiling and with a spring in my step when I thought about all I'd discovered that afternoon.

Nick had an alibi. He wasn't a murderer.

He also just happened to be the best darned kisser these lips had the pleasure of running into in a long, long time.

During the cab ride over to the plaza, the thought swirled through my head along with the possibility of what it might mean—and where it might lead—and I was still smiling when I got out of the cab. Something tells me I would have gone right on smiling if I didn't drop off the paperwork at the main tent and head over to our own tent so I could start getting things set up for that night's festivities and see a man I didn't recognize slip into the tent next to ours and start rummaging around.

Curious, I scooted behind a pallet of folding chairs that would soon be set up under the tents around the plaza and watched. The man was slim and of medium height with short-cropped dark hair and dark eyes just the same as—

"Teddi!" The name slipped out along with a breath of amazement. It was Teddi, all right, out of her drag costume and wearing a pair of khakis and a green and white plaid button-down shirt. No doubt she . . . er . . . he had just come from the Bexar County Medical Examiner's Office where Ginger told me Teddi—whose name when he wasn't in drag was Teo—counseled grieving families.

So what was he doing here at the plaza long before Ginger was scheduled to arrive?

And why was he rummaging around the tent?

It didn't take long for the little mystery to get even more curious.

Teo grabbed a piece of paper from underneath the counter where Ginger and Teddi would later set up their slow cookers, stuffed that same piece of paper in his pocket, and headed out of the plaza.

There was never any question in my mind that I was going to follow.

Keeping twenty feet in back of Teo, I trailed him down Crockett Street and all the way over to the River Walk where shops and bars and restaurants lined both sides of the San Antonio River and tourists milled around snapping pictures and climbing into the flat-bottomed boats that showed them the sights and took them from attraction to attraction. Here, one story down from street level, the humidity off the river was like a hand that strangled the air in my lungs, and between that and the fact that Teo kept up a brisk pace, I was tempted to drop into a seat at one of the outdoor cafés and order a pitcher of margaritas.

Instead, I kept him in my sights, tailing Teo down one small arm of the River Walk and into another. He finally stopped and went into a shop with a red front door, and, still wondering what was up and what he was up to, I parked myself behind a gigantic pot of flowers, my gaze on the door of the place called Tatiana's, and took a couple minutes to catch my breath.

When the door popped open and two middle-aged women came out, shopping bags swinging from their arms, the picture started to become clearer. It came into perfect focus when I closed in on Tatiana's and saw that the front window display featured an array of snazzy items: picture hats that dripped veiling and flowers, purses studded with sequins and rhinestones, shoes with tips pointy enough to skewer a vampire, and heels so high, even I wouldn't dare wear them.

I marched into the shop and saw Teo at the front counter, so busy checking out a long string of sparkling blue and purple beads, he never bothered to turn around when the little bell over the front door tinkled.

I sidled up next to him.

"Doing some shopping?" I asked.

He flinched once when he heard the voice right beside him and again when he saw it was me. "Oh, Maxie. What are you . . ." His surprise froze into a smile as stiff as a meringue. "Are you playing tourist this afternoon?"

"Just getting an idea of what's going on," I said, and I was trying to be cryptic and hoping he'd get the message, but he never had the chance, because a grinning clerk emerged from a back room with a gold lamé evening gown on a hanger in one hand.

"Here it is!" the woman crooned. "And isn't it just the most beautiful thing you've ever seen?" She ran a loving hand along the skirt and caressed the nipped waist, the tiny capped sleeves, and the deep, plunging neckline. "You, my dear, are going to be so glad you ordered this one. It's lovely, and you're going to look delicious in it!"

I moved before Teo could and intercepted the clerk when she was halfway back to the front counter with the sparkling dress. "Nice," I said with a look at the gown. I took a gander at the price tag that hung from one sleeve. "And expensive!" I whirled back toward Teo. "You've got good taste!"

"Well, of course I do." He tried for that little simper that looked so perfect when he was in drag. In street clothes, it came off as slightly sour and a little pathetic, too. He tossed his head. "Just wrap it up, Donna," he told the woman.

"You're not going to try it on?" She was honestly disappointed. "I've been waiting since you ordered this dress and that was . . ." She scooted forward and checked the sales receipt on the counter in front of Teo. I had no doubt it was the same piece of paper I'd seen him retrieve from the tent over at the plaza.

"It's been weeks," Donna said. "And I can't wait another minute. I want to see how lovely you're going to look in this little number."

"Wrap it up, Donna," Teo snapped. "I need . . ." He slid me a look. "I need to get out of here."

Donna might have been surprised, but she was not about to offend a paying customer. She went in back to wrap the gown, and that was just fine by me. It gave me a chance to close in on Teo again.

"You sure about this?" I asked him.

"About . . . ?"

"About buying a gown I'm guessing you can't afford? But then, you told me you were going to turn things around, didn't you? The other night, when I said you looked so yesterday, you told me, 'Not for long.' This is what you were talking about, right? This fabulous new dress."

His lips pinched. "So? So I ordered a new gown. It's what I do."

I shrugged. The better to look like I wasn't trying to intimidate him. "Fine by me. I can understand that you have to mix up your wardrobe now and again. And you have to make a big splash. I get that, too. That's what the whole drag scene is all about, and hey, I think it's great. Theater. Drama. Standing out in the crowd. I know you and Ginger appear at these kinds of charity fund-raising events all over town all the time, so I get it that you must need one heck of a wardrobe. I guess that's why I'm a little surprised you'd spend so much on just one gown. I figured you'd want to spread the money around, use it on more than just one outfit. You know, the money you've been stealing from the tip jar over at the fund-raisers."

Teo's mouth opened and closed. It opened again, and color shot into his cheeks. He was a good-looking guy, compact and wiry, but when he looked at me like that— his dark eyes wide with fear and his jaw hanging slack—I almost felt sorry for him.

Almost.

It's hard to be completely sympathetic with a guy stealing money from fluffy kitties, sweet puppies, and kids who can't read.

His left eye twitched. "You're not . . . you're not going to tell anyone, are you?"

I had to pretend to think about it. "That all depends."

He swallowed hard and his Adam's apple bobbed. "You can't."

"Can't tell anyone? Why not? Ginger already knows, by the way. She hasn't talked to you about it yet, though, has she? She was pretty broken up when she found out the truth. My guess is she's still trying to find a way to discuss this with you that's not going to break her heart."

He'd already taken his wallet out of his pocket, and he

turned it over and over in one hand. "I didn't mean to hurt anybody. That's not why I did it. I just . . ." He darted a look toward the back room, where I heard Donna fussing with tissue paper. "It's just that when that Dominic, when he found out I was taking some of the money . . ."

Of all the things I expected Teo to say, this wasn't one of them. Dominic knew Teo was stealing? Teo was desperate to keep his thievery a secret?

And then Dominic was dead?

My heart bashed my ribs. My blood went cold. I came to the River Walk searching for a thief.

And it looked like I'd found a murderer.

It was my turn to swallow hard.

"Are you sure you want to tell me about this here?" I asked him and hoped the answer would be no.

"I've got to tell someone." Teo's dark eyes welled with tears. "I've been holding it in all week and now . . ." He sniffed. "I've really made a mess of things. I know you'll understand once I explain, Maxie. We have to go somewhere else. So we can talk."

Go somewhere to talk.

With a man who'd just admitted that he was a murderer.

I was just about to tell him I had to get back to the plaza when Donna came to the front of the shop with a white shopping bag. "You let me know when you're going to wear this gown," she told Teo. "Because wherever you're going to be, I'm going to show up there so I can see you in it. It's gorgeous, and hon, you're going to look gorgeous, too."

His smile was a little watery around the edges when

he looked my way. "Thanks," he told Donna, "but I've changed my mind. I'm not taking the gown."

She flinched like she'd been slapped. "But this was a special order."

"It was. I understand that. You can keep the money I gave you for the down payment." He slid the receipt across the counter to her. "And if you don't sell the dress anytime soon . . ." Teo slipped his arm through mine. "Give me a call if nobody else wants it," he told Donna. "Maybe by that time, I can save up enough money to pay for the gown myself."

And with that, he walked me out of Tatiana's.

I'm not exactly sure what I expected. I mean, murderers are by definition bad people, right? But Teo didn't drag me into some dark back alley and conk me on the head. Instead, he led me to the nearest café and ordered mojitos for both of us.

"You're not going to . . ." It felt so crazy to even say it, I made a face. "You're not going to kill me?"

Good thing he'd just swallowed a mouthful of mojito or he would have spit it across the table. "What on earth are you talking about?"

"I'm talking about you. About your confession. You said . . ." It was hard to get the words out of a mouth that felt as dry as California, so I wet my whistle with mojito. "You said you felt guilty. About what you did to Dom."

"See? That's exactly what I thought would happen. It's exactly why . . ." He passed a hand over his eyes. "I didn't kill Dom," he said. "But I knew that's what the cops would think. I couldn't let anyone find out what really happened. I knew you were asking questions and poking around. And I can tell you're a smart cookie. I'm sorry, but that's why I went to the Showdown the other day and told you to mind your own business."

"You!" I sat up like a shot. "You're the one who grabbed me and—"

"Sorry, sweetie!" His smile was genuine enough, even though his bottom lip trembled. "I know it was a little melodramatic. But I had to do something. I thought if you found out—"

"Not about Dom? You didn't kill Dom?"

"Of course not. But the tip money . . ."

"You did steal the tip money. And that's what you didn't want me to find out about. Because you were afraid I'd turn you in."

"Well, maybe you would have. Maybe you wouldn't have. I really don't know you well enough to know what. But that's not it at all. What I was afraid of is that somebody would find out what Dom did and they'd think I really did kill him."

His words played over inside my head, twirling and whirling in there along with everything I'd learned about the victim and the case. "Dom had change and dollar bills in his pocket when he was killed," I said. "And you were stealing change and dollar bills. You gave Dom some of the money you took?"

"Not hardly." He clicked his tongue. "That Dom . . . well, he was cute enough, wasn't he? And charming, too.

At least that's what I thought from the little bit I talked to him on Monday evening. He was hanging around. Well, you know that. You saw him. And you know, come to think of it, every time I saw him, he was looking your way."

Before I knew Dom was a wife-stealing, partner-hurting creep who lied to Martha and Rosa and stole their recipes, I actually would have been flattered. The way it was, I really didn't care. Besides, cute or not, no way Dom could be as good a kisser as Nick.

But back to the matter at hand . . .

"So Dom was hanging around and . . ."

"And he saw what I did." Teo hung his head. "I thought I was being careful, but still, he saw what I did. He saw me take money out of the tip jar."

"He was going to report you?"

Teo nodded. "Unless I shared some of the tips with him."

Even I never imagined someone being that cold! Not only was Dom a wife-stealing, partner-hurting creep who lied to Martha and Rosa and stole their recipes, but he filched money from a charity, too.

"That explains the money Dom had on him when the police found his body," I said. "And you were worried that if the police made the connection, they'd figure out what you were doing."

"That," Teo said, "and they'd think I had a motive to keep Dom quiet. But I didn't do it!" he added before I could even suggest he did. "I'd never kill someone just to keep them quiet. Not over a few hundred dollars."

"That's what you've been worried about. That's why

you weren't as careful with your clothes and your makeup. That's why you were snappy and standoffish. You were scared."

He nodded. "I'll repay the money. I can now that I don't have . . ." He looked over his shoulder, back toward Tatiana's, his expression wistful. "The minute I saw that gown in a magazine, I wanted it more than I've ever wanted anything in my life. I knew I'd look spectacular in it, and it's so darned pretty. But you've shown me that it's not worth it." He turned back to me. "The guilt has been eating me up. Between that and being afraid the police were going to think I had a good reason to kill Dom, well, I haven't even been able to sleep a wink."

"That's because you're really a pretty good person," I told him. "And you'll pay back the money?"

He patted the pocket where he'd put his wallet. "All of it. As soon as I get back to the plaza. I guess I don't have to sneak the money into the tip jar since Ginger knows what's going on."

"She'll be relieved."

He smiled. "She's got a heart of gold. I'll have a talk with her as soon as I get back. Speaking of that." He checked the time on his phone. "I've got to head home and get changed. I'll see you over there later."

I hung around for a few more minutes, finishing my mojito, glad that Teo hadn't turned out to be the murderer. Thieving ways aside, he seemed like a nice enough guy, and I knew Ginger would be relieved to find out what had really been going on.

I was no closer to finding out who had murdered Dom,

and that was a bummer, but hey, I felt more relaxed and refreshed than I had since earlier in the day when I'd nearly been trampled by that bull. Ready to get to work, I headed back to the plaza.

And stopped on a dime not thirty feet from the café.

Here, the River Walk twisted and turned, and overhead—up on street level—a stone bridge crossed over the San Antonio River from one side to the other. Eleanor Alvarez—she of the willowy body, the flaming hair, and the gorgeous jewelry—was standing on it, and she was talking to a man with bulging muscles and golden hair.

They were so deep in conversation, they never looked over to where I stood, and that was fine by me. From this angle, I could see that Eleanor's hand was on the guy's arm. He flashed her a smile, and even from where I stood, I felt the sizzle.

Nice. Eleanor had a sweetie, and a hunky one, too. After what she told the Miss Consolidated Chili candidates about having her heart broken when her husband died, it was nice to see her happy, and I was smiling when I turned to head back to Alamo Plaza.

I would have gone right on smiling if there wasn't something niggling at my brain.

That sweetie of Eleanor's, there was no way I knew the guy. I mean, I'd certainly remember meeting a guy that good-looking.

But he sure did look mighty familiar.

CHAPTER 16

To tell the truth, I was actually relieved to find out that Teo was the one who'd grabbed me and warned me to stay out of the investigation.

I mean, in the great scheme of things, it pretty much proved he couldn't have killed Dom, right? Nobody who made threats that lame would have had the nerve to twist guitar strings around a guy's neck and pull tight.

This cheered me, because for one thing, Teddi the petty thief was repentant, and for another, what Teo had done back there at Tatiana's—walking away from a gown he wanted more than he wanted his next breath—told me that deep down, he was a good guy. And a good girl, too.

But all was not rosy. Sure, the field of suspects was narrowing, but I still didn't know who done it. Rosa and Martha certainly remained in contention. They both hated Dom for what he did to them, getting jobs at their restaurants and then stealing their recipes, and hey, I'd seen the two of them go at each other. They might be getting up there in years, but I had a feeling either one of them could have ambushed me and dumped me in the pen with that rodeo bull. To survive in the world of restaurants, food service, and hospitality, you have to be strong. Not to mention fearless.

And what about Eleanor and that hunky guy I'd seen her talking to? Honestly, I wouldn't have thought a thing of it (other than to be jealous) if not for the fact that he looked like . . . somebody. Somebody I'd seen? Somebody I knew? Somebody who might be somebody who was mixed up in murder? What with all the wrackin', my brain was getting tired.

Then there was the mysterious John Wesley Montgomery. If he knew the truth was going to come out about how he'd sent Dom to pilfer those recipes so he could condemn them to a can, he had every reason to want to keep Dom quiet—permanently.

It was hotter than blazes that night at Alamo Plaza, but still, a cold chill snaked up my back, and automatically, I glanced over my shoulder, then toward the Consolidated Chili tent. There was no sign of that shiny black limo I'd seen cruising the fairgrounds earlier or of Montgomery, and that was too bad. I needed to talk to the man. I would talk to him, I promised myself. And I'd get to the bottom of what he knew about Dom and why he was hanging around the Showdown and if he was the one who'd tried to kill me earlier in the day.

Just thinking about my close encounter of the bovine kind made another shot of iciness crackle up my spine and across my shoulders. I shrugged it away, or at least I tried, and since it was better to keep busy than to imagine all sorts of strange—and possibly deadly—scenarios that involved me and that black limo and how Montgomery didn't want anyone to know about his underhanded business dealings, I kept busy getting the tent ready. Sylvia would be at the plaza in just another hour with the chili she'd made for the night's event.

Vegetarian chili.

My stomach protested at the very thought.

What was the woman thinking? Carrots, zucchini, bulgur wheat, and corn? My plans that night were to grab dinner in someone else's tent.

And now that I thought about it, it was never too early to start.

Eating or investigating.

With that in mind, I strolled over to Martha and Rosa's tent and was glad to see their slow cookers were already plugged in and steaming away.

"Chili!" I announced as soon as I stepped foot in their tent. "I'm starving."

Rosa was closer to the slow cookers, and she had a bowl ready for me lickety-split. As soon as I sat down, Martha set another bowl of chili at my elbow. Since Rosa's was right in front of me, I dug into her chili first and sighed with delight when the first mouthful set off a barrage of delicious firework sensations on my taste buds.

Like with so many really good chilies, the taste intensified the longer it was on my tongue.

Then it exploded like a Molotov cocktail.

As if I'd been kicked by that rodeo bull, I sat up like a shot. My eyes streamed tears. My cheeks turned so hot, I could only imagine that they were the color of the matching fire engine red aprons Martha and Rosa wore that night. My tongue swelled to two times its normal size—I swear it did—and every last centimeter of it felt as if it had been painted with molten lava.

"Wow!" Understatement, but even I—who love my chili hot—could not think of a word that was anywhere near appropriate to describe the spiciness. Dragon's breath might do it. But only if dragons had learned to split atoms.

I sucked in a long breath in the hopes of cooling my tongue, and when that didn't work, I waved both hands, frantically motioning toward where I saw some packets of crackers on a nearby table.

"What's wrong with you?" Martha asked.

"Crazy girl." As if that was something right up there with a terminal diagnosis, Rosa shook her head. "Poor crazy girl."

I sucked and motioned some more, and Martha got the message. Or maybe she just finally noticed the tears that streaked my cheeks.

It wasn't until I polished off three packages of crackers and one of those short little cartons of milk that Martha said she'd brought along to put in her coffee that I was able to breathe. A few more crackers and I could finally talk. Except all I could say was "Wow."

Rosa screwed up her face. "Gringos! They can't take a little heat."

"Little?" I put a hand to my chest, grateful to feel my heartbeat, because I swear, this chili was hot enough to stop it cold. "I love spicy chili. But that . . ." With one finger, I pointed at the offending bowl. "You'll kill somebody with that!"

Rosa, it seems, was not willing to take my word for it. She grabbed a spoon from a nearby place setting and dipped it into my chili. I guess she found out what I was talking about, because as soon as she swallowed, her ears turned red and her eyes popped open.

"Ay, caramba!" There were a couple packages of crackers that I hadn't eaten, and she grabbed them and wolfed them down. Even then, she was breathing hard when she asked, "What happened to my chili? It tastes like there's too much lumbre pepper. Too, too much. But I added only two peppers." She pointed toward each of the three slow cookers on the left side of the table. "Only two peppers to each pot."

"Two peppers per pot! But those . . ." Martha gasped. "Those are my pots of chili! And I, I added two lumbre peppers per pot. Oh no." She dropped her face into her hands. "This is bad. This is very bad. Rosa, what were you thinking?"

"Me?" I guess that shot of spice put a little extra oomph into Rosa's step. She was up in Martha's face before I knew it, standing on tiptoe so that she could glare right into Martha's eyes. "You told me my pots were the ones on the left."

"I told you your pots were on the right," Martha said from between clenched teeth. "Right, right, right."

"Left."

"Right."

I popped out of my chair and squeezed between them to make sure this didn't come to blows. "It looks like we have some work to do," I announced and, in response to their stunned expressions, added, "You can't serve chili that hot. Not at a fund-raiser. We've got to get it toned down."

"Crushed pineapple." Rosa stepped back and crossed her arms over her chest. "It cuts the heat and blends nicely with the chili. No one will ever know it's there."

"Cider vinegar." Martha settled her weight back against one foot. "The acidity counteracts the heat."

"Oh fine. Great." Disgusted, Rosa threw her hands in the air. "It's not your chili. You should just tell me how to fix it. You're the one who ruined it in the first place."

"I didn't ruin it," Martha growled. "I'm not the one who added the extra lumbre. And I told you, I told you as soon as you got here, your chili is in the pots on the right."

"Left."

"Right."

"Ladies!" I put out both hands. Yeah, like that would stop them if they decided to plow right through me and go at each other. "We don't have time for this. And we don't have time to go grocery shopping." I glanced around the tent and saw what I was looking for. "Follow me," I told them.

They did, and I didn't even need to turn around to see it. I could hear the stomp of their footsteps as they trailed over to the serving table.

"This is Martha's chili." I spooned up some of the chili from the pots on the right, and believe me, I took a careful taste. It had some zing—and a nice kick from the beer she used in the stock—but it wasn't anywhere near as nuclear as Rosa's. "Okay, good." I pointed. "That empty pot," I told Martha, who went and got it for me. "And now, we combine."

Really, it was like I asked them to strip to their skivvies and pole dance in front of the Alamo.

Martha's mouth dropped and stayed open.

Rosa's jaw went up and down like a plunger. "You want to mix?" she stuttered. "My chili and . . ." Her eyes wide, she looked at Martha. "My chili with hers?"

"My chili mixed with . . ." I was pretty sure Martha was going to have a heart attack, so when she dropped into the nearest chair, I didn't stop her. Instead, I grabbed the empty pot from her, and since neither woman was in any shape to move, I started ladling. I filled the pot halfway with Martha's chili, then filled it the rest of the way with Rosa's and mixed, and when I was done, I tasted. The chili still had a kick, but not a fatal one.

"Done." I brushed my hands together. "You two can take care of mixing the rest of it. There will be no chili-induced deaths here tonight."

"And no authentic chili," Martha grumbled. "Not like my grandmother's."

"Not like *my* grandmother's," Rosa muttered. "She's turning over in her grave. I know this for a fact. She's thinking of her chili and her brave and noble ancestors and she's—"

"Please!" Martha threw back her head and groaned. "It's my ancestors who are offended. And who can blame them? Combining our chilies, it's an offense to nature. Like . . . like . . ."

"Like putting your family recipes in a can?"

Just as I hoped, this reminder of their common outrage settled both of them down. Martha let out a long, slow breath. Rosa took a seat next to her.

Now that they weren't going at each other and I had their attention, I looked from one woman to the other. "Any word from Montgomery?" I asked. "About Dom and your recipes?"

Martha sniffed.

Rosa snorted. "Not a peep. That no-good gringo . . ."

"Now, Rosa!" Martha wagged a finger at her. "We had that talk, remember, and you—"

"Said that not all gringos are bad. Yes, yes, I remember. But Montgomery is. Him and his factory and his cans and his chili. Him and his underhanded employees."

"Agreed," I said. "So what do you think? Is Montgomery underhanded, too? Underhanded enough to kill?"

I guess neither of them had thought of this before, because they both gasped, and while they were caught off guard, I closed in for the kill (bad pun, but it pretty much says it all).

"Or did you two do that?" I asked them.

Rosa fussed with her apron. "I told you. I tried to scare that Dom. I chased him with the knife. He deserved it."

"He did." Martha nodded. "But that doesn't mean Rosa killed him."

"But you might have," I suggested to Martha.

"She didn't," Rosa assured me. "She didn't, and I didn't."

I let a bit of silence settle between us. The better to let the ladies have some time to think about what they were telling me before I finally asked, "How do I know you're telling me the truth?"

It was Martha's turn to fuss. With her apron. With the rings she twisted around her finger. She stared at the ground. "The police know we're telling the truth. If they believe us, you should, too."

"I'd love to. But why should I? You admit that you were out to scare Dom. Rosa, you chased him with that knife toward the end of the evening. Right before he came over to my tent looking for Nick. And after that, how do I know what you two did? You might have waited until the fundraiser was over. You might have wanted to make sure there was no one around. Dom wasn't feeling good thanks to that spiked chili Tiffany gave him. He was weak. He was helpless. Then you two—"

"No." Rosa shook her head.

"Absolutely not." Martha mirrored the gesture.

"You weren't here? You weren't hanging around?" I asked them.

Martha hung her head.

Rosa turned ashen.

"Nobody is supposed to know," Rosa mumbled.

"Know what?"

"We don't want word to get out," Martha said.

"About what?"

The two ladies exchanged looks. Both of them nodded.

"We could have had a disaster here tonight," Martha said. "If you hadn't tried our chili . . ."

"And thought to mix our two chilies together . . ." Rosa added.

"It could have been embarrassing. And bad for business." She patted Rosa's arm. "Both our businesses. The least we owe you in return is the truth."

I pulled up a chair and sat down. "So . . ." I looked first at Martha, then at Rosa. "Somebody tell me what happened."

Martha sighed. "We were leaving the plaza on Monday night and—"

"And I was minding my own business," Rosa said.

Martha snorted. "You started it."

"Did not," Rosa insisted.

I waved them into silence before they could get into it again. "So you were already leaving the plaza on Monday night when . . . ?"

"She started it," Rosa said.

"Did not." Martha stuck out her bottom lip.

And I just about screamed. "What happened?"

The women exchanged looks and Martha gave Rosa a nod.

"We were on our way to our cars," Rosa said, "and one thing led to another and—"

"And we had it out with each other," Martha finished the sentence.

This did not seem unusual to me. From what I'd seen of the women earlier on Monday night and again here this evening, having it out with each other was second nature. Unless—

"It got physical?"

They both nodded. "And we . . ." Martha's cheeks shot through with color. "We got arrested."

"Both of you?" The question squeaked out of me. While Martha nodded in response to it, Rosa dug under the serving table for her purse.

"Here." She shoved a photograph at me. It was a police mug shot that showed Rosa with her hair mussed and her lipstick smeared.

"I've got one, too," Martha said. "The police officer, the one who took us in, he eats at both our restaurants. He said we should keep those pictures around and look at them once in a while. You know, just to remind ourselves that if we don't change our ways, we could end up in serious trouble."

"And you didn't want anyone to know!" It made perfect sense, so I didn't need them to confirm or deny.

"Bad for business," Rosa said, anyway. "And those nice police officers, they did us a favor. They lost the paperwork. They said, you know, that they didn't want to see us go through the public humiliation of, you know, a trial and the publicity and how it might hurt our restaurants."

"Which explains why you two were so chummy the next day." I nodded. "You did learn your lesson."

"We're trying," Rosa said. "Now if this one . . ." She tipped her head toward Martha. "If she'd learn to tell me which slow cookers are really my slow cookers—"

"And if this one . . ." Martha motioned toward Rosa. "If she'd keep her peppers out of my chili . . ."

It was as much of a truce as I could ever expect.

I left the two of them to sort it out.

CHAPTER 17

What with being shocked with a stun gun and having my head stuffed in a pillowcase, nearly being trampled by a bull, and almost going up in flames thanks to Rosa's incendiary chili, it was a long, long Friday, and by the time it was over, all I wanted to do was drag back to the RV, put up my feet, and have a little well-earned R&R.

Lucky for me, Sylvia went to bed as soon as we got back from the fund-raiser. That left me alone, and that meant I could indulge in one harmless pleasure that I knew she'd object to and another that I was pretty sure she'd put up a fuss about.

Her loss.

Because I'll say this much, that DVD that we found in Dom's apartment, the one I just happened to . . . er . . .

forget to leave behind when we raced out of there, that DVD was just the kind of eye candy a girl deserves at the end of a long, trying, and nearly deadly day.

Male models. A dozen or so different ones in the first thirty minutes of the DVD that I had a chance to watch. All of them gorgeous. All of them strutting their stuff in front of the camera and showing off abs and pecs and glutes—and other things.

Oh yeah, Sylvia would have gotten all prudish about it. And then probably watched it sometime when I wasn't around. She also would have lectured me about fats and carbs and blah, blah, blah, if she knew my dinner consisted of Twinkies and a beer.

Hey, Twinkies have plenty of redeeming nutritional value, not the least of which is sugar and empty calories, beer is perfectly appropriate at the end of a stressful day, and the naked guys . . .

I had just finished sighing as I checked out the six-pack on the dark-haired hunk currently on the TV screen when there was a tap on the door. I paused the video, scooped up the Twinkie wrappers I'd dropped around the chair where I was sitting, and went to answer.

"Nick!" When I stepped back to let him climb the three steps up into the RV, I dropped the Twinkie wrappers behind the coffeemaker on the built-into-the-wall counter in what passed for our kitchen. I might not care what Sylvia thought of my food choices, but I was too tired to explain my eating habits to Nick. "What's up?"

"I thought I'd stop by and see how you were doing." Nick is a tall guy with wide shoulders, and believe me, our RV is nowhere near as large or as elegant as the one Consolidated Chili was using to accommodate the beauty queens. With him standing next to the table and the two benches that flanked it, the RV seemed smaller than ever, like there wasn't room for both of us, and not nearly enough air.

That, at least, might explain why I felt a little lightheaded.

"I'm fine," I assured him. "I was just—"

He glanced at the TV screen and groaned. "You stole the DVD from Dom's apartment?"

The beer gave me courage. The sugar gave me enough energy to sound convincing when I protested. "What are you talking about? It's not the same DVD. It's—"

"The same DVD." Nick went over to the TV and tapped the screen. "Same background, see?" He poked a finger behind that hunky model toward a fairly ordinary (so how did he recognize it in the first place?) background of a bed covered with a white quilt and the powder blue chair beside it. "Same walls. Same—"

"Not the same guy. We didn't see this one when we watched the DVD at Dom's. See?" I pointed, too. Only not at the background, the white coverlet, or the blue chair. "Believe me, I would recognize this guy if I saw him before. In fact—"

The words froze on my lips. The blood stopped pumping through my veins. I stood paralyzed, staring at the screen.

"Maxie?" Nick waved a hand in front of my face. "Don't move. I'll call EMS. This is some kind of delayed shock. You're just reacting to what happened to you this afternoon. You'll be fine."

"I'm fine now." I batted his hand away and grabbed the remote, stopped the DVD, and started it again from the beginning. "In fact, I'm finer than fine, and in a moment, you're going to see why."

He stepped back and watched just like I did.

The first guy who came on screen was dark-haired and gorgeous. Oh yeah, I remembered him, all right: strong shoulders, narrow waist, an arrow of fine, dark hair that dusted his chest and went all the way down to—

"Why are we watching this?" Nick asked.

I shushed him and waited for the same funny flash we'd seen on the video back at Dom's. Just as I remembered, the picture flashed off, then came on again, and when it did, there was a slim, light-haired guy on the screen.

I slapped my forehead. "I should have seen it before," I wailed. "I would have seen it if I was watching closely and didn't get up to get another Twinkie the first time he was on."

"You're seeing it now."

"Not that *it*." I rolled my eyes because it was a pretty lame joke, and I pointed away from the *it* Nick was talking about and at the guy's face. "That *it*. This is the guy I saw Eleanor Alvarez talking to this afternoon."

"No way."

"Way."

Nick cocked his head. "A classy lady like Eleanor and him?"

"Well, he had clothes on down by the River Walk, so he looked pretty classy, too. His hair was shorter, too."

"And he was here? In San Antonio?"

"Obviously." I chewed on my lower lip and studied the

guy's face. "Definitely him. And you know what this means, don't you, Nick?"

"That Eleanor likes good-looking guys."

He was trying to get my goat, and I was so not in the mood. Sugar careening through my bloodstream, I whirled away from the TV screen. "That there's some connection between Eleanor and Dom."

"Really?" Nick scratched a finger behind his ear. "I'm pretty sure the DVD doesn't prove that."

"Don't you see? Dom had a video and this guy was on it. And Eleanor was talking to this guy."

"All right." He sat down on the green vinyl bench, and I slid into the one opposite. Lucky me, I was facing the TV screen. "But that doesn't mean Eleanor and Dom knew each other."

"But it could."

"It could also mean that this guy was visiting San Antonio and he was lost and he stopped Eleanor to ask for directions. It could mean that once upon a time this guy was involved in some sort of weird something that to me looks like a porn audition and that now, he's an upright citizen and he's involved in one of the charities that Eleanor works for. It could mean—"

"I get your point." Which didn't mean I had to like it. "You have to admit, it's a mighty big coincidence."

"It is. But you're jumping to conclusions again."

"Me?" As long as I was being accused of jumping, I jumped up and got myself another beer and I got one for Nick, too, and opened them both with the Consolidated Chili can opener Sylvia had left on the counter. Yes, it offended me no end, but desperate times, desperate measures and all that. "When have I ever jumped to conclusions?"

Nick took a sip of beer. And then another one. He set the bottle down on the table. He picked it up again. "When you heard I put Dom in the hospital, you assumed I was the one who killed him."

"I did. But that was only natural, right? I mean, really, when you hear that Guy Number One steals Guy Number Two's wife, and that Guy Number Two is so mad about it, he beats Guy Number One senseless . . . that's not jumping to conclusions. That's being logical. You know, like Sherlock Holmes or one of those detectives on TV."

"It might have been perfectly logical. And you might have been thinking like Sherlock Holmes or some other detective. Except I have a feeling those fictional detectives, they usually get their facts straight."

I can be excused for nearly choking on my beer. I slammed the bottle on the table. "Those aren't the facts? You didn't beat up Dom?"

"I did."

"And Dom and Nichole weren't sneaking around behind your back?"

"They were."

"Then jeepers creepers, tell me what facts I got wrong!"

"Maxie?" A bleary-eyed Sylvia dragged out of the bedroom holding her pink robe closed with one hand. "What's all the noise about? What's going on out here?" She blinked the sleep out of her eyes, realized Nick was there, and said, "Oh, it's you. Good night," and disappeared back into her bedroom.

I waited until her door closed before I eyed Nick across the table. "So?"

He made to stand up. "We really don't need to talk about this."

"We do." I put a hand on his arm to keep him from bolting. "For one thing, I just gave you a beer and you owe me for that. For another . . ." I don't do pitiful well, but I gave it my best shot. I hung my head and looked at him through the fringe of my dark bangs. "I did almost die today. That means someone doesn't want me to solve this case. And that someone . . . that awful, horrible, terrible someone might try again. You know, to shut me up." Since this was true and mighty disturbing, I didn't stop to think about it. "You wouldn't want me to die without knowing the whole story, would you? That would be—"

"Pathetic." He finished off his beer and got up, but he didn't leave. He got another beer and brought me one, too. "Not pathetic that you would never know, pathetic that you think you can get me to talk with that sorry act. You're not the helpless type."

I grinned. "Glad you noticed. I'm not the type who forgets, either. And you said—"

"That you didn't have all the facts. Yes, I know. It's just that . . ." He sat back down in the seat across from mine. "You're not helpless, and I'm not always comfortable getting too personal."

"Yeah, I've noticed."

He scraped a hand across his chin. "The thing is, I didn't beat up Dom when I found out what he and Nichole were up to."

This did not jibe with reality as I knew it. I crinkled my nose. "Sure you did. You told me—"

"That Dom and I were partners. That he and Nichole were fooling around. That I put him in the hospital. But that wasn't right away, not right when I found out what the two of them were up to. Actually, the first thing I did was move out of our apartment, then I requested a new partner. And then a couple years later . . ."

"You beat Dom up a couple years later? That's just weird. I mean, if you were still mad at him after all that time, that does make you look like a murder suspect! If you can still be mad at a guy for stealing your wife a couple years after it happened—"

"I didn't beat him up because of him cheating with Nichole. I was over it. Long over it. But see, I found out that Dom . . ." He took a sip of beer, and that was supposed to distract me, but don't think I didn't notice that his expression darkened like a thundercloud.

"He hit her," Nick said.

It took me a couple seconds to process and a couple more to get the words past the ball of outrage that blocked my throat. "He . . . Dom . . . he hit Nichole?"

Nick nodded. "When I found out . . . well, I talked to her about it and she gave the usual excuses: it was an accident, he didn't mean it, he swore it would never happen again. And I guess she really believed all that, because like I told you, she and Dom, they were talking about getting back together again. But I'll tell you what, the next time I bumped into Dom, I couldn't help myself. Nichole got a couple bruises and a black eye thanks to him. Dom ended up with a broken nose, a few stitches, and a couple broken ribs. That was thanks to me."

"And you lost your job because of it."

Nick's shrug wasn't casual enough to fool me. "A man should never lay a hand on a woman."

"Even a woman who ripped out your heart."

"Even a woman who ripped out my heart."

"That's—"

"Don't say it's crazy. Don't tell me I was wrong. That's just what I think. It's just what I feel. And I'm not going to let a creep like Dom Laurentius get away with something like that. I don't care if it was Nichole or some other woman. It's cruel and it's cowardly."

"And I wasn't going to say you were wrong." To prove it, I got up and scooted over to Nick's side of the table, and he was forced to slide over to make room for me. By the time his back was against the wall, he couldn't retreat any farther, and I closed in.

I looked into his eyes, and yeah, that put my lips dangerously close to his. But then, that was the whole point.

"I was going to tell you that you're pretty special," I said, and hey, why bother trying to explain what's impossible to put into words? Rather than waste my time, I kissed him.

Believe me, I was glad when Saturday finally rolled around. What with working the Showdown and the Chili Queens fund-raisers, nearly getting killed, and investigating a murder, I was dead on my feet. I would be glad when Sunday—and the Miss Consolidated Chili pageant—was over and we would head to New Orleans for the next Showdown. At least there, I would no longer have to worry about spending my evenings on Alamo Plaza and my days fearing for my life. Plus thanks to my bet with Sylvia, I'd have Saturday off, too.

But Sunday wasn't over. In fact, it hadn't even started, and for now, Alamo Plaza was the place to be. Saturday's was the last of the Chili Queens fund-raisers, and this one promised to be a doozy. Eleanor and her society pals were raising money to help support a city school of the arts, and all things artsy were in the air. The students who helped act as hosts and hostesses for the night's event had been encouraged to show off their style and their spunk, and when I arrived at the plaza, I was greeted by two of them dressed as pink flamingos—complete with feathers. Another couple had come as giant chilies that wore sombreros and ponchos. Cute, but not as cute as the Chili Chick.

In fact the whole plaza took on a festive atmosphere the likes of which it hadn't had all week. If I had the energy I would have joined in the line dance going on outside Teddi and Ginger's tent.

Instead, I slipped over to the Women's League tent and headed straight for Eleanor, who was grooving to the line-dance beat while she rolled plastic silverware in paper napkins.

"Maxie!" She smiled when she saw me. "What can I do for you?"

"Not much." I was wearing that cheap black wig, and I took a moment to toss one of the braids over my shoulders. "Unless you want to explain how you knew Dom."

She needed a moment to think about it. "Dom? Oh, the man who was killed here the other night. I think I told you, I talked to him on Monday. But other than that, I didn't know him."

"Except that you and Dom have the same taste in porn."

This time, she needed more than just a moment to compose herself. She looked gorgeous that evening in a slim black dress with short sleeves that were dusted with beading. Her flaming hair was pulled back and tucked into a chignon at her neck, and her makeup was flawless. Still, I couldn't help but notice that she went ashen.

"What on earth are you talking about?" She pressed a hand to her heart, and again, I saw that blue sapphire ring she wore on her left hand. It winked at me in the glow of the twinkling overhead lights. "I can assure you that I don't know anything about . . ." She looked left and right and lowered her voice. "Porn."

"The guy," I said. "The one you were with at the River Walk yesterday. I've seen a video. And he's on it."

"And it's . . ." Again, that furtive look. "Porn?" Eleanor fanned her face. "Oh my. Are you sure?"

"I could be if I saw him naked. For now, I'll have to trust my memory of faces. It was him all right; honey hair, chiseled features, big—"

"Oh my!" Eleanor dropped into the nearest chair. "Does anyone else know?" she asked.

I figured Nick did not fall into the *anyone else* category since he didn't buy into the Eleanor/Dom connection. "Just me. And it's not like it's a big deal or anything. Hey, you're a young woman. And from what I hear, you had an old husband. I get it. Really, I do. I enjoyed watching the video, too."

She shook her head as if to clear it. "Video? What are you talking about? And as for my husband . . ." Eleanor sat up, lifted her chin, and inched back her shoulders. "Jacob Alvarez might have been a bit older than me, but he was man enough, I assure you. I don't need to indulge in prurient interests."

"Even though ol' Jacob is dead and gone?"

"And don't you think that I don't miss him every single day!" She sniffled. In a ladylike sort of way. "But you're telling me that . . . James?" Again, she looked around just to make sure no one was listening. "James Faragut, he's the man you saw me with. He's not a friend, if that's what you're thinking. We have a business relationship."

She didn't give me a chance to dispute it.

"Strictly business," Eleanor said, and whispered, "James is a model and an actor. He was hired to emcee the Miss Consolidated Chili pageant tomorrow. If word gets out that he's been in porn videos . . ." She got so pale, I thought she was going to pass out, but with a shake of her shoulders, she composed herself. "My goodness, I'd do what I could to get him fired if there was time to find another emcee. I hope no one recognizes him."

"You're probably safe if he leaves his clothes on."

She did not see the humor in this. In fact, she gave me a squinty-eyed look. "You've actually seen one of these videos? With James in it?"

"Sort of. I've got what I think is a DVD of an audition."

"So maybe he never got a part in a movie!" Eleanor's face was transformed by an angelic smile. "Maybe there's no way anyone is going to recognize him, because maybe he never appeared in a movie. Any kind of movie." As if the weight of the world had been lifted from her shoulders, she rose from her chair. "That's it. That's what I'm going to believe. I'm not going to let baseless worries get me all upset. It might be nothing, right? And there's no use worrying about nothing."

"Absolutely. But you might want to talk to him about it. And while you're at it, ask him how he knew Dominic Laurentius."

"Did he?" Eleanor's bowed lips opened into a perfect O of astonishment. "You don't suppose he's the murderer, do you? And we have to appear at the pageant with him tomorrow? I know, I know," she said, and she patted my arm and turned away. "I shouldn't worry, and I shouldn't jump the gun, and I'm not going to say anything that points any fingers at anyone, but I've got to let the girls in the pageant know that they need to be very careful tomorrow."

I watched her hurry away, and I actually might have gone after her if something didn't catch my eye. Sleek, shiny, black. John Wesley Montgomery's limo slipped by in the shadows along the far end of the plaza and stopped.

I waited for the driver to zip around to the back door and open it, and when he didn't and that back door didn't open, I made my move, zigzagging through the crowd and coming at the limo from behind. By the time I got there, the driver was out of the car, leaning back against the closed front door, puffing on a cigarette.

"Why have you been following me?" I demanded.

The man was maybe fifty, short and hefty, and he eyed me and then glanced around. I liked to think that I intimidated him and he was checking to see how far away help might be. Tell that to the rumba beat that started up in my chest, the one that told me that he was looking around to make sure that when he came at me there wouldn't be any witnesses.

It was too late to think about that. In fact, it was too late for anything but a little bravado and a whole lot of sass. In the hopes of looking a little less goofy, I pulled off my wig.

"Me." I pointed a finger at myself. "Do you recognize me now? You've been at the Showdown and you've been around here and you almost ran me over on Monday night. Why have you been following me?"

"Sorry, ma'am. You must have me mixed up with someone else."

"I don't have your license plate mixed up. Tri-C. How many big black limos have that license plate?"

"You'll have to excuse me, ma'am." He wasn't wearing a hat, but he touched two fingers to the curl of dark hair that fell over his forehead. "I need to get back to work."

"Following me."

His smile was so gosh-darned honest, I nearly believed it was real. "I don't even know who you are. Why would I follow you?"

"I have a feeling you don't do anything your boss doesn't tell you to do. Is he in there now?" Since the windows of the limo were tinted, it didn't do me any good to try and look inside, but I pressed my nose to the back window, anyway. The only thing I saw was my own reflection.

"What are you up to, John Wesley Montgomery?" I knocked on the window. "What are you trying to hide?"

"You'll have to move away from the car, ma'am." The driver moved toward me.

I stepped back. "Tell him I know," I said. "Tell your boss I know he had something to do with Dom Laurentius's murder. There was a trail of your cheap Consolidated Chili giveaways near the body. Tell him that for me. Tell him I'm onto him."

Without another word, the driver slipped into the car and the engine purred to life.

"Tell him I'm onto him!" I yelled when he inched the limo out of its parking space.

If I wasn't careful, he'd run right over my feet, and I jumped back and looked down to make sure I was well away from the back tires. I guess I was so busy not getting smooshed, I wasn't paying attention to anything else.

Which is why I didn't notice the back door pop open until it was right next to me.

And the arm that reached out and snaked around my waist.

Or anything but the dim lighting and dark shadows inside the limo when I was dragged inside and the door closed behind me.

And by that time, it was too late.

CHAPTER 18

I kicked and I screamed and I pounded on that arm wound tight around my waist, and when that didn't work, I bucked back in an attempt to butt my head against the face of the man who had a hold of me.

"Hold on there!" the man cried out. At least that's what I thought he said. What with all the noise I was making squirming and yelling and fussing and fighting, I could hardly hear. And even if I could, there was no way in hell I was going to listen, anyway.

I thrashed like a hooked fish, and I was all set to sink my teeth into my attacker's arm when he tried again to simmer me down.

"Hold on! Maxie! Maxie, it's me!"

The words penetrated through the layer of terror that

wrapped around me like a clammy hand. The voice was familiar, and finally listening—and hearing—I froze. Too afraid to turn around and see that I was wrong, too afraid not to turn around and never know, I pushed away from my attacker, spun on the buttery leather seat, and sucked in a breath.

"Jack!" I stared across the foot of space that separated me from my dad, Texas Jack Pierce, and questioned my eyesight and my sanity. But then, the interior lighting of the limo was dim and my eyes were suddenly hot with tears. I leaned closer for a better look. "Jack?"

"Yup, it's me, darlin'!" He opened his arms to me and we came at each other and he crushed me in a hug. "Sorry to cause you conniptions, but I didn't know what else to do. I couldn't have you worryin'. I had to talk to you."

I pushed myself away from him. Jack was a big man: big shoulders, big voice, big ideas. The top of his head brushed the roof, and there was a white ten-gallon hat—that same ten-gallon hat I'd seen on John Wesley Montgomery, the president of Consolidated Chili—on the seat next to him. I gulped in a breath to steady myself, but let's face it, there was no way that was going to work. My dad had vanished after a Showdown in Abilene months before, and since then, I'd been searching for any clue that would point to where he'd gone and what had happened to him.

And now, this.

And the *this* I'm talking about didn't make even a little bit of sense.

"You're not John Wesley Montgomery!" I said.

Jack laughed, and just like that, all the fear and anger

that had built inside me melted. Jack's laugh, his boisterous nature, and his never-ending supply of optimism had gotten me over every bad thing life had ever thrown at me. Every one but the one that hurt the most—the one where I had spent months not knowing what had happened to him and worrying every minute of every single day.

I smiled like a fool.

That is, right before I burst into tears.

"Oh, sweetie, I'm sorry." He pulled me into another hug. "I think maybe you're a little mad at me."

"A little?" I soaked his dark suit coat with tears. "I thought . . . I thought . . ." There was no way I could admit the truth, not if I wasn't looking into his eyes, so I pushed away and said the words I'd refused to say—even to myself—since the day I got the call that he was missing. "I thought you were dead!"

"I know. I'm sorry." He patted my hand. "There was nothing else I could do. I shouldn't even be talking to you now, but—"

Remember what I said about how all my anger melted away? Well, it had. At least for a couple minutes. That is, until it reared its head and washed over me like a tsunami.

"What do you mean you shouldn't be talking to me?" I demanded. "What do you mean by disappearing and letting me worry and having me think the worst? What were you thinking? Or maybe you weren't thinking. Maybe you were so busy with some woman that—"

His baritone laugh cut me short. "Not a lady. Not this time. This time, it was all about chili."

Chili.

Consolidated Chili.

John Wesley Montgomery and Consolidated Chili.

I'd like to say that the pieces fell into place, but the way they swirled and whirled through my head, nothing made sense. "You're . . . you're using the name John Wesley Montgomery? And you're the president of Consolidated Chili?"

He chuckled. "Ain't that a kick in the head! I'm walkin' in the tall cotton. Got me a limo and a driver and fancy office and a seven-figure salary!"

My throat closed over the outrage that boiled up inside of me. "Consolidated Chili?" I looked at him hard and knew that the Jack Pierce I had known and adored all my life would read my mind and know exactly what I was getting at. For the first time, he didn't, and I gasped. It was like I was looking at a familiar face but didn't know the person behind it. "You . . . you put chili in a can!"

"Well, not me personally, sweetheart. I got a few thousand people who work for me who take care of the details."

"But . . ." Again, my eyes filled with tears, and this time, relief and happiness had nothing to do with the waterworks. "But it's canned chili!" I wailed.

"You see, that's just the problem." Jack slapped a hand against the empty seat next to him. "I knew you'd be fit to be tied. That's exactly why I dragged my feet telling you the truth. I knew the way you love chili, you'd go up like a bottle rocket. But then, that's always how you deal with things, ain't it?" His chuckle was deep and long; he didn't hold any of this against me. As a matter of fact, I knew it was just another reason he loved me.

"I admit," he said, "that's why I was as afraid as a grass-hopper to talk to you. I knew you'd get all swole up, and I didn't want to see you mad. I tried to make myself fess up a couple times. You probably saw the limo over at the Show-down. But dang it, Maxie, I just couldn't get up the nerve. I guess I just didn't want to see the disappointment in your eyes. I knew it wouldn't be that way with Sylvia, and I was right. Sylvia, she understood."

Those last three little words turned my world upside down. My stomach clenched and froze. I couldn't catch my breath. "S-S-Sylvia knew? She knows? She knows you're all right? She . . . she knows you're here? You . . . you talked to Sylvia? First?"

Jack has a heart as big as all of Texas, but that doesn't mean he's a sucker. Or naive. He lowered his chin, puffed out his cheeks, and gave me the look I'd seen a thousand times before, mostly when Sylvia and I were kids and going at each other as only half sisters can. Part of what sparkled in his dark eyes was understanding. He was her dad, after all. He knew how annoying Sylvia could be. But don't think I had Jack wrapped around my little finger. He adored me and I knew it, but sometimes, he just wouldn't take any nonsense. Even from me. Sure, he was a pushover when it came to his two daughters, but he was a pushover who wouldn't tolerate stupidity.

"It was only just tonight I talked to Sylvia," Jack said. "Just a little while ago. I had to talk to her first. She's the oldest."

I was offended to the bone and pulled my hand away from Jack's and wrapped my arms around myself. "The only reason Sylvia's traveling with the Showdown is so that she can use your recipes and publish a cookbook."

He didn't look especially hurt by the news. Or surprised. "I figured as much. It's kind of nice, really, that she thinks so much of my cookin'."

"Your cooking?" I practically choked on the words. "Sylvia doesn't think about anybody but Sylvia. She didn't even care when I got her off a murder rap!"

"Back in Taos!" Jack slapped his knee. "You showed some spunk there. That's for sure. I always knew you were the smart one."

I should have basked in the glow of the compliment. I would have, back in the day. Right about then, I was so busy sitting there with my jaw flapping, I didn't have time to feel anything but outrage. "You knew? All along? You knew what was going on and you didn't—"

"I couldn't. As much as I wanted to. But I did keep tabs on you two. You bet I did. Where do you think that bail money came from when they had Sylvia in jail?"

I remembered the night I'd found five thousand dollars in the RV, money I used to spring Sylvia from the clink. "It was Gert Wilson, wasn't it? She's the one who's been helping you out all along. She told me—"

"She told you exactly what I told her she could tell you. Nothing more, nothing less. Don't blame her. She's a good woman."

I had spent a lifetime hearing Jack talk about his women. In his book, they were all dolls and babes and honeys. They were good for a laugh and he romanced each and every one of them like no other guy could. Once in a while one of them—like Bernadette Kromski, who'd I'd run into on our recent trip to Las Vegas—got a little closer than the rest and threatened Jack's free-and-easy lifestyle and the individualism he valued so much. In all that time, with all those women, I don't think I'd ever heard his voice warm the way it did when he mentioned Gert.

"You and Gert—"

"Too soon to say," he told me, and this, too, was weird, because with Jack, too soon was never soon enough. "We'll see what happens down the road. For now—"

"For now, you've got plenty of explaining to do. Why are you using the phony name?"

"Well, I couldn't risk hurting the business at the Palace, could I? And if Jack Pierce suddenly started running the largest canned chili manufacturer on the planet—"

"I can't believe it." My stomach clenched and I pressed a hand to it. "I can't believe you'd do such a thing. Canned chili is against everything you ever taught me. It's wrong!"

"It is. It's also mighty profitable."

This did not sound like the Jack I knew, either. Jack cared about quality, not net income. He cared about carrying on hundreds of years of chili tradition and creating a spark of interest in chili and peppers and spices everywhere he went. It had worked with me; I'd bought into the lifestyle and the love of chili, body and soul. So what was he telling me? And what did it all mean?

It didn't make any sense. None of it. I needed more time to process, and more information.

"What does all this have to do with you disappearing,

anyway?" I asked him. "Why are you suddenly John Wesley Montgomery?"

"Lawyers." Jack's mouth twisted. "Non-compete clauses and secrecy clauses and enough legal hoo-ha to fill a convoy of semis. I shouldn't even be talking to you now. Revealing who I really am violates my contract with Consolidated. But there's no way I could have you and Sylvia here in San Antonio and not get in touch. I knew I couldn't get too close. I knew I shouldn't talk to you. That's why I had Dom following you."

"You? You told Dom Laurentius to—"

"Keep an eye on you. Sure. Shoot, he was on the payroll. Figured I might as well make him earn his salary. I wondered how you two were getting along, and I'll tell you what, from what I've seen myself and what Dom told me, it's worked out right as rain. You and Sylvia make a pretty good team. I knew you girls could do it. I knew you could put aside your differences and—"

"Don't get carried away," I told him. "You're not the one who's been working with Sylvia!"

Jack's grin lit up the interior of the limo. "She's got a good head for business. She keeps the books shipshape, doesn't she? And there's nobody better when it comes to orderin' and working with suppliers."

He was right, and it stung more than I wanted to admit. "And me?" I asked him.

"You? Oh, Maxie, don't you get it? All that stuff about price points and economics and the best return on the dollar . . . sure, it's all important. Without paying attention to all that, a business would sink like the *Titanic*. But you know it and I know it, the Palace is about more than that. It's about the chili. It always has been. And you . . ." He beamed me a smile the likes of which I hadn't seen since I graduated from high school and he admitted he was extra proud because he had spent the first seventeen years of my life convinced I'd end up in jail before I ever had a diploma in my hot little hands.

"You've got the soul of the Chili Chick! All those years ago when I first thought of the Chick, I never imagined there would be one woman who would embody her to perfection. But you do, Maxie, honey. You do. And I couldn't be any prouder."

It was almost enough to make me forget that he had talked to Sylvia before he talked to me.

Almost.

"I still don't get it," I admitted. "You and Consolidated Chili? It doesn't make any sense."

"It doesn't. It wouldn't. Except that when they waved that big, fat salary under my nose . . . well, I'll tell you what, darlin', after years on the road with the Showdown, the thought of ridin' high and settlin' down in this kind of comfort was too good to pass up."

I swallowed the sour taste that rose in my throat. "You've gone over to the dark side?"

"Thought you'd see it that way." He gave my knee a pat. "Sylvia, she looked at it from a financial point of view. She saw the benefits. But not my Maxie. You look at things with your heart."

"Not possible," I insisted. "Ask anybody. I don't have a heart."

He wagged a finger at me. "You've got the heart of a Pierce and don't you let anybody tell you that's not true. You've got a fierce determination, too, and you've got all the imagination and the cleverness and the resourcefulness you need. Some of that stuff came from your mother, by the way. I won't take credit for it all."

He settled back, and for a couple minutes, I listened to the smooth purr of the limo engine and tried to make sense of everything that just happened.

"So back in Abilene, Consolidated Chili offered you the job and—"

"They've been after me for years," he said. "They'd come sniffing around now and again, and every time, I told them to get lost. But you know, they really did make me an offer I couldn't refuse."

"But it's wrong! Chili in a can is—"

"Against the very laws of nature. Oh yes, I do know that. But I got to thinkin', you know, about folks who aren't lucky enough to ever come to a Showdown and try all the different chilies and all the different peppers and the spices and the sauces. All those folks who never have a chance to eat really good chili. And I decided that if we could give them that experience right there in their own homes . . . well, then chili in a can wouldn't be such a bad thing, would it? Not if we put really good chili in a can."

It was a terrific plan.

But . . .

"That really good chili you want to can, you could have helped the company develop the recipes. You're the best chili cook in the whole world!"

"Thank you, darlin'." He smiled, but let's face it, the compliment didn't come as much of a surprise. Jack *was* the world's best chili cook and he knew it. "That's exactly what I've been doing. I've had to tone down some of my favorites. That one with the scorpion pepper, that little bowl of flaming madness I came up with when we were visitin' Omaha, you remember that one?"

I did, and my mouth watered at the very thought.

"That didn't work." Jack grinned. "Every time we put a label on a can, the heat of the chili would cause it to peel right off!"

I knew he was teasing, but I couldn't smile back. Not until I knew the whole story. "So if you're developing your own chilies, why did you have to resort to stealing Martha and Rosa's recipes?"

"You know about that, huh?" Jack cleared his throat. "I should have known a smart girl like you would find out the sorry facts. But here's the story, darlin', and you know I wouldn't lie to you. I might not be the best father in the world—"

I sat up like a shot. "You are!"

Jack's cocky smile melted at the corners. "That's the other difference between you and Sylvia. She sees the world just the way it is. Black and white. No shades of gray for her. You look at things the way you'd like them to be. It ain't always good from a business point of view, but it means you've got real spirit, Maxie. It also means you're likely to get your heart broken more than most."

There was a time I would have instantly thought of Edik and everything that happened back in Chicago.

These days, none of it seemed so important—especially Edik—and realizing it, I traded Jack bittersweet smile for bittersweet smile. "You are the best dad in the world."

"And since you believe that, you'll know I'm telling you the truth when I tell you I had nothing to do with what happened to those nice ladies, Martha and Rosa. Dom, he was working for the company long before I signed on. It was the guy who was president before me who sent Dom over there to those restaurants to steal chili recipes, not me. Dom!" Jack twitched his broad shoulders. "I didn't trust the guy. I didn't like the guy. In fact, after the Showdown left San Antonio next week and I didn't need him to check up on you and Sylvia, I was all set to fire his sorry ass. So you see, sending him to steal those recipes . . . well, you know I'd never do a thing like that, Maxie."

"But you were giving out samples and—"

"Yes, we were. But that's because there's no use wasting perfectly good chili, and the chili, it was already made when I found out where those recipes came from. Rest easy, darlin'." He patted my knee. "Southwest Glory and Texas Favorite are not going into production. In fact, I had my research and development people destroy the hard drives those recipes were stored on, and all the files related to them have been shredded. My research and development people!" He barked out a laugh. "Sure does sound funny sittin' here sayin' things like that."

"Have you told Martha and Rosa yet?"

He gave me a wink. "They'll find out tomorrow at the big Miss Consolidated Chili shindig. That's when I'm presenting each of them with a dozen roses, a heartfelt apology, and a whopping big check for all their troubles."

"You're not a crook!" Of course I knew this deep down in my soul, but it never hurts to have these things confirmed. A wave of relief washed over me and I sighed. "I'm so glad. And it means you didn't have any reason to want to keep Dom quiet. You didn't kill him!"

Jack laughed so hard, he had to stop and catch his breath. "You didn't really think I did, did you?"

"Well, I thought John Wesley Montgomery might have. Before I knew he was you. Or you were him. Or whatever. I know you wouldn't do a thing like that."

"But that doesn't help your investigation much, does it?"

"How did you—"

"Well, give me some credit there, girl! I've been following you around for days trying to find the right moment to talk to you. I've seen what you're up to. You just promise me you'll be careful."

"You know I will."

"And I know you're smart and as tough as a boot, too. You'll figure out this here little mystery."

I hoped he was right, but at that moment, I didn't really care about who'd killed Dom and who tried to kill me as much as I did about what Jack was up to. We'd never had secrets from each other, and I'd grown up knowing I could talk to him about anything. Still, butterflies filled my stomach and I gulped a breath for courage.

"You sold out," I told him.

He made a face. "I did. Like I said, the board of Consolidated came a'courtin' and there was only so long I could resist. They said they wanted my chili expertise. They said they wanted my marketing genius. And the paycheck . . . well, heck, Maxie, I didn't think I'd ever see anything like it in my life."

"But canned chili!" I shivered.

Jack laughed. "Right now, it's regular ol' canned chili, but believe me, darlin', I'm going to change all that. Besides . . ." He drew in a breath and let it out slowly. "After all those years on the road with the Showdown, I was thinkin' that I wanted to leave you two girls more than just a food truck full of peppers."

"You've already done that," I assured him.

I knew I'd missed his smile, but it wasn't until that exact second that I realized just how much.

"I've left you a love for chili and life on the road," he said. "I've left you recipes and stories. Now you'll have an inheritance, too. Who cares if the money comes out of a can! I'm finally going to be able to take care of my two girls."

CHAPTER 19

By Sunday afternoon, I should have been exhausted. We finished up the last of the fund-raisers over at Alamo Plaza on Saturday night, and even though my feet hurt and my back ached and it was late by the time I got back to the RV, I didn't sleep a wink.

How could I after what happened?

Sylvia, it should be noted, tried to play it cool about the return of our dad. Not that I believed her cucumber attitude for a minute. When it comes to Sylvia, it's hard to recognize the signs of excitement since she's so darned reserved anyway, but I knew what to look for. She had a cup of coffee with me when we got back to the RV. And a chocolate cupcake. Sylvia and chocolate? Oh yeah, I could tell that like me, she was walking on a cloud.

We talked until the wee hours of the morning, speculating about everything from what would happen to the Palace now that Jack had returned to how he'd turn Consolidated Chili around, and I had an extra chocolate cupcake just for the heck of it and because there seemed no better way to celebrate.

I don't think I'd ever been giddy in my entire life. Not until that night, anyway. Sure, I was still a little confused as to how my father—ever the rebel and always a believer in the joys of small business ownership—could have sold out to a big, bad corporation. But that, I told myself, was a problem for me to consider another day.

For now, all that mattered was that Jack was safe and well. He was back.

And yes, I was giddy.

My euphoria carried into the next day as we wrapped up our final afternoon at the San Antonio Showdown. The Chili Chick had an extra kick in her step that day, and who could blame her! I danced to attract customers to the Palace. I danced to celebrate chili in all its varieties and all its glory. I danced because for the first time in months, my worries didn't weigh heavy on my heart. The last thing on the day's agenda was the Miss Consolidated pageant, and once that was done, we'd take a well-deserved night off, then head to New Orleans and the next Showdown, and when I wasn't driving the RV, something told me I'd still be dancing. Just for the hell of it.

And if by the time we pulled up stakes and left town I hadn't managed to find out who killed Dominic Laurentius?

In spite of the stifling afternoon heat, a chill like the

touch of icy hands tickled its way up my back. It sure would be nice to put this case to bed, I reminded myself. Just like it would be nice to find the low-down snake in the grass who'd tossed me in with that rodeo bull.

But call me crazy; right about then, my heart was so light and my spirit so buoyant, the case was the last thing on my mind.

"Nice dancing, Chick!" Apparently even Nick noticed the extra kick in my step, because when he walked over to where I danced outside the Palace, he was smiling. "You've been at it all day. Shouldn't you get some rest?"

"Don't feel like resting." I shuffled and kicked and, just for good measure, spun around with my arms out at my sides. "I feel like flying!"

Nick knew why. I'd told him as soon as I got out of the limo and back over to our tent in Alamo Plaza. After all, Jack said that thanks to his contract, he was forbidden to reveal his true identity to anyone, but that didn't mean I had to keep the news a secret. Besides, I'd only told Nick, Tumbleweed, and Ruth Ann, and they weren't going to spread the news, anyway.

As for Gert Wilson . . .

I'd made a quick stop at Gert's setup before I donned the Chick costume, and though I didn't tell her how I knew what I knew, I did let her know I knew it. I also told her that I understood that she'd been sworn to secrecy and that we'd talk later. When I left her, she was smiling, so I guess that didn't exactly put the fear of God into her.

"Don't wear yourself out before the pageant tonight," Nick said when I was done spinning and came to rest in front of him. "If they're short a beauty queen, maybe you could be Miss Consolidated Chili."

Since I was lost inside the Chick costume, he missed the face I made as well as my crossed eyes. "Not interested in a sparkling tiara or a sash. Got everything I need!"

Nick moved in close, the better to peer beyond the mesh and into the costume. "Everything?"

The Texas heat was nothing compared to the sizzle generated by his smile. "Well, now that you mention it—"

"All right, you two. Break it up!" Sylvia rolled down the aluminum window on the front of the Palace. "It's time for the pageant, and Maxie, I've got to believe that's not what you're planning on wearing."

She was right.

And I was late.

I told Nick not to move a muscle and zipped into the back door of the Palace so I could change out of the Chick and into my street clothes and met him back outside in record time.

"I can't wait for you to meet him," I told Nick as we headed for the main building where the pageant would be held. "But you're going to have to call him Mr. Montgomery, remember. At least while there are other people around."

"I remember."

Hard to believe, but when we got to the pageant, there were plenty of other people around. Ginger and Teddi were at the front of the line, dressed as elegantly as any of the contestants would ever be. Ginger was in a pale blue gown with a plunging neckline and a diaphanous skirt, and Teddi . . .

I took a careful look just to make sure she hadn't pulled a fast one on me when he walked away from Tatiana's.

True to her word, no gold lamé for Teddi. This afternoon, she looked splendid in a mid-calf-length white dress adorned with giant red poppies, a red picture hat, and matching heels.

Martha and Rosa were there, too, chatting it up with the people in the crowd around them.

"People actually come to watch these things?" I wondered out loud.

"Hey, beautiful girls showing off their legs and their talents." Nick grinned. "What could be wrong with that?"

The good news was that because the pageant was sponsored by Consolidated Chili, security was being handled by Tri-C and the fairgrounds and Nick didn't have to work. He was free to be an audience member, just like me, and we took our seats along the aisle about halfway back in the auditorium. The red velvet curtain was down, and right in front of it was a gigantic Consolidated Chili can surrounded by bouquets of pink and white carnations.

"Nobody knows tacky promotions better than Jack," I said.

"It's probably one of the reasons they hired him." Nick made sure to keep his voice down. "Promotions and publicity translate into sales."

A few minutes later, the lights in the auditorium dimmed and music filled the air. James Faragut walked out from behind that giant chili can and welcomed everyone to the Miss Consolidated Chili pageant.

"That's him." I elbowed Nick. "He's the one from the video, remember?"

Nick squinted. "It could be."

"It is. I remember him from the video. He's the one with the big—"

"Shh!" From the row in front of us, Sylvia shushed me.

When she turned back around I made a face at the back of her head. "He's the one," I grumbled, but I doubt Nick heard me. On Faragut's signal, the red velvet curtains whooshed open, the music swelled, and all seven of the Miss Consolidated Chili contestants paraded in. The crowd burst into applause.

"See, swimsuits." His gaze was on the stage and the leggy women who graced it when Nick elbowed me. "I told you there were reasons people came to these things."

Maybe he was right. Like everyone else in the audience, I settled back and tried my best to enjoy myself.

After the parade of swimsuits came the first round of chili trivia.

Tiffany—Miss Texas Chili Pepper—missed two answers out of the five questions she was asked. Miss Texas Triangle—Bindi Monroe—missed one. The other girls were pretty much clueless.

I knew every answer.

"You're pretty proud of yourself, aren't you?" The auditorium lights came on for intermission and Nick smiled my way. "Maybe you should be up there competing."

"I don't think so." I popped out of my seat and grabbed Nick's hand. "Come on," I said. "I know he's backstage." Notice I was being careful and didn't say who I was talking about. "I can't wait any longer. I want you to meet him."

"Now?" Nick got up, but only because I was already out in the aisle and still hanging on to him. "Won't he be busy? There's lots going on and—"

"Never too busy for me," I assured him, and of course, I was right.

Backstage, we located John Wesley Montgomery in a small room off the main stage where he wouldn't be likely to be seen by anyone from the Showdown, and when the door was closed behind us, I gave my dad a hug.

"Enjoyin' the show?" he asked Nick. "Plenty of pretty girls out there."

"There are, but you see, sir, I—"

"Sir!" Jack threw his head back and roared. "Now that's going to take some gettin' used to. So . . ." He gave Nick a knowing wink. "You were about to tell me, son, about how you weren't really lookin' at all those girls because you've only got eyes for Maxie here."

Nick grinned. Which is the only reason I didn't slug him when he said, "Maxie's not exactly my type."

"But . . ." Jack egged him on. "You were gonna say that even though she's not your type, she's the sort of woman that just worms her way into your heart, whether you want her to or not, right?"

Color touched Nick's cheeks. "I'm pretty sure that's what happened."

"Well, from what I can see, it looks righter than hen's feathers to me. That is . . ." Jack looked my way. "If it's what Maxie wants."

I never had a chance to answer. That's because from out in the hallway, I heard Eleanor Alvarez's voice. I opened the door just in time to see her come sweeping through the backstage area barking orders.

"I need those girls out here now!" Poor Eleanor struggled between projecting a note of authority in her voice and keeping it down so those on the other side of the red velvet curtain couldn't hear. "They need to be lined up before the curtain goes up." When no one jumped, she looked at the nearest stagehand and waved a hand backstage. "Go!" she ordered. "Get them! And get that useless director, too! Where is she? Isn't this her job?"

He did. Within a minute or so, a line of evening gown–clad, giggling beauty queens hurried onto the stage. They were followed by the middle-aged woman whose job it was to direct the logistics of the show, looking even more frazzled than she had when I watched her work at the rehearsal.

Eager to see how the whole behind-the-scenes thing worked, I told Jack we'd see him later, and Nick and I trailed into the wings. From that vantage point, I was nearly blinded by the twinkling of sequins and beads.

But even that didn't equal the flash when Eleanor waved a hand and blue sparks shot from that gigantic sapphire ring of hers.

"The curtain's going to go up in just a few minutes," she told the girls. "So let's make sure you all look your best. Stand back. Now turn to the left. Now to the right."

"Turn to the left. Turn to the right." I followed her direction as I repeated what she'd said.

"What are you mumbling about?" Nick asked.

I waved away the question.

But then, I was a little busy feeling amazed.

"Come on." He put a hand on my shoulder. "Let's get back to our seats while the auditorium lights are still on."

"I'll be . . . I'll be right there. Going to find a ladies' room." I lied, and once Nick was out front, I took a quick look around, racing through the maze of backstage corridors, hoping to find the dressing room.

"Looking for something?"

I hadn't planned on running into Eleanor Alvarez so early in my search, and when we nearly crashed into each other in a narrow hallway, I skidded to a stop.

"Just looking for the dressing rooms," I told her. Completely true, since I'd hoped to make it there before she got back so I could rummage through whatever she might have left there in search of clues. "Tiffany borrowed my blusher." Not so completely true, but Eleanor didn't need to know that. "You know the girl's as dumb as a box of rocks. Just thought I'd get it back before—"

"You can do better than that, can't you?" Eleanor's smile was angelic and tinged with just the slightest bit of pity. "Tiffany would never use your blusher. Number one, because I suspect you buy your makeup at the drugstore and she has far better taste than that. Number two, the color would be all wrong for her."

"Like that brownish lipstick she's always wearing!" I shivered like it actually mattered. "I told the girl to go pinker, but like I said, box of rocks."

Eleanor stepped to her right. It was a casual enough

move, but I couldn't help but notice that because of it, she completely blocked the hallway.

"What are you really up to?" she asked.

"Not a thing." I stepped forward, but she didn't give way. "I just wanted to look around. You know, to soak in some of the glamour of the—"

She laughed. "I really don't think so. You weren't going to do something you shouldn't do, were you? All the girls left their purses in the dressing room. I can't believe it, Maxie! Should I . . . Do I need to call security? We've got our money and our credit cards in our purses. We all need to protect that."

"And you've got a reputation to protect, too, right?"

She tossed her head. "Really, I don't know what you're talking about. My reputation is—"

"As pure as the driven snow." I took a tiny step to my left, nearer to where Eleanor stood looking as gorgeous as ever that day in a trim black suit. I'd never realized just how much she towered over me until that moment. "That was the idea, right? To keep your reputation nice and squeaky clean."

"I don't need to do anything. My dear, late husband—"

"Yeah, yeah. Blah, blah. Your dear late husband was what, like a hundred years older than you? And when he died, he left you a pile of money, didn't he? He bought your way into society, and I bet you're willing to do anything to make sure nothing ever upsets that applecart." I managed another careful step to my left just as Eleanor stepped forward to further block my path.

"Whatever you think," she said, "it isn't true. And your crazy lies . . . well, you could never prove them."

"Pretty much. Except for that ring of yours. And the DVD. You know, the one I took from Dom's apartment the night I was there."

"You? What were you doing at that poor man's apartment?"

"The same thing you were doing there, I imagine. I wanted to have a look around and see what the police missed. You wanted to make sure there was no incriminating evidence left behind. By the time you got there, there wasn't. See, I took that DVD with me."

"Number one, I've never been to that man's apartment. Why would I have been? And number two, what DVD are you talking about?"

"The one I told you about. You know, the one with James Faragut in it. It shows actors auditioning for porn movies, and I'm pretty sure you were the one directing them."

Eleanor's laugh was as sharp as broken glass. "Do you know who I am?"

"I do. And hey, it's not like I hold the whole porn thing against you or anything. My bet is that it all happened before you met that old husband of yours. And a girl has to eat, right? I'm sure you made more money making porn movies than you would have waiting tables."

Her top lip curled. "You're talking crazy. And besides, even if it was true, you could never prove it."

"I can. Because, see, at one point in the video, we can hear your voice in the background."

She sloughed this off like the nothing it was.

"And for another . . ." I gauged the distance between me and Eleanor, and the distance from there to the intersecting hallway that would take me toward the wings and back out front. "There's that ring of yours. There's no mistaking that. See, you held out your hand at one point in the video, and the ring flashed nice and bright and blue, just like it's been flashing in the stage lights."

She glanced down at the sapphire. "It isn't in the video. That's impossible!" She spoke too quickly and realized her mistake the moment the words were out of her mouth. "You don't know what you're talking about."

"Maybe not. But if that's true, then you won't mind me giving the cops a copy of that DVD. We'll let them decide if I'm right."

"Or not."

Eleanor closed in on me, her eyes flashing sparks much like her ring. Only these sparks were icy cold.

Before she could get any closer, I raced forward, rammed her out of the way, and ran.

I wasn't at all surprised that she came after me, and I looked left and right, trying to make a split-second decision about which was the best way to go and the quickest way to find help.

From out front, the music swelled, and I imagined the curtain getting ready to rise on all those smiling beauty queens.

"Nobody's ever going to find out." Eleanor was right behind me, her growl punctuated by the upbeat rhythm of the music. "No one's ever going to know what I did in my past. It's none of their business."

I spun to face her, back stepping the entire time. "But Dom found out, didn't he? And since I know Dom was a lowlife who blackmailed Teddi, I'm guessing he blackmailed you, too, right? He wanted money or he'd let everyone know you directed porn movies. And once your society friends found that out—"

"They weren't going to find out. Nobody was ever going to find out. That's why I paid Dom. That's why I paid him a whole lot of money."

I thought back to our visit to Dom's apartment. "Enough for him to buy a Porsche."

"Enough for two Porches," Eleanor snarled. "But that doesn't mean I killed him."

"Oh, come on!" I guess the stage decorations had been changed since the first part of the pageant, because, still backing up, I bumped into the giant can of Consolidated Chili that had been moved into the middle of the passage-way, and was trapped there between the can of chili and Eleanor.

"You're not going to ruin this cushy little life," she growled. "I won't let you."

"Oh, but I am." This sounded plenty brave, but with any luck, she couldn't see that I was shaking. "I'm going to tell the world. Everyone's going to know that Dom was black-mailing you and why. Everyone's going to realize you had a great reason to want to shut him up. I bet he ran into you back in LA when he was a cop and you were shooting those porn movies. And then he shows up years later here in San Antonio and sees that you're this queen of society. Dom was the kind of guy who didn't bat an eye at stealing seventeen dollars from Ginger and Teddi's tip jar. I can only imagine that when he saw what you'd become, his mouth started to water."

Eleanor rumbled and came at me. My back plastered to the can of chili, my arms out at my sides, I slipped to the other side of the giant can and took off running.

There was only one place to go. I raced onto the stage just as James Faragut stepped up to the microphone and the curtain rose.

"I might have been producing porn videos, but I didn't kill him, you little bitch!" Eleanor screamed and skidded to a stop just a foot or two away from me, and when she realized where she was and that there were seven beauty queens onstage and a couple hundred people in the audience staring at her with their mouths open, she offered them a grand and gracious smile.

It might have been more convincing if her eyes didn't spit fire, she wasn't breathing hard, and her fingers weren't curled and ready to go around my neck.

I wasn't about to wait around and see if she'd succeed. I ran, bowling over Miss Chili's Cookin' and Miss Hotter than a Chili Pepper in the process. Before I made it to where James Faragut stood with his mouth hanging open, Nick had already jumped up onstage and subdued Eleanor.

Well, physically, anyway.

"She made me say that!" Eleanor screamed. "She made me say that stuff about the porn movies. You can't believe it. None of you . . ." Her eyes wide and her hair mussed, she pleaded with the audience, most of whom had their phones out and were busy snapping pictures. "None of you can believe that. I would never . . . I would never . . ."

It was almost enough to make me feel sorry for her.

"You okay?" After he handed Eleanor off to fairgrounds security, Nick hurried over. "Good thing you're fast."

I wound my arm through Nick's. "Let's get out of here. I think I've had enough excitement for one day."

"No! No, you can't!" Tiffany stepped forward, waving toward the people in the audience who were thinking the way I was thinking and had already gotten to their feet to head to the doors. "You can't leave. The pageant isn't over! We have to crown a Miss Consolidated Chili!"

I glanced at the seven assembled beauty queens. Miss Chili's Cookin' and Miss Hotter than a Chili Pepper were back on their feet and looking none the worse for wear, and one by one, each girl raised her chin and smiled.

"I guess the pageant isn't over yet," I told Nick, and like everyone else in the auditorium, we returned to our seats.

"Well . . ." Sylvia spun in her seat so she could see me, and really, I couldn't decide if that gleam in her baby blues was one of begrudging admiration or all-out envy. "Looks like you've solved another murder."

At the risk of looking like a beauty queen, I pulled back my shoulders. "Looks like I have."

Nick slipped an arm around me. "You should have told me you had an eye on Eleanor. There's no way you should have gone after her alone."

He was right, but hey, it turned out okay, didn't it? When

the house lights dimmed, I sat back and watched Miss Texas Spice twirl baton, Miss Chili's Cookin' sing (yikes!) opera, Miss Hotter than a Chili Pepper juggle, and on and on.

"Will it never end?" I groaned when Miss San Antonio Chili Queens finished her sign language rendition of the Declaration of Independence.

"Only one more," Nick whispered back. "Miss Texas Triangle."

Bindi Monroe.

I will admit that when she walked out onstage holding a guitar painted in a wild pattern of red, white, and blue stripes, I held my breath and prepared for the worst.

Until she opened her mouth and started to sing.

The girl had a good voice and a sense of style. I sat back and enjoyed her jazzy interpretation of "The Yellow Rose of Texas."

For like twenty seconds.

"Nick," I tugged at his sleeve just as Bindi started in on a second chorus. "Do you remember the murder scene?"

His wrinkled nose conveyed his *huh?*

"The murder scene . . ." I grumbled, mad that I couldn't explain, not with the music and the singing and the swirls of painted colors on Bindi's guitar that I found so distracting and so revealing.

"Dom had a plain guitar," I said.

Nick gave me another *huh?* look.

"Dom had a plain guitar," I whispered. "When he came by the tent to check on me and Sylvia, he was holding a plain, ordinary guitar. It was probably some piece of junk he picked up at a pawn shop. But at the murder scene—"

The song ended and the audience applauded, and I knew I didn't have much time.

Before Nick could ask where I was going and long before he could stop me, I popped out of my seat and went around to the far side of the auditorium to head backstage. Oh, sure, he made to follow me, but got waylaid by fairgrounds security who wanted to talk to him about Eleanor's apprehension. Fine with me. I didn't have to explain myself.

The dressing rooms were down a corridor to my right, and I made sure everyone was still busy onstage and raced that way.

The long, skinny dressing room featured a row of mirrors on the wall with a small vanity and a chair in front of each. Those familiar makeup cases were parked in front of the dressing tables: black, purple, leopard print, pink sparkles, gold sparkles, photo-collage covered.

Just what I was looking for. I bent closer for a better look at the photographs and homed in on the one that had jogged a memory when Bindi was onstage.

Teenagers in a garage band playing brightly painted instruments.

From out front, I heard James Faragut's voice. "Now for the moment you've all been waiting for . . ."

I didn't have a second to lose, so I popped open Bindi's makeup case and stared at the single photograph pasted on the inside cover.

"What are you doing?"

When I heard Bindi's voice, my head came up. For the

second time that night, I'd been surprised doing what I had no business doing. The first time—with Eleanor—I'd been quick and I'd been smart and I'd been lucky.

I was about to find out if my luck would hold again.

"What are you doing back here already?" I asked Bindi. "Faragut is just announcing the winner."

"Yeah, well he just announced the three semifinalists and I wasn't one of them. I was supposed to stay there onstage and simper and smile, but when I saw that you'd left your seat . . ." She shrugged like it was no big deal when it was actually a pretty smooth piece of deductive reasoning. "I had a feeling you might be poking your nose where it didn't belong."

"Good thing, or I never would have found this." I pointed toward that photo on the inside of the case. It showed a young man with shaggy hair as dark as Bindi's. He was holding a brightly painted guitar, and the line of handwriting under the photo listed his name as well as a birth date and a death date, just a couple years before. "Tommy Monroe. Your brother, right?"

"My twin. So what?"

"He painted guitars."

She set her own brightly painted guitar down in the corner. "It was his hobby. So what?"

"So I should have noticed right away, but by the time I saw Dom the night of the murder . . . well, the guitar was all smashed. There was no way I could have known that it wasn't the same guitar he'd been carrying around earlier. That explains that trail of Consolidated Chili souvenirs near the body, too."

She twitched a shoulder, and the beading on her sky blue gown twinkled. "Really, I don't know what you're talking about."

"I don't, either," I admitted. "But I bet it won't be hard to find out. Your brother is dead and I'm sure there's a way the cops can find out the circumstances. He died young. That's too bad. And his death had something to do with Dom Laurentius, didn't it?" I took another gander at the photos on the outside of the makeup case. "I'll bet that beach isn't a Texas beach. I bet you lived in LA. That's where Tommy ran into Dom. He must have, and whatever happened, I bet it wasn't pretty. It's the only thing that would explain why you killed Dom."

"You think so?" That perfect smile firmly in place, Bindi closed in on me. She stopped at her dressing table, slid the drawer open, and pulled out what I thought was a pink cell phone.

That is, until I realized it was the stun gun she had used to knock me out before she dumped me in with the bull.

I looked into her eyes. Better than concentrating on her hands and letting her know I was scared to death she'd come at me with the stun gun. "Pink? How cliché!"

"But effective."

"I should have known Eleanor would never get her hands dirty with rodeo animals." I could have kicked myself for not thinking of it sooner. I glanced at the photos again, and the one that showed Bindi and her brother on horseback. "You're not afraid of big animals."

"Or of anything else," she assured me. "Let's get moving." She flashed the stun gun toward the door. "I don't

want to do this here. We'll find a nice dark corner somewhere where they won't find your body for a few hours."

It wasn't hard to pretend this scared me, but I cranked up
the drama a notch. I can cry at the drop of a hat. Ask Jack.
He'd given in to me plenty of times thanks to the waterworks.

"All right. Okay." I scooted toward the door, sniffling
all the while, but careful to keep just out of Bindi's reach.
"But the least you can do is tell me why you killed Dom.
It was because of Tommy, right?"

"Of course it was because of Tommy. He was railroaded
back in LA by none other than Dom Laurentius. He was
sent to prison and he was killed there in a fight. So much
talent! So much potential. And it all got wasted because of
that lowlife Dom. He was more interested in closing a case
than he was in finding out the truth, and poor Tommy was
in the wrong place at the wrong time. Laurentius planted
evidence. He made up a story. He arrested my brother and
he pinned a burglary on him that landed him in jail, and
when Tommy was killed . . ." Bindi pulled in a shaky
breath. "When Tommy was killed, I swore I'd do whatever
it took to make sure Dom paid for what he'd done. When I
went to my first meeting at Tri-C and saw him there . . ."
Her eyes flared. "It was like a gift from the gods, and there
was no way I was going to waste the opportunity.

"You were right about the guitar," she added. "I used
one of Tommy's to kill him. It was painted with a skull,
and you know what, I thought that was pretty funny. Too
bad I don't have something nearly as appropriate for you."

I was at the door, and it was now or never. I threw it
open and took off just as I'd taken off a little while earlier

when Eleanor was after me. But this time, I never made it as far as the stage. I got as far as that giant can of chili and ducked behind it.

"You can explain the whole thing to the cops," I said, sticking my head from behind the can of chili to see what Bindi was up to. "They'll understand. They'll take your brother's death into consideration. But if you kill me, too—"

"If I kill you, then nobody will ever know what happened." She made a stab at me with the stun gun just as I dashed back behind the chili can. "I didn't win the Miss Consolidated Chili pageant," she growled. "I have nothing else to lose."

My back flat against the chili can, I slipped around to the other side of it.

Bad timing.

I found myself toe to toe with Bindi.

"Hold still," she said, and poked the stun gun at me. "This is only going to hurt for a second. Then—"

Then a dull thud interrupted whatever she was going to say.

I looked up, stunned, to find Jack standing not ten feet away.

And the can of chili he'd thrown and beaned Bindi with at my feet.

CHAPTER 20

What with the police and the handcuffs and Tiffany crying because everyone was paying more attention to Bindi than to her even though she'd just been crowned Miss Consolidated Chili, it was late when we got out of there.

Not too late, though, to celebrate.

Jack took me and Sylvia and Nick to dinner, and he invited Gert and Tumbleweed and Ruth Ann along, too, for a reunion that had been a long time coming.

It was a chichi restaurant, and Jack picked up the bill for really good wine and steaks the size of San Antonio. By the time the waiter brought over a tray of what he called Texas Brownies, we were all pretty relaxed and in a good mood.

"The Showdown will be leaving town tomorrow." Jack

took us all in with a glance. "I wish I had more time with y'all, but since I don't . . . Nick, Tumbleweed, Ruth Ann, Gert, you'll excuse me if I talk a little business with my daughters."

I guess Sylvia had been expecting this, or at least hoping for it; she sat up like a shot. Me, I didn't have a clue what was going on. I took a sip of coffee and held my breath.

"I've got a big ol' company to run," Jack told us. "And there's a bit of what I'd call a divide between what I want to do with it and the current corporate culture. I could use a couple good assistants."

"Yes!" Sylvia practically jumped out of her seat. "Work here in San Antonio? For Consolidated Chili? In a real office? Yes, yes, yes! Count me in."

Jack gave her a smile. "I knew I could." He turned in his seat to look my way. "What about you, Maxie? I'm thinking of puttin' Sylvia on the business side of things, you know, prices and strategies, that sort of thing, but there's a PR department that could use a little shakin' up. With your experience and your head for promotions, I'd say it was a perfect fit."

It would be perfect.

A steady job and a reliable paycheck.

Working with Jack day in and day out.

I wasn't sure which of those things appealed to me most.

Which was why I grimaced when I told my dad, "That would mean leaving the Showdown, and the Showdown . . ." I took a deep breath and let it out slowly. "If it's all the same to you, Jack, I think I'll stay on at the Palace. The

Showdown wouldn't be the same without me, and I wouldn't be the same without the Chili Chick."

I don't think I was imagining it when I saw Nick sigh with relief. Jack, on the other hand, didn't look the least bit surprised.

"All rightee then." He shook hands with Nick and Tumbleweed and gave Ruth Ann a big, smacking kiss before he looped his arm around Gert's shoulders. "We'll see each other again soon. And Sylvia, you report to the office bright and early tomorrow and we'll get you all settled."

He didn't need to tell her twice. Sylvia was up and out of her seat in record time, heading for the door while she mumbled something about a double-breasted pin-striped blazer and matching pants.

"Maxie . . ." When I stood up, Jack grabbed my hand. "You're all right with this?"

"With staying with the Showdown and leaving Sylvia behind? It's like a dream come true. Well, except that I won't get that day off in New Orleans like I was supposed to."

"And you don't mind that she'll be working directly with me?"

There was a time I would have, and Jack knew it.

I stood on tiptoe so I could kiss his cheek. "This Chili Chick doesn't need a big paycheck or a fancy title. And now that she knows you're back and that you're happy . . ." I smiled at Gert. "I'm going to be just fine."

I slept in late the next morning, and hey, it's not like I didn't deserve it. I'd had a week of working the

Showdown plus the fund-raisers at Alamo Plaza, a week of investigating, getting bushwhacked, nearly being killed, burgling Dom's apartment, and solving a murder, not to mention a week of realizing that everything I'd ever been looking for was right there at the Showdown—including Nick.

When I got dressed and went outside to hitch the Palace to the RV, I was smiling.

At least until I rounded the corner and saw Sylvia standing there dressed in jeans and a Texas Jack golf shirt.

"What are you . . . ?" Since I wasn't sure I could believe my eyes, I pulled my phone out of my pocket and checked the time. "Aren't you supposed to be at the office?"

"Yeah, I am." My half sister stepped back and crossed her arms over her chest. "But I was thinking about it and . . . well . . ." As if even she couldn't believe what she was about to say, she threw her hands in the air. "You don't think I'm going to let you head out on your own with the Palace, do you? You'd get it all wrong. The way things are going, you'd be out investigating when there are customers lined up and bags to pack. The way I see it . . ." Even Sylvia could only look as gloomy as a thundercloud for so long. "Oh heck, Maxie, I talked to Jack this morning. He understands. I'm coming along! Of course I'm coming along."

I'm pretty sure she was just as surprised as I was when I smiled. "Well, don't get any ideas about being pushy," I told her. "About raising prices without talking to me first or changing our packaging or telling the Chili Chick what she can and can't do."

Sylvia pulled her slim shoulders back. "Well obviously somebody needs to be in charge. Your head is always in the clouds, and your common sense goes along with it. Now, let's get the Palace hitched and get on the road. I've got some things I want to talk to you about. I've been thinking about ordering spice jars that are just a little smaller than the ones we're using. If we can use one less ounce in each jar—"

I cut her off with a laugh. That is, right before I wound my arm through Sylvia's. "Oh yeah?" I asked her. "Who died and left you boss?"

No one can say for sure that they have an authentic chili recipe from the Chili Queens. Every Queen had her own secret recipe and every family had its own chili tradition. If you search online, you'll find endless versions that claim to be the real deal. Here's one Maxie would approve of. Enjoy!

ALMOST-AUTHENTIC CHILI QUEENS CHILI

A small amount of flour
2 lbs beef shoulder, cubed
1 lb pork shoulder, cubed
¼ C suet
¼ C pork fat
3 medium onions, chopped
6 cloves garlic, minced
1 quart water
4 ancho chiles
1 serrano chile
6 dried red chiles
1 T comino seeds, ground
2 T Mexican oregano
Salt to taste

Lightly flour the beef and pork cubes and put them in a pot with the suet and the pork fat. Sauté, stirring often. Add onions and garlic and cook until they're soft. Add water and simmer slowly. In the meantime, remove the stems and seeds from the chiles and chop very fine. You might want to wear gloves while you do this to keep the spicy capsacian off your skin. Add to the pot along with the ground comino seeds, the oregano, and the salt. Simmer two hours. Remove suet casing and skim off some of the fat. Serve with condiments of your choice.

Turn the pages for a preview of the next entry in
Kylie Logan's League of Literary Ladies series . . .

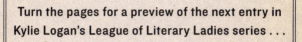

AND THEN THERE
WERE NUNS

Coming in early 2016 from Berkley Prime Crime!

"There's a penguin on my front porch."

Truth be told, that statement doesn't sound any less crazy to me now than it did that early spring morning when I muttered it through a fog of sleep.

But then, it had been a long and interesting night, and since I'd just rolled out of bed, I couldn't really be certain that I was thinking straight.

I was pretty sure I wasn't seeing straight.

Just to confirm this to myself, I brushed my long, dark hair away from my face and rubbed my eyes. Nothing changed. From the doorway of my private first-floor suite there at the B and B, I looked to my right and toward the foyer. There was a row of long, thin windows on either side of the front door and the glass in them was as old as the house. Through those windows, the scene outside always looked as rippled as the waves that lapped against the Lake Erie shore beyond the tiny strip of rocks and grass just across the street.

Between the antique glass and the glare of the early morning sunshine reflecting off the lake, it was impossible to see clearly, but I knew this much—I'd come out of my bedroom to make a pot of coffee and I saw what looked like a penguin on my front porch.

Black head.

Torpedo-shaped body.

White at the front.

Outlined with black.

"Very large penguin," I mumbled.

"What did you say? There's a big peregrine on the porch?"

From back in my bedroom, Levi Kozlov sounded as sleepy and confused as I felt.

Yeah, that's right, Levi, the guy I'd felt an instant attraction to the moment I met him. The one I swore I'd never get involved with because I'm convinced good relationships are all about honesty and for reasons I wasn't ready to divulge to Levi or to anyone else, I couldn't be honest.

We'd been dancing around our feelings, me and Levi, for months, taking two steps back for every one we took forward, weaving and bobbing and dodging every hint of intimacy like old pros.

That changed just hours before the penguin porch encounter.

Blame it on what I made the mistake of calling my "world-famous Bolognese" when I was chatting with Levi earlier in the week. Blame it on him for daring me to prove how good my pasta sauce was and me for taking him up on the challenge. Blame it on the fact that I didn't have any guests staying at the B and B and on the soft glow of the candles on the dinner table and the dancing fire in the parlor fireplace. Heck, blame it on spring fever. Or just go ahead and blame it on plain ol' stupidity. Whatever the reason—the alignment of the stars, the overwhelming power of passion, the weakness of human nature—we'd finally stopped side-stepping each other the night before and finished the dance.

And yes, just for the record, Levi is as good a dancer as I always imagined him to be.

All of which was incredibly exhilarating to remember.

None of which changed the fact that Levi and I had some serious talking to do.

After I took care of the penguin.

"Not a peregrine," I told him. "It wouldn't be weird to see a falcon on the island. This is a . . ." I had always prided myself on my good eyesight. In fact, I didn't need the glasses I'd chosen to hide behind ever since coming to the island and I'd left them on the nightstand next to the bed. I leaned forward and squinted. "Penguin. Definitely a penguin."

When Levi came up behind me, the temperature shot up a dozen degrees and my heartbeat quickened along with it. He wrapped his arms around my waist, propped his chin on my shoulder, and looked where I was looking, his bare chest brushing my terrycloth robe.

"It's a nun," he said.

A wave of memory washed over me like the slap of a cold Lake Erie wave and I groaned. "The nuns! The nuns are coming to the retreat center today. Elias told me . . ." I spun around and raced back into the bedroom, collecting the clothing we'd discarded in disarray hours earlier.

"Not my socks. Yours." I'd already scooped them up off the floor and I tossed them to Levi and found my purple panties and bra, then pulled on jeans and a sweater in record time. My shoes were . . .

When I didn't see them I settled for what I could find; I slipped my feet into the fuzzy bunny slippers next to the bed. "Elias Weatherly, the guy who runs the retreat center. He said the nuns were coming today."

"Right." Levi had a blanket wrapped around his waist and in the glow of the brilliant morning sun just peeking in my bedroom window, his chest looked as if it had been sculpted by an artist with a keen eye for both the gorgeous and the tempting. "You're helping with the food."

I raced to my 1930s-vintage dressing table and dropped down on the bench in front of it, the better to see myself in the mirror when I combed my fingers through my hair. "Yeah, but what I didn't tell you was that he called yesterday to tell me his mother-in-law was really sick over on the mainland, and I promised I'd help with anything else he needed. The nuns must have just arrived. They must need something." I whirled away from the mirror. "How do I look?"

A slow smile spread over Levi's face. Have I mentioned tall, golden-haired, chiseled chin? Oh, what that smile did to me! Before my heartbeat raced out of control and took my common sense along with it—again—I popped off the dressing table bench. I had every intention of heading for the front door. I would have done it, too, if my conscience didn't pick that moment to prick.

"Look . . ." Feeling suddenly as awkward as I definitely hadn't been all night long, I scraped one bunny slipper against the carpet and stabbed my thumb over my shoulder in the direction of the front porch. "I need to take care of this. Then I'll make that pot of coffee and some breakfast. We need to talk."

He pursed his lips. "Talk. Sure. But not now." Levi reached for his jeans. "Twelve years of Catholic school," he said. "And I'm not about to let a nun know that we—"

"What?" My shoulders had already shot back before I could remind myself that the stance was altogether too confrontational. "You're having regrets?"

His head came up. "That's not what I said."

It wasn't and I knew it. Conscience, remember? And I could have kicked myself for letting mine get the best of what should have been a punch-drunk morning of simmering smiles and sizzling shared memories. Damn conscience!

"No, it's not what you said," I admitted. "I'm sorry. I just didn't think you'd be leaving so soon."

"I've got a delivery coming in for the bar this morning so I really do need to get over there." Levi sat on the bed to put his sneakers on. "But Bea . . ." He looked up at me through the honey-colored curl of hair that fell across his forehead. "You're right. We do need to talk. There are a few things—"

The doorbell rang.

"Penguin at the door," I said and heck, who cared if I was running away from whatever he was going to say to me or simply dodging what I knew I had to tell him? I spun around and raced out into the hallway.

With any luck, by the time I took care of the nun at my door, Levi would be out the back door and gone.

The thought stabbed at my heart and the memories of what had been a perfect night. Rather than dwell on it, I pasted on a smile, threw open the door, and came face-to-face with one of the most formidable-looking women I had ever seen.

I had been right about the body type. Stout and tapered. Like a hoagie sandwich. I had been right about the penguin similarities, too. The nun who stood at my door wore an old-fashioned habit, a black wool robe that touched the floor, and was covered by a panel of creamy white. She wore a very shiny silver crucifix over that. Her head was covered by a black veil; her face was framed with a stiff white contraption I knew was called a wimple that covered her forehead and her ears.

She had dark eyes, thick lips, and the kind of eagle-eye stare that my imagination told me had intimidated school children for decades.

"Good morning. I hope we didn't wake you." Her smile was bright enough to rival the morning sunshine and instantly, her forbidding face was transformed. If she was a teacher, I had no doubt she was a kind one. "I'm Sister Liliosa and this . . ." She waved a hand toward the stairway and for the first time, I realized there were two other nuns waiting there, both of them wearing much the same kind of old-fashioned habit as Sister Liliosa. "Sister Mary Jean," she said, gesturing toward a lean-faced, ruddy-cheeked nun. "Sister Gabriel." This nun was far younger than the other two. She didn't look at me when she was introduced. "And this is Sister Margaret." That particular nun had been standing off to the side at the base of the porch stairs, checking out the daffodils just peeking their heads out of the front beds. Her dress was black, too, but shorter than the ones worn by the other sisters. Her veil was a simple square of black fabric, pinned back on her head to reveal a glimmer of silvery hair. She took the stairs carefully and stepped up to Sister Liliosa's side.

"Elias Weatherly told us we could contact you if we needed help," that sister told me.

"Of course!" I stepped back to allow the nuns into the B and B. They came inside and clustered in the foyer, Sister Liliosa nearest to me and the others lined against the wall. I closed the door behind them just in time to catch a glimpse of Levi's black Jeep backing out of the driveway.

An inglorious finish to what had been a splendid night, and maybe I wouldn't have felt so disappointed if I reminded myself that it was bound to end this way.

"The others who were with us on the ferry this morning have gone on to the retreat center," Sister Liliosa informed me, shaking me out of my thoughts. "They rented golf carts down near the ferry dock. We thought . . ." The sister slipped a quick sidelong glance toward Sister Margaret, who, rheumy blue eyes wide, studied the stained-glass window in shades of peacock, teal, and purple above the front door. "They dropped us here because we thought it might be best if we didn't ride all the way in an open golf cart." Another furtive look in Margaret's direction. "You know, with the morning air being a little brisk. We didn't want to take a chance of getting sick. Not when we've got such an exciting week ahead of us."

I had no doubt "they" weren't worried about anything at all except their elderly companion and I couldn't blame them. Sister Margaret was short and so stick thin, I was sure a stiff southern breeze could have blown her clear across the lake to Canada.

"You stopped here because you need a ride to the retreat center."

Sister Mary Jean grinned. "You're reading our minds."

"Could we be so bold as to ask?" Sister Liliosa asked. "Mr. Weatherly said we should contact you for anything we needed."

"I have to go over there today anyway," I told them, though I left out the part about how I'd been hoping it wouldn't be until later, long after the time Levi and I might have done a little more of what we'd been doing the night before. "I can bring over the salads I made for your lunches and that will save me the drive over at noon. Elias asked me to help with the food," I explained and headed into the kitchen for the salads that I'd already prepared and put in ten separate containers, one for each of the nuns who would be attending the week's retreat. I loaded the salads into carry bags and added the extras I'd packaged: cheese and ham and turkey, pickled beets and chopped hard-boiled egg and bacon bits, along with a variety of dressings. When I got back to the foyer, I put the tote bags on the floor and grabbed my jacket from the nearby coat tree. "Elias was called away. His mother-in-law is very sick. Over on the mainland. The house that's being used as a retreat center—"

"Old and fabulous, from what we've been told," Sister Mary Jean said, and I caught the trace of a Southern drawl.

Fabulous. That's what I'd always heard, too. The lake-front home now officially known as Water's Edge Center for Spirit and Renewal had once been the home of wealthy island recluse James Scott Findley. Findley died right before I came to South Bass Island—about a year earlier—and in his will, he left the house to a nonprofit with the requirement that it be used as a retreat facility. All were welcome and since its opening, the Center had already hosted a group of rabbis and a meeting of Buddhist monks.

"Old and fabulous and still a work in progress," I told Sister Mary Jean, who'd already reached for one of the bags of food and hefted it up in her arms. "From what I've heard, the kitchen isn't exactly up to snuff. That's why Elias asked me to help with the food." I didn't add that the original plan was for me—or, more likely, Meg, who helped with cooking for my guests—to prepare the meals and for Elias to come get the food every day and take it back to the center. That had changed when Elias went to the mainland. Now I'd need to schlepp the meals up to the center, but there was no use mentioning that and making the nuns feel guilty.

"Actually, I've been looking forward to checking out the house," I admitted instead. "Everyone says it's amazing and when Mr. Findley lived there, no one was allowed near it."

"Oooh!" Sister Mary Jean shivered. "Sounds like something out of a Gothic novel. I can't wait. You don't suppose it's haunted, do you?"

Sister Liliosa laughed and picked up the other bag of salads. "If it is, I think we can handle it, right?"

Sister Mary Jean nodded.

Sister Margaret, her eyes wide and her steps shuffling, mumbled something about extra prayers and angels.

Sister Gabriel didn't say a thing. In fact, when she followed the other sisters toward the door and I stepped in back of her, she flinched and shot a look over her shoulder. Like she'd just remembered I was there, she offered a thin smile.

"No worries," I told her. "I'm not much for ghost stories, either."

"Things that go bump in the night?" From out on the front porch, Sister Liliosa's silvery laugh flowed through the house on the tail of a spring breeze. "There are ten of us at this retreat, remember. And if there's one thing I know for sure, it's never bet against ten nuns."

I stepped out onto the front porch just as Sister Liliosa stepped back to allow the other nuns to go down the steps ahead of her, and I would have followed right along if I didn't stop to shoot a dirty look at Jerry Garcia. Jerry? He's the cat that lives next door and loves to lounge (and do other less sanitary things) on my front porch. I glared at Jerry. Completely unconcerned and ever unrepentant, Jerry tossed his head and went right on doing his cat thing.

The momentary pause gave Sister Liliosa a chance to step in front of me. Her grin melted. "I hope you'll convey our apologies to that handsome young man who left here in such a hurry when we arrived," she said. "I'm sorry if we interrupted anything."

My jaw had already dropped when she gave me a wink and allowed her gaze to slip to my feet.

"He has your head in such a whirl, you're leaving the house in your bunny slippers."

Searching for the perfect mystery?

Looking for a place to get the latest clues and connect with fellow fans?

"Like" The Crime Scene on Facebook!

- Participate in author chats
- Enter book giveaways
- Learn about the latest releases
- Get book recommendations and more!

facebook.com/TheCrimeSceneBooks

Obsidian

M884G1011

The delicious mysteries of Berkley Prime Crime for gourmet detectives

Julie Hyzy
WHITE HOUSE CHEF MYSTERIES

B. B. Haywood
CANDY HOLLIDAY MURDER MYSTERIES

Jenn McKinlay
CUPCAKE BAKERY MYSTERIES

Laura Childs
TEA SHOP MYSTERIES

Claudia Bishop
HEMLOCK FALLS MYSTERIES

Nancy Fairbanks
CULINARY MYSTERIES

Cleo Coyle
COFFEEHOUSE MYSTERIES

Solving crime can be a treat.

penguin.com

M7G0610

FOR THE LATEST IN PRIME CRIME AND OBSIDIAN MYSTERIES, VISIT
berkleyobsidianmysteries.com

- *See what's new*
- *Find author appearances*
- *Win fantastic prizes*
- *Get reading recommendations*
- *Sign up for the mystery newsletter*
- *Chat with authors and other fans*
- *Read interviews with authors you love*

berkleyobsidianmysteries.com

M2G0610

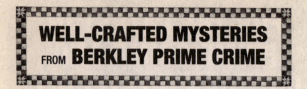

WELL-CRAFTED MYSTERIES
FROM BERKLEY PRIME CRIME

- **Earlene Fowler** Don't miss these Agatha Award–winning quilting mysteries featuring Benni Harper.

- **Monica Ferris** These *USA Today* bestselling Needlecraft Mysteries include free knitting patterns.

- **Laura Childs** Her Scrapbooking Mysteries offer tips to satisfy the most die-hard crafters.

- **Maggie Sefton** These popular Knitting Mysteries come with knitting patterns and recipes.

- **Lucy Lawrence** These brilliant Decoupage Mysteries involve cutouts, glue, and varnish.

- **Elizabeth Lynn Casey** The Southern Sewing Circle Mysteries are filled with friends, southern charm—and murder.

penguin.com

M5G0610